THE
LIFE
ASSISTANCE
AGENCY

THE
LIFE
ASSISTANCE
AGENCY

BY
Thomas Hocknell

URBANE
Publications

urbanepublications.com

First published in Great Britain in 2016 by Urbane Publications Ltd
Suite 3, Brown Europe House, 33/34 Gleaming Wood Drive, Chatham, Kent ME5 8RZ
Copyright ©Thomas Hocknell, 2016

A CIP catalogue record for this book is available from the British Library.

ISBN 978-1-911129-03-5
EPUB 978-1-911129-04-2
MOBI 978-1-911129-05-9

Design and Typeset by Julie Martin
Cover by Nikki Dupin

Printed in Great Britain by
CPI Group (UK) Ltd, Croydon, CR0 4YY

urbanepublications.com

"A marvellous neutrality have these things mathematical, and also a strange participation between things supernatural – immortal, intellectual, simple, and indivisible – and things natural – mortal, sensible, compounded, and divisible."

Dr John Dee. 1570.

Who really wants to live forever? Once the fishermen left the pub for afternoon naps, leaving *The Crown* smelling of cuttlefish and fishy stories, Scott and I used to ponder this, at least after we'd washed the glasses. Living forever means you could listen to every Bob Dylan album, even the ones he couldn't. Hell, you could even learn to play them on every instrument known to man, *and* those not yet invented. If playing Dylan wasn't already bad enough, you'd see all your friends die. Life has enough death. Who would want more?

From *Mirrors and Lies* by Ben Ferguson-Cripps

Chapter 1

I sat on my own in the corner of *Vampires and Garlic*. Daisy had suggested we meet there. She had taken a shine to Goths, although not keenly enough to be punctual. Presumably punctuality was missing from Gothic dating criteria. I was surprised they still existed. Spending my time unaccompanied was risky. It meant obsessing about the imminent sales figures of *Mirrors and Lies*. My book had finally been released in paperback, and needed to be a success, because for someone writing a mildly popular blog and a published book, I spent more time gumming envelopes in a windowless City room than my ego could handle. I sipped my beer, even that tasted of glue. Writing the book had taken longer than I care to admit without taking heavy sedatives. I flicked a business card left on the table into the air. It landed face-up: **The Life Assistance Agency**.

My *Mirrors and Lies* was your typical semi-autobiography of growing up with a fortune-teller mother, and bullies unfailingly finding humour in 'Bet you didn't see that coming.' I started writing young, showing my mother frequently enough for her to develop appreciation of at least my commitment, but not before she warned me of 'ice-cream dreams'. Mind you, writing a good line is like smoking after masturbation; no one else cares. My school friends were sporty, and I should have pretended to like football, in the hope it might grow authentic. It's generally the first thing men talk about, particularly when bashful about interests in esoteric practices of the 19th century. I sipped more beer, but not enough to require another pint before Daisy arrived. I wondered why she was late, and if I had time to write a blog about it.

Blogging is basically emptying your head of all the things deemed uninteresting enough to say aloud. At least that is what a 'commentator' said, before I deleted his comment. It's like Speakers Corner with less excuse for sounding like a lunatic, and better opportunity to use a flattering avatar.

I started promoting myself before *Mirrors and Lies* was published. I wanted to be easy to find, which made the lack of people seeking me even harder to bear. I worked so hard at promoting my book that I actually spent more time pre-empting the promotion of the book than actually writing it.

The blog was related to the book, so it predictably attracted readers who took offence at me suggesting that crystals lacked transformative powers, or my criticising pre-life regression for its uncanny ability to identify people as Lords and Ladies rather than peasants who died of teeth decay during adolescence.

I glanced again at **The Life Assistance Agency** business card, and marvelled at the optimism of a business plan that involved punters not mocking such speculative services. I recognised the card's Impact font. The KLF used it on their record sleeves.

YOUR PROBLEMS, OUR ASSISTANCE

**Where telephone banking and dietary supplements fail,
The Life Assistance Agency succeeds.**

Private investigation, sick day excuses, situation manipulation, people: lost and found, Life advice,, coincidences arranged, hits arranged, soul mates found (special rates apply), final Will and testament re-writing, fear of death minimalisation, account

**massaging, Swimming lessons, Feng Shui
and Bonsai trimming.
0208 333 21-0
07873 643 338**

"Hey," Daisy said, interrupting my thoughts as she arrived with the subtlety of a gale at an origami convention. She retained the trace of an American accent picked up in San Francisco. To compensate for lack of punctuality she was unwinding her scarf like there was no time to waste.

Daisy was obviously new to the Goth world. She wore a billowing black and white top she'd be advised to not wear in the wild. She looked like a Scandinavian superhero; the flower in her hair perfectly angled above a geometrically cut fringe.

She smiled, "How *is* my favourite writer?"

"Pleased to have *a* fan," I replied, glad to be finally finishing my drink.

"Well, most people don't know any published authors."

"Probably because they're unbearable."

"Well, there is that." She smiled. "So, let's celebrate," she said, looking at me, "The paperback *is* out today isn't it?"

It was, which put me in a good enough mood to buy the round. Apart from Jehovah Witnesses, no one was stopping me in the street yet, but no one gets published for the fame. Daisy took a slug of beer, before putting the glass down like it had been the shag of her life.

"Wow," she declared breathlessly, "*That's* better."

I had spent the previous day moving belongings from her parents in Kingston back into town, where I was now inexplicably buying *her* drinks. Town is what Londoners call London once they know which side of the platform trains arrive on for at least 50% of stations. I'd been calling it Town for fifteen years.

"What's this?" she asked, taking the business card. Daisy believed in anything and everything. Deep below us a Piccadilly line train rumbled towards Heathrow.

Daisy read the card. "Wow, it looks like they can help with *anything*." She picked up her phone.

"Like the A-team?"

"Well I need a job."

"Are you calling them? Be careful, they might get you one."

We shared her iPhone's headphones, and she dialled the number. The answer phone stuttered congratulations for contacting the Life Assistance Agency, before disappearing into a wail of technical incompetence.

"Don't put the phone down," said a voice apparently locked in a cupboard. "How can we help?" it said. "I mean assist?" It coughed professionalism into its tone, but still sounded like it had been given the wrong change. "*Assist*, how can we assist?" The voice scrambled into feedback.

"What's up with your voice?" Daisy asked. "It sounds treated."

"Treacle?" it asked.

"*Treated.*"

"I thought I'd turned that off." There was squealing noise followed by silence, before the voice returned sounding like *Speak and Spell*.

"Now, how can we help? *Damn* it. Assist?" It went quiet, before the calculator returned. "How may we *assist*?"

Daisy frowned like she regretted calling. "I need a job, but I'm not entirely sure you can help...."

"Perfect, in that case you can't be disappointed. Let's book you an appointment."

"Tomorrow at 11?" she suggested.

"Yes," the voice agreed without pretending to have other bookings. "We're in Hanway street. It's near Tottenham

Court Road, above the record shop. It's very supportive of our Agency. We'll see you tomorrow."

The line went dead. Daisy looked like a child told it could roll in sugar

"You're easily pleased." I said.

"It's the secret to life Ben. That and coughing when opening crisps."

I bought more drinks.

"Kathleen got the sales yet?" she asked on my return.

I guessed she hadn't, but my stomach knotted with hope. Kathleen was my literary agent. Someone introduced to me a long time ago by a mutual friend Scott Wildblood.

"We'll know the early sales figures tomorrow," I said.

After more drinks than I intended, I left Daisy. She caught the tube home, but I decided to walk back to Deptford. The streets were full, pleasure-seekers wanting more drinks to regret in the morning. I paused to lean over Hungerford Bridge and stare into the Thames, which I did for long enough to encourage a policeman to enquire after my suicidal intentions. I was so drunk I'd have missed the water, but kept this to myself. A RNLI lifeboat bobbed below us. The officer informed me they were watching me. The lifeboat had found a flashlight, so I moved on before the copper handed me one of those Life Assistance cards.

Chapter 2

I woke up remembering the lifeboat, but little else. I groped for a glass of water, but there wasn't one. Apart from being something to better grope for, the best thing about girlfriends is their interminable bedside water. My mouth was glued shut by dehydration. I sat up, to grip my forehead like I'd been shot.

I had been single for six months, reward for allowing my ex-girlfriend to find my bank statements revealing restaurants I had not taken her. You'd think that shared ownership of fitted curtains would have meant I treated the relationship with greater emotional maturity than that of a stag party. I had now been single for long enough to rediscover that dating involves being told that the perfect evening, followed by the shag of your life, wasn't mutual, and that requests to never text again isn't playing hard to get. I had ticked 'Anything' in my preferences, which provided matches with the precision of a D-Day flailing tank.

I checked my phone for messages from Kathleen, but there were none. I remembered how excited I'd been when I met her. Meeting a literary agent had inspired me to start the book I'd always planned. We had met when Scott, Daisy and I worked at *Vital Marketing (-Putting YOU into YOUr market)*. Scott had found me a job there after my mother died.

Kathleen was married to Eustace Morelock, our sales manager. Like Scott he was ex-army, but when surveying the sales-floor, hands on hips, he looked more like a cricket grounds-man. Morelock had fought in several military campaigns, none of which killed him quite like low sales. It was a tough sell. Cold calling to sell marketing space was harder than flogging diaries in August. Sales had suited Scott. 'He'd win with a cat at a dog show' Morelock repeated in the hope that his good fortune might rub off on us. I didn't even have a dog, but my mother and I had once owned one in Hastings. It woke us up by staring at us, like a Spaniel alarm clock. I cursed it, but I overslept after it died. I still do.

I downed a pint of water, before putting jeans on over my pyjamas and leaving my flat. A steady drizzle did little to flatter Deptford, but I needed milk for tea. An impatient Ford Fiesta with 'Little Princess on board' almost ran me over. I gave them the bird.

I got back to the flat and sent some speculative emails pitching article ideas to newspapers, before accepting that I needed to attend a new locum job. I rang them to claim train delays had disrupted by journey and left the flat.

Typically, actual train delays caused even further lateness to a job I hoped to no longer need once the *Mirrors and Lies* sales figures came in. I was so confident that I considered calling Kathleen, but someone once told me literary agents should be the ones doing the chasing. The hardback sales had measured me for a suit and I hoped the paperback would pay for the cut.

I wouldn't recommend writing a book. Unlike rock music, you never stare into the impassioned eye of an audience, which is fine. The audience isn't girls ravaged by hormones in overpriced tour T-shirts, but someone struggling to finish the page they failed to complete before falling asleep the previous night. I had soon abandoned writing novels, and instead turned my eye to non-fiction. Already familiar with the effect of their empty promises on my mother, I researched occult, religion and pop psychology, and typed arguments defending rationality in the face of so-called spirituality. *Mirrors and Lies* came together as a semi-auto-biographical treatise with surprising ease. It felt good kicking sand in the face of everything that deluded my mother. Mind you, it was good she never read it. She would have blamed my cynicism on my father. I had apparently inherited his eyes, the noise he made when indignant, and his pessimism. I never met him. It sounded like no great loss, but that was probably my bravado. The problem with an absent father is you idealise him.

I slipped into the cramped temp office I had been given to transfer data from some ancient mainframe onto a contemporary IT system in London's Barbican. Any plan B alternative to my literary career needed more work than the North Korean nuclear project, but instead of addressing this, or compensating for my late arrival, I read the *Metro*, searching for mention of my Radio 4 interview from the previous week.

I had been invited to participate on a panel to discuss the debunking of popular myths. I feared the microphone would only pick up my thundering heartbeat. I was introduced as the author of *Mirrors and Lies*, and the programme had actually gone so well that I expected my sales to have increased. They did not. The audience you're debunking doesn't buy a book lambasting the scrying for angels and other new age idiocy, and nor do the cynics, who don't need telling.

At lunchtime, a tap on my shoulder interrupted me as I practised what I hoped looked like an autograph.

"Busy?" the manager asked.

I stared into a face I had previously reassured of my ability to work old mainframe computers. His features had grown far less friendly.

"Mr Ferguson-Cripps," he said. "You've never done this before have you?"

I looked from him to the blank screen. "I'll get my coat."

Ben Ferguson-Cripps sounds like an arranged marriage between tractor manufacturers and a tailor. But my father disappeared long before talk of wedlock, and before I was old enough to focus. My mother wanted nothing more to do with him, or his surname, which I believe had been Kaley or something, but which he changed with the frequency of headlines to stay ahead of local bookies and loan sharks. So, she affixed the randomly chosen Cripps to the feature in a magazine about Massey-Fergusons. I was grateful it was not from her beloved *Fortean Times*.

My father brought nothing to the relationship but drunkenness. 'Useless as radio subtitles' my mother said to anyone still listening. If she missed him, I glimpsed it only when she arrived home from work, sitting in our front room, passers-by shadowing across the net curtains. She unfailingly nursed two brandy glasses, as though he had simply left the room. 'Never drink alone,' she advised, whilst steadily ignoring her own advice.

I decided to simmer over my dismissal from the Barbican at Soho's *French House*. I looked around at men apparently having last worked in the 1960s, in *their* 60s, or possibly both. Perhaps this is how my father started, or ended up. The lunchtime swell ebbed, exposing the low tide mark of those with nowhere else to be. They cradled pints, their ticket in from the wet. I ordered a bitter. It seemed appropriate. I sat in a corner, and admired a cluster of drama students chatting away oblivious to the effect they were having on the male clientele. The beer filled my emptiness, but barely. I was afraid to go home. I knew what my flat had in store, that sinking feeling accompanying a low tally of visitors to my blog, or a half-hearted Google; a mouse-sniff from *everything*, but finding interest in nothing.

Research shows increases in people working from home, presumably because they've got time on their hands to complete the necessary questionnaires. It has its upsides – the closest you get to the rush hour is watching it on BBC London- but most of the day is spent moving between rooms forgetting the reason why. I used to go swimming, until all that confirmed was that swimmers are so full of themselves that it's amazing they don't sink.

The *French House* reminded me of working in *The Crown* in Hastings, where I first met Scott Wildblood. Scott was someone better at tucking in the front of his shirt than the back. He had been twenty-something, whilst I wasn't old enough to drink in pubs, much less serve in them. Even then, Scott struck me as someone good at leaving, not in a cowardly way, like my father, but in noble obligation to keep moving. He was pretentious enough to say he liked film, as opposed to films, and slept with the ease of well-exercised spaniel. But, he was as elusive as a rainbow. He was so full of plans that no one else needed any. One of his better ideas was suggesting the only place worth metal detecting for coins was the Glastonbury festival site. When I say better, I mean only.

The beer was making me angry, as were the students overusing the word "awesome". My phone buzzed with a text from Kathleen. A text was bad news, so I rang her.

"Hello, Ben," she said in a tone even spaniels would question. "The paperback sales are disappointing."

My hand gripped the pint glass. "How disappointing?" I asked.

"I'm afraid they're disappointing enough for us to question representing you."

I stopped listening. I felt myself drop into a pit apparently without bottom. It felt so unfair I wanted to cry. Disappointment flooded back: rejections, poor interviews and ejection from

Hastings' buses. I had now lost the agent I *had* secured. Every 'Fuck it' I'd ever silenced exploded. I raised my pint jug, and smashed it onto the table. The beer splashed my face before I heard shattering glass. I looked down. From somewhere I heard Kathleen asking if I was still there. I wasn't. Beer dripped from my nose. The jug I was holding had somehow broken across the table. The jagged seam from its base staring at me matched the tide of self-hatred. I heard someone scream. I looked at my hand, which was gushing with blood from a cut deeper than I had ever seen before. The students stopped saying "awesome". I gasped and then groaned. My eyes closed and I fell off the chair.

I spent a day in Guy's Hospital's neuropathy department enjoying a soul holiday courtesy of morphine and bedside service. Beneath the sound of floor polishers and medical hum I heard the world bustling outside without me. I knew I should care, but the painkillers suggested otherwise. Someone once told me you should earn your age; I wish they hadn't. As a left-hander, I had at least destroyed my right hand. I was kept in for a day of 'obs.' It was worryingly easy to reassure the psychiatric nurse that any risk to myself had passed. I roamed the hospital looking for signal, holding my phone up like a prison warden looking for drugs or weapons. I found a single bar of reception leaning into a stairwell. The first message was from my recruitment agency sacking me following the 'unprofessionalism' in the Barbican. Rejection by people I didn't even want to impress hurt more than losing Kathleen, although admittedly less than my hand.

Thankfully, following bicycle mishaps and a ballet foray, Daisy understood hospital discharges. She carried my bag home and poured wine. The flat seemed emptier than ever. My hand felt like a table tennis bat. A nurse had taken my watch off, to accommodate the swelling. Daisy strapped it to my left wrist. When she departed, I wanted to grab her so she wouldn't leave.

The next morning embraced me like damp washing. I made tea and checked my Twitter to discover I had lost four followers. I followed a link to Denzel Washington's top ten badass moments, before checking my emails, which confirmed the inclusion of my article on trees in *The Guardian*. It had been a final favour from the Editor that wouldn't pay the rent. I emailed her replacement, but knew she would be bringing her own nepotistic freelancers. I wandered into the sitting room, fooling myself there was reason to. I felt panic rise at not having a job. I had a £5000 advance for *Mirrors and Lies*, which I had never cashed. I took the cheque from its frame. A lot of money that wouldn't last long – a few months rent. Then what? The TV darkened the corner of the room. I intended it to stay that way; I was not going to fall into the daytime TV trap.

Advertisements for cheap loans and stair-lifts jerked me awake.

The phone rang.

"You *have* to visit that life assistance place." It was Daisy. "It's amazing," she said. "I'll tell you tonight. You need to manipulate your situation sweetie."

Situation manipulation was on that damn business card. I quickly Googled them, but nothing came up.

"But, they don't even have a website."

"Well, that's about to change," she said, "*I'm* designing it." She paused. "They'll change your life. Ben."

Such positivity was typical of Daisy. Since working at *Vital* she encountered new jobs like planes collide with migratory birds. That is not to say she did not have hard times. Her inability to find a suitable man flew in the face of *Eight ways to make Mr Left, Right.* She didn't really fit London; she didn't have sharp enough elbows. Then I imagined that once she found something to retire from she would live in Brighton or Hastings. She had been most proud of *Mirrors and Lies*, despite utterly disagreeing with it. I put the phone down and wondered what to do.

Chapter 3

For someone claiming to predict the future, my mother spent a surprising amount of time in her shack on Hastings Pier awaiting customers that never arrived. She combated the English Channel's wind gusting between the rotting boardwalk with nips of sloe gin earlier and earlier in the day. She returned home drunk, although always denied it, yet never enough to forget those two glasses. I followed her path for a while, taking so many drugs that I lived in fear of their long-term affects.

My mother's death brought one advantage. I could dismiss her beliefs without upsetting her. *Mirrors and Lies* early success was clearly an anomaly, related more to the atheist zeitgeist sparked by Richard Dawkins than my writing skills. Western rationale was destroying remnants of an older, more magical world. It set fire to the shadows and I was glad to be part of the light. My mother would have recognised herself within the pages, even if I had changed her name, which I did not. There was little point in disguising names, although I later wish I had. She would have been less familiar with the anger at my absent father. I tended not to dwell, but on drug-comedowns and lonely weekends, it was his lack of name that scarred deepest. 'He lied about that too,' my mother insisted, leaving me guessing as to who was lying.

I visited St Thomas' hospital to have my hand re-bandaged. Afterwards I wandered into the West End. I found myself in the Mind, Body and Spirit department of *Foyles* bookshop.

I exhausted my marketing expertise by surreptitiously moving *Mirrors and Lies* from the wasteland of A-Z to front of house. I was tempted to buy one, but even I wasn't going to sink to that level. I left the shop with *Great Expectations*, an ironic gesture that no one was privy to, and two copies of *Mirrors and Lies*. As I paid, I found the advance cheque in my pocket. If I were to survive, I'd need to bank it. I headed towards Tottenham Court Road glowing with the sort of shame unique to authors having not only repositioned their book in a shop, but also having bought it. I passed Hanway Street and thought of the Life Assistance Agency. I guess the devil finds routes for idle feet.

I strolled down the narrow cut-through. Boxes were stacked in the window above the first record shop, presumably unsold copies of Oasis' *Be Here Now*. Either way they were stored in the most expensive real estate in the country. I stepped over a dog in the gutter. I paused to check my iPhone. It found nearby Wi-Fi connections: *Boots*, *McDonald's*, and a record shop, but no sign of a Life Assistance Agency. I reached *Sly's Records* where T-Rex's *Jeepster* blared from a shop empty of customers. The owner, in a leather cap, read the newspaper with the concentration of a bookie, oblivious to his volume and unsecure Wi-Fi. A paint-peeled door with three buzzers faced the street to the left of his shop front. A slim woman disappeared through the doorway, heading I presumed, to the Russian modelling agency on the 2nd floor above the shop. Next to the 1st floor button I recognised the enigmatic Impact: **LAA – Life Ass**. The agency even needed assistance in choosing a smaller font to fit properly. What did I have to lose? The door remained open. I did not buzz, and climbed the narrow stairs.

Chapter 4

The first surprise was Scott wearing the suit I had last seen him in, a brown number once intellectually tailored, but now losing interest, unlike its owner. His eyes could inflate party balloons from a distance. And, unlike an increasing number of my friends, he still had hair. In the eight or so years since I'd seen him it had greyed, which typically suited him. He was as slim as a postman and looked like England's answer to David Hasselhoff. He was holding a small bottle of medication, which reminded me of the last time I'd seen him. Seeing me, it quickly disappeared.

"Is this the life ass?" I asked.

Scott Wildblood had not been the sort suggesting frailty, but heart attacks prefer surprise. The *Vital* sales floor had been the usual reclining in chairs at angles implying important conversations that were actually with friends. Scott, returning from his morning swim, was striding across the room when he halted. His *Cadburys* bar fell to the floor, followed by him. Initially I thought he was joking, with the rush of people caused by the chocolate. More phones clattered to rest like gunfire, as he remained sprawled on the carpet. Everyone approached, like pigeons investigating an abandoned sandwich that was too good to be true, but before anyone touched him, the Groundsman yelled from his office.

"Leave him!" He knelt to hold Scott's head. "Death sweats," he muttered. It was apparent Scott was suffering heart failure; his handsome face realising how little pain he had hereto experienced. I was shocked. A pillar of my world wobbled. People like Scott did not collapse. We looked on stunned, as the ambulance crew stretchered him away. We missed him like a punch line.

"So, you're why Daisy insisted," I said, recovering from the shock of seeing him again.

"Good to see you too, Cripps," Scott Wildblood grinned. He remained a man calling a moth a butterfly. He stood up. His smile was the best thing the shabby room had seen since it had presumably closed as a massage parlour.

"I knew you'd come." He winked. "Never chase rainbows. Let 'em chase you."

"Well, I've been called worse things than a rainbow." As various bad reviews flashed through my mind.

He laughed. "Actually," he said, considering what he'd said, "That motto should be on my business card."

"It's about the only thing that isn't."

"That's true, we offer unlimited assistance in peoples' lives."

Looking around at the dilapidated room I decided to be diplomatic. "So, what's Daisy's involvement with all this?"

"Confidential I'm afraid." He resisted tapping the side of his nose, but barely. "She's webbing our site. It was good to hear from her."

He hugged me. He felt *fit*. He had only been in the army for a week, and a long time ago, but long enough to instil admirable commitment to morning sit-ups and ironing. He had been medically discharged due to eczema, which is apparently hard to treat in the field, and which miraculously disappeared once he left.

A poster of people wearing unfeasibly large sunglasses clung to the wall. The room smelled of latex, sex and purchased promises.

"*This* is the Life Assistance Agency," he announced proudly. I looked around, at a life assistance agency apparently unable to help itself.

"A Life Assistance Agency?"

"It's like a detective agency, but without detectives. It's more flexible."

He indicated that I take the chair opposite him. There was a phone on the floor where a desk should have been. Clocking my surprise, he tutted, "I still need a desk; this is doing business during a bloody lull in musical chairs."

Before I could laugh, the phone actually rang. I say *actually*, because I suspect even Scott had forgotten it worked. It turned out to be BT, which Scott endeavoured to pretend wasn't.

"What used to be a brothel is now the Life Assistance Agency," he explained, having got rid of BT. Hoping a life assistance agency, whatever that was, might be more profitable than a brothel tells you everything you need to know about Scott. His business plan involved the sort of optimism spaniels use to chase squirrels up trees in parks.

"Now, to business," he said. "How's your book doing?"

"Middling…"

"That bad?"

"Worse actually."

He nodded. "Daisy said you needed help." He leaned back in his chair a little too smugly for my liking.

"I do need a job," I admitted.

"Is that all? Why can't people be more demanding? How about eternal life, or stopping Peter Jackson from making more Hobbit films?" He paused for what I feared was dramatic effect. "Want to work here?"

"Not while I've got this." I pulled the advance cheque from my pocket. I was unsure what was worth more; the security it represented, or the three months it bought me in rent.

"How long's that going to last?" He read my thoughts.

He had a point. I looked at his business card. Private investigation, situation manipulation, hits... "Hits? You don't mean..."

"It's a typo, at least that's what we tell unwanted enquiries," he smiled. "Although you *could* help there."

I was chuffed he remembered I knew which end to hold a pistol. "*You* were the one in the Army."

"Gone before the fun stuff I'm afraid."

"Is there much demand for life assistance?" I asked.

"There's a *huge* gap in the market."

"Because there is no market?"

"People don't dare ask for it, *actually*." Scott sounded defensive. "It's chaos theory. Throw eggs and flour in enough rooms and you'll open one to cake."

"Got any assignments?" I asked.

"Assignments. They sound good."

"Well, have you?"

"No."

He looked well. There had been a time, seeing him in a hospital bed, when I was unsure I'd see him again. Fittingly, an ambulance broke my thoughts as it screeched through Hanway Street. His phone rang again, and he answered it, sounding like a sheep.

"LAA. We're a Life..." Scott paused. "Sorry, we're *the* life assistance agency." He listened. "A missing cat? No, sorry." He terminated the call, looking disappointed. "So, what're your plans?" He asked. I think he meant longer term, which I couldn't face.

"After this? I'm seeing my agent."

Scott's positivity had bolstered my mood enough to visit Kathleen. When I left, he handed me a business card, which I used as a bookmark in *Great Expectations*.

I sat in the reception to Kathleen's Bloomsbury office. The usual copies of the *Literary Review* were scattered with purposeful carelessness across a low table, but I was too nervous to read. Kathleen appeared, to invite me into her office. She looked like she had been up all night celebrating awards success. It was a good look for a literary agent, if only the success had been mine. I took a chair, and the moment I saw her face I knew it was a mistake to have visited. She circled her desk, and sat like she'd been felled.

"Sales haven't picked up Ben," she said in a tone impossible to misinterpret. "We'll give it the weekend." She looked regretful, and we shared the moment, until her glancing at the phone willing it to ring suggested it was time I left.

Leaving her offices, I squeezed through Soho gearing up for a Friday night. The banks were shut, so it was too late to deposit my cheque. Once I was on the train back to Deptford I realised I'd left *Great Expectations* in Kathleen's reception. I was grateful it hadn't been the two copies of *Mirrors and Lies*.

I was pleased to see Daisy later that evening in Greenwich's *Trafalgar Tavern*. I was early again, so I fetched drinks, while Daisy untangled her scarf. I hope Daisy appreciated the last round I could afford to buy.

"How's the hand?" she asked on my return.

I raised it like a trophy, almost spilling my drink.

"Scott called me," she said. "He really wants you to work for him. Have you got any journalism?"

"An article about yew trees," I smiled. "It's considered a potent channel for connecting with ancestors and the otherworld."

"Who by?"

"By idiots, mainly."

When I got home I sat on my sofa, missing my mother and ex-girlfriend. I put the cheque back in its frame. I was determined not to use it.

I rang Kathleen on Monday morning.

"There's no improvement on the sales I'm afraid," she said, followed by a silence suggesting that she had breakfast on her desk that she was desperate to eat. "You got published Ben. Most don't." It went quiet.

"Did I leave *Great Expectations* in your reception?" I asked. We ignored the irony.

"Oh yes, he took it."

"Who?"

"Oh, someone came in asking about *Mirrors and Lies*, after you left on Friday. He must've heard the radio show. But he didn't wait."

I thought of the reception I'd never see again, and wondered who the visitor could be.

"He didn't say who he was," she continued. "A journalist I think. He's got your Dickens." It sounded like my last chance had left the room, yet Kathleen had more to say.

"Ben, there's something else." Her voice took the sincere tone of a donkey sanctuary leaflet.

"There is?"

"We need to discuss your advance. As you know, we fronted the marketing of *Mirrors and Lies*, and I fear we didn't recoup our outlay."

If she hoped I'd take this well, she was wrong. "I thought that was my money?"

"It would have been, had the sales made enough money to cover it."

I sensed the floor beneath my feet disappearing.

"Ben?" she asked.

"I'm here." We were lucky I had no jug of ale in my hand.

"Minus the percentage of book sales," she paused, "I'm afraid you owe us four thousand, six hundred and fifty pounds." There was silence. "But, we can make it a round four thousand six. It's best you don't cash that cheque."

Crisis unfailingly exposes weak scaffolding in your life. I threw away the frame holding the cheque. It smashed in the wheelie bin at the bottom of my block's communal rubbish chute. I looked for the Life Assistance Agency card, but I'd left it as a bookmark in *Great Expectations*. Rather too conveniently I found myself needing Scott's help.

Monday's West End had lost its weekend shine. Refuse lorries competed with hassled commuters. Scott was a little too pleased to see me for my liking.

"Daisy said you need assistance?" he said, smugly sitting back in his chair again; I wished he'd fallen over backwards. All he needed was a desk to put his feet on.

"I do, but I can't imagine how you can help." He raised an eyebrow. "Or assist," I added.

He looked as though he already knew I had no choice but to work for his joke of a business.

"I'll pay you," he said, appearing surprised at his own suggestion.

"How much?"

"What were you on?" he asked.

"Enough to pay the rent."

This caused momentary panic, but he pressed on with his offer.

"How about three months rent on completion of our first case?"

Even without a first case it was worth more than my smashed cheque languishing in a wheelie bin. However, I had worked with enough salesmen to request his offer in writing.

After a farcical search for a pen, he agreed.

So, I officially joined the Life Assistance Agency, that's if financial promise for unspecified services to an unsecured case scrawled across the back of a sports shop flyer was legally binding.

"We're stronger together, Ben," he argued. The circle's complete."

Logic from *the Lion King* was hard to counter, and Scott re-entered my life with the subtlety of Elton John's birthday.

"The kettle's on the landing, which pretty much completes your induction."

"A cup of tea then?" I suggested.

"Excellent idea, your first of many as an LAA agent." He paused. "Or operative? What d'you think?"

He was interrupted by the intercom buzzing; he leaned out the window. Parked downstairs on the curb was a UPS van.

"Promotional key rings for Mr Wildblood?" The driver shouted up, holding a package that Scott eyed with suspicion. The deliveryman put them in the doorstep. "I'll get the rest," he called up.

"What do you mean, the *rest*?" Scott asked, as he adopted the confusion familiar to anyone who's got up from a beanbag in a hurry. His overheads had just outstripped even his projected earnings, spending £2000 on company key rings. 10,000 of the bloody things, as opposed to the 100 he had ordered. The supplier's Customer Services Department was less well staffed than its Sales department. However, his despondency did not last.

The following day, I arrived at Hanway Street in more need of life assistance than an operative, consultant, or agent probably should. A tall man, failing to duck coming down the stairs, cursed as his head struck the gas cupboard. I asked if he was

OK, but avoiding eye contact, he paced off towards Tottenham Court Road. I thought I recognised him, but you get that a lot in London. He had disappeared by the time I presumed we had met at one of my three book signings. I climbed the stairs to find Scott wiping away what appeared to have been a family tree from the whiteboard.

"One down then," I said.

"What's that?"

"That tall bloke just leaving with a Life Assistance card. Was he a client? He certainly wasn't a Russian model."

"Oh yes. No one leaves Hanway Street without a card." His smile looked forced. "He'll be in touch."

But, the rest of the day dragged into a week requiring no life alchemy, coincidence arranging, or bonsai trimming. We took shifts in pacing Soho's streets with the Life Assistance Agency sandwich board, which was something Scott had neglected to mention as part of our duties. Nothing screams that you need help quite like wearing a Life Assistance Agency advertising board.

"It takes *one* phone call." Scott argued. I began wishing the woman with the missing cat would call back.

"Are you sure there's a need for a life assistance agency?"

"Of course. You build a wishing well, and people'll drop in coins."

The sandwich board hurt my shoulders and I was cursing Scott's business plan based upon Kevin Costner's *Field of Dreams*. An afternoon pint in the *Harp* seemed a good idea, when my mobile rang. It was Daisy, asking how the assisting was going.

"If *we* don't get any we're out of business." I explained. Everyone was OK, although my reflection in *Patisserie Valerie* suggested otherwise. "We need a millionaire missing his parrot, or just a missing millionaire..."

"I don't know if he's a millionaire," she interrupted. "But there's someone missing from Mortlake. My parents live near there."

"How d'you know?" I asked.

"I've known them all my life," she laughed. "No, there's a wanted poster..."

Back at the office I told Scott, who instantly looked happier than a baby swimming in dummies. I rang the number Daisy's parents had found and was about to cancel the call, when a woman finally answered.

"Hello," I said. "We saw the poster." There was silence. "For the missing person...?"

"Yes, for my husband." She hesitated. "My friend posted them up."

This was awkward. I asked if he was still missing, aware we needed him to be.

She sounded tired. "Yes. He is. The police aren't interested," she said, "They're more interested in keeping custody suites empty." She sighed. "Anyway, who are you?"

"We're a life assistance agency."

"*The...*" Scott hissed, "*The* Life Assistance Agency."

"The what?" she asked, like I was selling chocolate kettles. "Can you help?" she asked.

For a moment my friend's enthusiasm sparked my own and I agreed we could. She provided an address in Mortlake and we caught the Piccadilly Line.

Chapter 5

While London had gone to shit, Mortlake hadn't. TVs were turned up against the jets of Heathrow's flight path, but the streets had manners; litter walked itself to the bin. The smell of hops hung in the late afternoon air. A weak wind was refusing to budge the intoxicating cloud from *Budweiser*'s brewery. We passed women in gut wrenchingly short dresses. It felt like being in a Bentley showroom with a Boots advantage card. Life's sickest joke is erosion of novelty. Admittedly, preservation of novelty would leave mankind still giggling at mobiles in playpens, but a homeless man given a room soon wants a house.

We found a handsome Edwardian house stood back from the road. A garden ran to the Thames behind. We rang the bell. A middle-aged woman dyeing against grey introduced herself as Mrs Foxe. Scott, always a man proffering a hand to shake from a hundred yards did not disappoint.

"Hello, Mrs Foxe." He said, charm un-holstered and handing over a business card. "I'm Scott Wildblood. Proprietor and," he glanced at me, "operative at London's Life Assistance Agency."

Mrs Foxe appeared to be dressed in Knightsbridge, in that country/city fashion of Barbour jackets and designer jeans.

"Call me Connie," she said, her eyes widening as she read the card's services. She was accustomed to money, but was friendly and no snob. She invited us in. She looked worn. The house smelled of town halls. We passed through a panelled hallway, past a grandfather clock and hallway doors leading into a sitting room that overlooked an unkempt garden backing onto the river.

"My husband's the gardener," she explained. "Tea?"

"Definitely," replied Scott like his life had been depending upon it.

Still recovering from Scott's enthusiasm, she left us in a room lined with enough books to pull down the walls. The clock chimed from the hallway.

"Does operative sound more efficient?" Scott whispered. "Better than agent? Deputy?"

I feared he was about to look for a thesaurus in the bookcase, when Mrs Foxe returned. Scott stood to help her settle the tray – the chink of China a long way from London's grime. She tapped the teapot and asked if the Life Assistance Agency had good testimonials. I guessed the chipped cups were for tradesmen. Scott cleared his throat.

"This is our second case. We're hoping *you*'ll be our first testimonial."

"The previous was unwilling to provide one?" she asked. "I don't know why I'm trusting a two-bit operation like yours, but I am desperate."

I thought 'two-bit' sounded generous, but said nothing, restricting my contribution thus far to that of a singer on an instrumental.

Scott flipped open his notepad. He actually licked his pen, before asking how long Mr Foxe had been missing.

"It's been exactly two weeks," she replied. "He'd like that, the synchronicity of your arrival. He'd probably like your Agency too."

"Has he disappeared before?" Scott asked, evidently warming to this Mr Foxe.

"He disappears all the time, into his own head, the pub,

or brass rubbing his way 'round Europe. You know, psycho-geography. You know what they're like."

Scott didn't, so I saved him.

"Wandering around finding poetry in topography, architecture, that sort of thing," I explained, "It's more wondering than wandering."

"Unexplored mews keep him awake at night," Mrs Foxe agreed, looking surprised I had spoken. "I'm afraid his interest doesn't stop at mews. But he's never disappeared for this long."

"He tells you everything?" Scott interrupted.

"Of course not. No one needs to know *everything*. People are entitled to secrets."

My ex-girlfriend would have disagreed.

"*Particularly* in marriage," she added, "But most things, yes." She sipped her tea. "He left a note." She handed it across. 'Back soon'. Scott read it, before surprising us by asking the colour of Mr Foxe's hair.

"Black," she replied, "But he's not a man you'd describe by hair colour, but the fact he still has it. He's bright, with faith, a potent mix."

"And there's no one else?" Scott asked awkwardly.

"Good Lord no, I don't see other men."

"I meant *him*."

"No." She laughed. "He's devoted. I'm his riverbank."

"You have children?" Scott asked.

She shook her head. "No. That was a stipulation I had to accept." She went quiet. "Despite that, he likes life. It's surprising how many people don't. He's always reading. To know one's heart is to know the world, apparently." She smiled. "He's a lecturer, at UCL. He looks after their Renaissance history. I do the shopping." She winked, handing over a small mirror. Its top was etched: 'As above, as below'.

"What provoked his disappearance?"

"I had a scare. Septicaemia. I was on a drip. They caught it in time. But Thomas wasn't happy."

"With the hospital?"

"With me." She hesitated. "I've never seen him so worried. And I've never felt so loved." She blinked, as though to brace herself. "Can I trust you?"

Troops would have followed Scott's nod over the top.

"The London Stone's disappeared," she said, "Not that anyone noticed, but it's too much of a coincidence." She stood to find a book with librarian ease and read aloud. "The London Stone, an ancient and mysterious object mentioned by Shakespeare, Dr. Dee, William Blake and Dickens. It's one of the capital's greatest relics since the Middle Ages, and earlier." She paused. *"So long as the stone of Brutus is safe, so long shall London flourish,* says the proverb."

She watched Scott struggling with his pen. He approached technology with the competence of knitting one handed. She found him one that worked.

"You remind me of him." She paused. "Now, how much is this assistance?" she asked, too interestedly to strike a bargain.

"We certainly can assist," Scott assured her. "And Ben misses nothing."

"An accountant?" she asked.

"No, a writer."

She looked at me with renewed sympathy, glancing at my numb hand. "More dangerous than it looks?" She asked, before taking a deep breath. "Well, Thomas was listening to Radio 4, or dictating in the study. It was a day after the letter arrived."

"Letter?"

"The letter I opened. When he recognised the handwriting, he snatched it from me. The torn bit's here."

She fetched it from a bureau. Fragments of indecipherable

writing covered the torn corner. It wasn't language we recognised. Scott squinted.

"Dear Mr Foxe..." he attempted to translate. "Nope, we'll have to take it to our people." Scott pulled a paperback from his bag. "If that's ok?" She nodded, and he placed the ripped corner of the letter carefully between its pages.

"It was from Oliver Turner," Connie explained. "They worked briefly together a few years ago now. It ended badly. They're both members of the Society." She clocked Scott's immediate interest. "The Society of Psychical Research. They look 'round corners."

"Another life assistance agency," exclaimed Scott.

"There's room for another?" she asked.

"Probably not, we *are* unique. "We provide..."

"Thomas and Oliver Turner fell out after they were introduced by the Society," she interrupted his pitch. "It was soon after Thomas and I met," she admitted. "I didn't like Turner, or what they were up to."

"What were they up to?"

She hesitated. "I'm not sure I fully understood."

We waited for her to continue, but she did not.

"What happened to Oliver Turner?" Scott asked.

"I don't know. He was an arrogant sod, bit of a banker, if you know what I mean. He stormed out of here twenty years ago, and didn't come back. Went abroad I think."

There was little else she could tell us, so she saw us to the door. A huge, blacked out SUV was parked opposite.

"Our people?" I laughed, as we walked back to the station.

"Yes, we need a linguist. Obviously we'll outsource. Unless your esoteric language knowledge is up to scratch?" he asked, as the blakeys in his heels clicked purposefully. "Do you think Mr Foxe *has* disappeared?" He pondered. "You think she's made it look like he has? Isn't it always someone in the family?"

"You don't think she's knocked him off?"

Living with a heartbroken-mother had schooled me in noticing female heartache, and I recognised Mrs Foxe's desperation. I was ready to go home, but Scott was apparently unfinished for the day

"Let's visit Cannon Street, to confirm the London Stone is missing," he said.

"Really? Surely we have better things to do than go and see something that isn't there?"

We took the tube across town and emerged with St Pauls looming over us. Its limestone stood bone-like against a darkening London sky. As expected, the London Stone wasn't there. There was a grille, fronting a small hole in the side of a non-descript banking building that swallowed daily lives. The London stone kept a profile even lower than the suits passing it each day, but not low enough to avoid being stolen.

"So *that's* why things are buggered." Scott said, looking up at the building above. I must have made my doubting noise, because he looked at me.

"Ben," he said, "Who knows what mysteries keep the world together. Like Mrs Foxe said, so long as the Stone of Brutus is safe, so London shall flourish."

If that was proof, then Mars bars really did help you work, rest and play. Was the Stone London's kryptonite, reducing the capital to a shy, bumbling city-on-work-experience? We stared at the gap in the wall like one gazes at historic sites, wishing they would repair themselves, for Norsemen or monks, to stream from their arches.

Chapter 6

I took the morning tube into Soho. It was packed with passengers failing to disguise their distaste for each other. However, I had discovered a disconcerting sense of purpose. I passed through Tottenham Court Road's barriers like a regular, and found Scott already in the office. He was staring at the whiteboard, wearing the expression of someone about to announce excitable political policies.

London Stone
Mr Foxe
Oliver Turner
Society for Psychical Research (THE SOCIETY)
Translate letter

Ain't Nothing Going on but the Rent drifted through the floor from downstairs.

"Oliver Turner. He's a writer, so he'll have made sure he's google-able."

That was hard to dispute. Writers spend so much time ensuring they are google-able that they neglect to actually write. Turner was an exception. There wasn't much on him. There was a book published by the Society for Psychical Research, but it was out of print. There was some blurb about him having disappeared, to pursue other interests, but anyone who's written a book entitled *Crystal Balls and Crystal Bowls; the art of modern scrying and ancient seership* is unlikely to have other interests. Readers hoping for a sequel would need to be patient, and apart from a dusty website, advertising his ability to scry for angels in a font mostly used by primary education, there was nothing.

At Scott's suggestion, our translation people turned out to be a client of Kathleen's. Explaining to the receptionist that I was after a linguist and not to plead for representation got me put through. Kathleen was offish in a way only ex-literary agents can be. However, she provided me with the linguist's telephone number, before asking if the man enquiring after me had been in touch. I'd forgotten about that. I lied by saying he had, and abandoned any hope of seeing *Great Expectations* again.

I called the linguist. She agreed to look at the language and gave me her fax number. Our Life Assistance Agency obviously had no fax machine, but the local newsagent did, although the owner had apparently forgotten. He removed a stack of newspaper returns, and punched in the number to dispatch the torn corner of the letter.

"What's that bleeping?" I asked Scott on my return to our office.

"It's my stick'n'find tracking device. I've lost it. Its battery's dying."

"You've *lost* a tracking device?"

He handed me his iPhone so I could study the display indicating the bug's location. It flashed co-ordinates.

"Are these longitude and latitude?" I asked.

Scott nodded vaguely. I looked around, before finding it magnetised to the back of the empty filing cabinet.

"You think Mr Foxe is ok?" Scott asked, taking the device back without thanking me.

"How do I know?" I said. "It's all rather far fetched isn't it?"

"So's life, Ben, you *know* that. Writers' don't make stuff up, they just write it down."

"This one doesn't."

"So, we'll assist with that too."

Mrs Foxe was less sure about our return to Mortlake, and who can blame her. Allowing life assistance agencies into your home is the sort of idiocy making newspaper headlines. She showed us into the study.

"Mind your head.' She tapped the doorframe. "Not that he ever does."

There was a mantelpiece, and disused fireplace. It was an ideal room for writing, with ceiling mouldings and overlooking the lawn. Mind you, nothing demolishes creativity like the perfect environment in which to express it. The bookcases were overflowing. A *Roberts* radio sat on the desk.

"He's read them all," she said. "What're you looking for?"

"Everything. Then we whittle down," Scott reassured her like someone unaccustomed to whittling. I spotted a quote pinned to the wall, and read it aloud.

"Two conflicting impulses rule our short time on earth. One draws us forward, towards the distant horizon, curious to find out what lies beyond; the other roots us to one place and weds us to the sky. Both impulses are ours; they define us, as human beings."

Scott transcribed it into his notebook, before seeing the desk.

"Nice desk," he said, unable to keep envy from his voice. With a desk's top drawer being the first place to look, Scott went to the bottom. It was locked.

"Life *assistance*," he reminded me, as cavalier use of a penknife assisted the drawer open.

I was uncomfortable looking through personal papers. Men have scarce privacy, and intruding upon it betrayed something. We found a photo of a man in a military uniform. It was dated 1944. He was standing on the footplate of a Willy's jeep holding a Bren gun. There was also a feather from some country walk, keys long forgotten by their locks, and a corkboard pin with a tiny flag, on which was written Swift.

"An uncle of his. He was in the war," Connie called from the door. "There's a strong similarity."

I noticed Scott frowning, before pulling out the drawer entirely, and lifting it onto the desk.

"Look," he observed. "It's shorter than it should be." He kneeled down, to reveal a safe box embedded into the wall behind the drawer. It had a small keyhole.

"Did you know about this?" he asked Mrs Foxe.

She looked impressed for the first time, but shook her head. "I had no idea, nor where the key is, before you ask."

The study was where the sitting room's books graduated. The titles alone would melt a spell check: Alistair Crowley's *Magik*, Thomas Val's, *Dark Pools: The Art of Scrying*.

"What's scrying?" Scott asked me, and Mrs. Foxe groaned before I could answer.

"It's the calling of angels through reflective surfaces," I explained.

She nodded, "He gave it up, thank God." She sat on a sofa worn in places that betrayed a familiarity with afternoon napping.

"I can't be the first woman with an ear to the door of their husband's life." She sounded tired. "It was a long time ago. They were still building the Piccadilly line extension to Heathrow. The works traffic was louder than that bloody grandfather clock. Thomas and Turner had been up for days-"

"Oliver Turner?"

"Yes, the retired City trader I mentioned. Some bright young thing. He made stacks of cash on the metal exchange. After that I guess he had time on his hands, and got involved with Thomas' hobbies. Look-" She looked at us. "Thomas is a lecturer, so an inability to find reading glasses, occasional mumbling, and student affairs I can deal with, but his angel nonsense was too much. It's why I listened in on them. I sensed something wrong, so peered through the door. They were too distracted to see me."

"What did you hear?"

"I heard Thomas flattering Turner that he was a better scryer than even the Society had claimed." She closed her eyes. "There's a reason I remember it so well." She began talking, but Scott suggested she pause, so I could make notes. This is what she told us, or at least what I wrote down:

"The windows were shaking from them building the Piccadilly line. The fire in the hearth was dying. They'd been in the study with a large crystal ball for three days. It stood on a slab of black obsidian. Thomas had all his stuff out, even the rosewood disc that he'd engraved with precise tables. He was ready for the younger man's arrival. He'd even brushed his hair. I think Thomas had a standing arrangement with the Society to alert him to promising scryers. Once Turner arrived, I didn't really see them, but when I bumped into Thomas he was excited, telling me they were nearer than anyone had been for years, maybe centuries. However," she paused. "It wasn't enough. Turner wasn't who he was looking for."

"Who was he looking for?" Scott asked

"He's never told me, but someone with the sort of skills you apparently can't learn, but only inherit. And it always takes two people to scry. Anyway, Turner started asking too many questions, about where Thomas had got Dr. Dee's grids to translate the angels' language. Thomas was getting irritated, I heard him repeating that Dee wrote 'every new line has a start.' Turner was arrogant enough to think that it referred to him, but Thomas told him he lacked the skills. However, he suggested that Turner might help him find the person who was assigned the Angel stone. Turner said that he had better things to do than chase someone who was assigned the stone but died four hundred years ago. To be honest I sympathised." She smiled.

"So, Thomas starts saying how the angels choose who see them, but he's aware Turner is looking at the rosewood disc, as though trying to memorise the tables. Frankly, it'd be easier to memorise computer code. So, Thomas puts his foot through the disc and throws it on the fire. Turner grabs a poker to rather hopelessly salvage it. 'Don't worry,' says Thomas. 'The tables survive elsewhere. The angels aren't interested in us.' But Turner was furious. '*I* saw them clearly enough.' he says. And starts swearing about how scrying burns his mind, not that Thomas would know. He suggests that perhaps *he's* the weakest link. At this point I opened the door.

"Breakfast?" I asked like someone who'd slept, probably to rub it in. Turner winced at the light. I ignored the crystal balls, ancient symbols and choking smell of charred wood.

Thomas stood away from the fireplace, "Good morning Connie. Oliver was just leaving..."

Turner found himself in the panelled hallway clutching his bag. He muttered farewell, adding that he intended to cut through to the river for a walk behind the house. He waved, and departed. The grandfather clock struck 7am. Thomas stared glassily at the front door. My hand found his. He clutched it and smiled.

"You didn't reach them?" I asked

"No," he hesitated. "But perhaps I should propose

anyway."

"I had no idea wedding proposals depended upon seeing angels." I paused, "And please don't say I am one, it's early, and I may vomit."

I kissed him, but he had stopped listening. He rushed back into the study, and frowned. The curtains were billowing into the room. He pulled them, to find the window wide open. Turner must have doubled-back alongside the house and hopped the fence. Thomas turned back to the room. The crystal ball was missing.

"*Fuck.*"

I don't know much about cars, but the shredded roar of a V8 is unmistakable. Oliver Turner's Aston Martin was probably in Brentford before Thomas could get his Jag out of the garage.

Chapter 7

I suspected it was the first time Mrs Foxe had told anyone this. I stopped taking notes, but Scott suggested I keep going.

"So, they were calling angels?" Scott asked. "And that letter he snatched from you? You say it was from Oliver Turner?" Scott sat down behind the desk, making himself more comfortable than was polite.

"Yes," she nodded.

He picked up a Dictaphone, while I looked more closely at the books.

"He's more scared of me dying than I am. He wants to cure the fear of death." She explained.

"It's like losing your shadow," said Scott.

"Pardon?"

"Sorry," I apologised on Scott's behalf. "He does that. Scott had a near-death experience," I explained. "And saw nothing," I added, before she could ask.

Scott held up a book on alchemy.

"It's harder than it looks," she commented. Professionalism prevented me from asking *how* alchemy is harder than it looks

"He used to practice," she said, "but Oliver Turner was his last scryer. There were no others. They were obsessed during their time together. Thankfully it didn't last long. Them corresponding again bodes badly."

"The letter," Scott interrupted, "Was it unsolicited? Did it *cause* his disappearance, or was it a *reply*?"

"I don't know. I like to think Thomas chose me over

Turner, but who knows, maybe things changed. Turner never forgave Thomas for drawing a line under their endeavours. He wasn't used to people saying no. Wealthy people never are."

Scott held up the Dictaphone, "And this?"

"He thinks out-loud," she warned, "Into that. He was using it when the Society visited." She smiled, "They're an old man's youth club that Six Foot fell out with."

"Six Foot?"

"Sorry, yes, Thomas' nickname. He actually *is* six foot, but it's from the 60s. Six foot was standardised distance between hospital beds."

We looked confused.

"He keeps his distance," she explained. "He doesn't let people close."

I noticed a copy of *Great Expectations*. Momentarily, I thought it was mine, although there was no LAA business card bookmark. It was then I also noticed a hardback copy of *Mirrors and Lies* on the desk. It was unsigned, and already dog-eared, with pages torn out, mainly autobiographical sections about my mother. Perhaps I should have changed her name. I felt a puff of pride, seeing it out in the wild.

"See, I'm not the only person who's read it," said Scott. He looked at Mrs. Foxe. "Ben wrote that," he explained.

"*You* wrote that?" Mrs. Foxe looked annoyed. "He was reading it before he disappeared."

She left the room to squealing voices as Scott pressed rewind on the Dictaphone. He rewound it to the beginning, and pressed play.

Mr. Foxe was murmuring complicated equations to himself in an evenly paced voice when he was interrupted by a knock at the door. The Dictaphone clunked as Mr Foxe put it down. There were muffled voices.

"Good evening Mr Foxe," said a London accent.

"What engenders this visit?" Foxe asked.

"You know the reason." There was silence. "Your renewed interest in old matters. As you know, we did as you asked. We located him for you twenty years ago."

"For which I'm grateful."

"Practices of *his* nature are hard to conceal."

"Well I couldn't find him."

"A single man lacks the reach of many Mr Foxe, you'd do well to remember that." More silence. "So why the interest in Oliver Turner again?" The same voice asked. "You two haven't been close since we introduced you."

"Let's just say he owes me something. As do you." Foxe replied.

"Your work has been invaluable to us, I'll grant you."

The grandfather clock could be heard chiming in the background.

"And why the request for our storage item?" The voice continued. "You'd assured us of your retirement..."

"Consider it a comeback."

"You're a little old for comebacks." He coughed. "And the London Stone?"

"You think I have it? You think it has powers?" Foxe said.

"Evidently it has powers, look at London." They paused, as though to consider the state of the city. "*Thomas*, come now," his tone was softer.

"Surely, you don't heed Brutus' old proverb? The *mythical* King of old Briton? Blaming London's decay on the London Stone is preposterous."

The silence gathered menace. Mr. Foxe did not answer.

"Very well," said the voice, "But we'll be watching." The words landed like hammer falls. "We're now less concerned that the item you requested from our European storage depot was stopped at Customs."

"It's been held?" Foxe sounded worried for the first time. Chairs scraped the floor.

"Goodbye Mr Foxe. We'll keep ourselves informed."

We heard the door close and Scott pressed stop, as Mrs Foxe returned with some photos.

"You've found something?" she asked.

"The forecast's clearer," Scott replied.

"It's *always* clearer if you wait long enough."

Scott gave the photos a cursory glance, before passing them across. A tall man stood against a cabinet. His tightly cut grey hair showed little sign of balding. His eyes reflected a wry smile, incongruous amongst the scholarly background. The resemblance to the uncle standing on the jeep was remarkable. Scott asked about the cabinet we'd passed in the hallway that matched the one in the photo.

"He collects Second World War guns. Family heirlooms." Mrs Foxe explained, as she saw us to the door. "The key's probably in the same place as the one for the safe behind the drawer."

This recently discovered secret was clearly bothering her.

"Does he own a corkboard?" Scott asked. I guessed he was thinking of the *Swift* flag pin we had found.

"A corkboard? I don't think so. Do you?" she smiled.

"I have a whiteboard." Scott shook his head. "We'll take this though," he picked up Mr Foxe's copy of my *Mirrors and Lies*. "If you don't mind?"

"Take it." She smiled. "It's too cynical even for me."

From the train Scott called his girlfriend Ronnie, who invited us for a drink.

"Who was your bird at Vital?" he asked, when he was done. "What happened?"

Was I so obviously single?

"Claire. She found my bank statements. Restaurants I hadn't taken her to," I admitted, shuddering at the memory.

I seldom enjoy other people's houses. Like regulars at *the Crown,* I prefer neutral environments. Ronnie was a writer, photographer and artist. Her converted warehouse in Silvertown, beneath the flat skies of east London, amongst disused docks and rotting jetties, was large enough to house her studio. Final clocking-outs echoed in the air. We edged past canvasses stacked in the hallway.

"I'm in here," she called and, rounding crumbling brickwork into the kitchen, we met a staggeringly shapely behind wearing sprayed-on jeans. She emerged from a fridge.

"Is that you Borrowed?" she asked, as she reversed out with a plate of cheesecake.

Ronnie stood and stretched. Her breasts momentarily pressed against her t-shirt. She leaned in for an introductory kiss. I brushed her cheek, breathing her in. I prayed she could not hear my thundering heart. She looked after herself, the sort of woman with lip-balm in every pocket.

"I'm too hung-over to get out of a fridge," she laughed.

She looked better hungover than anyone should. She said something, but I didn't hear. Her eyes grinned even when her mouth was not. Scott was looking at me, apparently for an answer, but I had no idea to what.

"Ronnie asked about your hand?"

"Oh, an accident," I said.

"Careless," she smiled and my heart inflated. "I'm Ronnie."

"Hello. And what's that you call Scott? Borrowed? Borrowed money?"

"It's his nickname. Borrowed Time."

Scott handed me a beer. "Although Ronnie *is* one of the Life Assistance Agency's capital venturists."

"One of? You mean *the* only." She laughed.

"Well, meet our latest recruit. Ben's joined the Life Assistance Agency."

"Congratulations." She looked at me with undisguised pity. "The A-team really is back in business isn't it?"

"That's what I said,' I smiled, sounding like I deserved a medal.

"Well, we can argue over who's Face at the first weekly meeting," Scott said, popping open my beer.

"Well, Murdock's obvious." Ronnie winked at me.

Sodium streetlights complemented the candles in her sitting room. Books were stacked everywhere. I wandered over to a bookcase. There were various novels and books on Feng Shui, Bonsai trimming, fear of death and even swimming.

"Did you just put the titles of Ronnie's books onto your business card?" I asked Scott.

"Not *just* Ronnie's."

I spent most of the evening as a spectator, trying to understand their relationship. Scott found women easily, or rather they found him, and the day Ronnie struggled to get a man was the day I beat Denzel Washington's top ten badass moments. I eventually left drunk but lonely.

Chapter 8

In Hanway Street's office, Scott stood back to admire the whiteboard on which was now written:

The letter
A secret society
The London Stone
A show stone?
Hidden safe
Oliver Turner

"Remember Foxe's bookcase? *The Sceptical Chymist* by Robert Boyle, *Opus Majus* by Francis Bacon? They're alchemical texts. I've checked. And he's evidently read *Mirrors and Lies*." Scott made it sound like the obvious anomaly in a police line up.

"And that two conflicting impulses quote-" he continued. "It's Alberto Manguel. It's from *the Eternal Wanderer*."

He had been busy. Scott stared at the letter torn from Mrs Foxe's hand. He shook his head impatiently, and handed it over. The strange letters were archaic; like nothing I had seen before.

"Get that linguist on the horn," he suggested. "She'll have got your fax by now."

I phoned and she sounded relieved at human contact. I ignored pleasantries about us sharing a literary agent, because we no longer did. She had received the fax, and suspected the

letters were hieroglyphs, but she rubbished my theory it was
Egyptian.

"It's Enochian. A medieval language used to commune with
angels." She continued. "I don't know much about it. Enochian
appeared in the 1580s. It suggests both Sanskrit, and ancient
Egyptian roots. It's been attached to medieval alchemists,"
she paused dramatically. "Dr Dee and Edward Kelley mainly.
However, Egyptian and Sanskrit were *completely* unknown
in medieval times. No one can explain where Enochian came
from. It's unlikely it was made up. It'd be impossible." She
paused. "But the alternative's equally implausible. That angels
dictated it." She allowed this to sink in. "It's difficult to
translate, all I could make out was: *You've found him?*"

"And-?"

"No, that's it."

What we should do with this development was unclear,
which Scott varnished over by suggesting I visit the University
of London, where Mr. Foxe lectured, to see if they had any
clues as to where he had gone.

A suffocating awareness at my own lack of education
accompanied me as I crossed the university campus off Gower
Street. In Hastings, further education was the High Street.
Scott felt it best if he remained to man the office phone. I
suspected this coincided with potential for a post-lunch nap.

Students wafted around giggling and gossiping. They
were at an age with something *to* gossip about. They were
simultaneously acutely aware of themselves, and yet not. A
flock of girls was ignoring me when the receptionist asked,
possibly for the second time, if she could help. I introduced
myself as Ben Ferguson-Cripps. She was unimpressed, so I
persevered.

"Does Mr Foxe work here?" I asked.

She nodded like it cost her. I handed her a LAA card, refraining from adding a key ring. She studied it blankly.

"I'm looking for Mr Foxe," I explained. "He's missing."

"Mr. Foxe?" interrupted a young man who was loitering nearby. I had not imagined students modeling themselves on Cary Grant. His confidence and unshakeable demeanor annoyed me immediately. He clutched papers like a lawyer fearing commotion on courtroom steps. He waggled a finger, unable to offer a hand.

"Foxe is my tutor," he explained.

It occurred to me that he might be useful, so I offered him a drink. With an eye for a bargain that Cary Grant may have missed, he led me to the Refectory. We sat down, distancing ourselves from the crisp-fuelled gossip.

"Foxe is a star around here," he smiled. "I'm lucky to have him as my tutor. At least I was until he vanished. He's probably at some conference claiming that Dr Dee actually did speak with angels."

I bit my tongue.

"Probably in Europe," continued Cary, blowing on his coffee. "He's obsessed with medieval Prague."

"He is? Why?" I asked.

He looked at me with sympathy. "Because its courts were full of cool shit like alchemists and magicians. 1580's Prague was the centre of new science. The Emperor collected astrologers, alchemists and thinkers. He had *everything*. Tigers, lions, even a bloody dodo."

"Alchemists?" I asked, ignoring my interest in the dodo.

"That was big stuff then," he said, "It was early chemistry." He sipped his coffee. "Does anyone know where he is?"

"No, not even his wife."

"Well, he might be researching another Dr. Dee biography."

"Dr. Dee, the scryer?" I asked. My rudimentary knowledge

of Dee was growing by the day.

"Yeah, a man in desperate need of a Kindle. Dee owned hundreds of books, most of which he took to Europe," he continued. "Holiday reading that needed its own bloody carriage. Dee was a founding fellow of Trinity College. He suggested England adopt the astronomical calendar two hundred years before it did. And wanted a national library before anyone could even read. He'd be better known if he hadn't indulged Kelley's nonsense. He found the north passage to America for Chrissakes."

"Kelley nonsense?" I asked.

"Edward Kelley was his scryer."

"And they summoned angels with crystals?"

He nodded. "Dee couldn't do it alone. No one can. It takes two to scry. You think Foxe disappearing is to do with Dee's stuff being stolen from the British Museum again?"

"I think so," I lied, before noticing the receptionist approaching. She had probably realised I was in a student area. "Stolen *again*?" I asked quickly.

"Yeah, there was a theft in 1892, at the auction of Dee's stones. There was a ruckus in the auction room. The purchaser had to escape in a cab…"

"Stones needed to contact angels?"

He confirmed the need for a specific table to filter the angels' words, and that it had been missing since Dee died, when the receptionist interrupted, reading from the Life Assistance Agency business card.

"Mr Wildblood," she announced. "Mr. Foxe is in Reception."

"What?" Cary was more surprised than I was.

"I've strongly advised he wait," she said, before turning round. "And visitors are *not* allowed in the Refectory area."

Cary was ahead of me as we ran up the steps.

Chapter 9

"He must've left," the receptionist peered around the Reception area. "He was picking up his passport he'd left for I.D." She looked the sort requiring pediatrician statements to secure a library card.

"If he's heading home, he'll be headed for Tottenham Court Road," she continued. "You'll want to know what he's wearing I suppose? The usual trench coat, umbrella..."

I thanked her, and took Cary Grant's number. I reassured him I'd let him know when we found Mr. Foxe. I flew out the door dialing Scott, demanding he station himself on the corner of New Oxford Street. He tried to sound like I hadn't woken him up. Weaving through pedestrians, I described Foxe's clothes, and passed Hanway Street to find Scott already loitering where it joined Oxford Street.

"Trench coat?" he smiled. "He's there." Scott nodded towards *Sports Direct*. There was no one there. "Shit..."

We pressed on, scanning bobbing heads for our quarry. Then I glimpsed a man in a trench coat crossing the road between two buses. He was heading west, his umbrella flicking as he walked. Scott and I split, taking each side of Oxford Street. No one ever looks behind them, so we stayed close. Uncertain why we weren't introducing ourselves, we followed Foxe to Hyde Park Corner, where he crossed towards Marble Arch just before the lights turned green. Lucky timing, or had he seen us? We spotted an underpass, and shot down it before we lost him on the other side.

We galloped up the steps, into a square that was empty, apart from Marble Arch. Foxe had disappeared. It was inexplicable: footprints leading to a cliff edge. The square accommodating Marble Arch was effectively a traffic island. We were looking around, when two men emerged breathlessly from the underpass. They stood a few yards away, struggling to pretend they weren't following us. As I said, no one looks back for a tail, including Life Assistance Agencies. We made eye contact. They seemed less bewildered than us.

"You appear to have lost him," announced one, in a London accent I recognised from Foxe's Dictaphone.

He was squat, wearing a Canadian tuxedo of denim jacket and matching jeans. A beard compensated for his baldness. His expression suggested he was biting foil; though it was probably gum that he was too old for, but was nonetheless chomping at 180 bpm.

"Lost him too have you?" Scott asked, sidestepping mind-games by stating the obvious. They studied us, while scanning the square keenly. There was the unmistakable sound of shit yet to hit the fan.

"Where is he?" asked the other man, who had been saying a lot by saying nothing. He was muscular, wearing a Fred Perry T-shirt beneath a suit. He looked the sort who worked out before the gym; the sort you wouldn't enjoy asking to marry his daughter. He held my gaze. I looked away. Scott was unperturbed. Fred Perry found a cigarette and clicked a Zippo. He inhaled, before blowing vanilla smelling smoke in our direction. He smoked cocktail cigarettes? I felt like the loser in a race to the prop cupboard.

"You the Psychic Society?" asked Scott. Fred stepped forward, but Beardy indicated for him to stand down.

"It's Society of Psychic*al* Research. Where is he?" said Beard, in a tone implying he wouldn't be asking twice. "I suggest this is left to professionals."

"Know some do you?" Scott asked.

I glared at him, but the men left to pace around Marble Arch. There was nothing but restoration work behind billboards. A generator throbbed, but no workers. They returned looking as if they'd had a chat. Fred flicked his cigarette at our feet, before leaning in. His breath was strung with vanilla.

"We're worried for Mr Foxe..." his tone had softened. "He's flipping stones he shouldn't be." He smiled and I wish he hadn't. "If you *do* find anything, keep us looped," he said, as they buttoned up their jackets. "Should've stuck to writing, Ferguson-Cripps."

We watched them leave, before hailing a cab.

"Looped?" I shook my head in disbelief. "What the fuck does that mean? I need a proper job, and how the fuck does he know my name?"

"Ben, *this* is your career now—"

"Career's when you lose control of a car..."

Back in the office, Scott was taking the involvement of an agency significantly more sinister than our own with the shock of someone mislaying his slippers again. He was more interested in the arrival of his second-hand desk. The sound of loud Russian swearing from upstairs suggested the modelling agency was unhappy our deliverymen had abandoned it in the stairwell. We forced it up the stairs, prioritising momentum over communal paintwork. The desk was covered in tea stains and indented with writing. Scott ran his fingers over the indents, before sitting down. He already looked happier.

"Something has to be in that safe behind Foxe's desk. We should visit Mrs Foxe again."

"Sounds like a wasted trip without the key."

I was concerned that Fred knew my name, but it was Scott

who sounded breathless, which in light of his medical condition I was unsure was promising. I watched him as he searched for his medication. I was impressed he had it with him. Scott looked good, but his heart condition lingered backstage. An ambulance fittingly screamed through Hanway Street. Scott swallowed his tablets, before heaving a PC salvaged from the Ark onto the desk.

"It's not the latest kit, but…"

We finally connected to Sly's Wi-Fi, as rockabilly rattled the floorboards from downstairs. We found the website for the Society of Psychical Research. It was founded in 1882 to advance understanding of events and abilities described as psychic or paranormal. They quoted Jung: '*I shall not commit the fashionable stupidity of regarding everything I cannot explain as a fraud.*' They looked respectful enough, although fell out with Sir Arthur Conan Doyle for defending a spirit photographer in the twenties.

"He understood the power of creating someone who didn't exist," I said.

"So, the Society needs Foxe and the London Stone returned."

"Scott," I interrupted, "Aren't you even a little bit disturbed by their agents?"

"You mean societal *members*? Perhaps Foxe is testing a myth."

I left Scott to swear at the Internet and went to fill the kettle.

"Seems Foxe isn't the first to be interested in the London Stone," Scott called. "William Blake, Shakespeare, and this Dr Dee…"

What was it with Dr Dee? It was like trying to drown a duck; he kept popping up.

"He was fascinated by the London Stone," Scott read. "He may have sampled it, for alchemy."

I took a deep breath, bracing myself for Scott's enthusiasm, and told him what Cary Grant had mentioned about the theft of Dee's possessions from auction in 1892.

It was growing dark outside; streetlights hummed on. Scott put on a CD, and stood to write on the whiteboard. *Racing in the Street* by Bruce Springsteen filled the room.

"Foxe is missing," Scott yelled over the music. "So's the London Stone. Foxe is an alchemist, as was Dr Dee, who *also* borrowed the Stone."

"What is it with you and Springsteen?"

"It's hard to explain," he grinned. "People run when I start."

I remembered the Cary Grant student also describing the theft from the British Museum. We searched and found an article from *the Telegraph*:

RARE 16th-century artifacts that belonged to a maverick consultant to Elizabeth I have been stolen from the British Museum in London. A man dressed in a long leather coat smashed a display case and ran out of the Museum before security guards could catch him. The wax discs, believed to be used in conjunction with a crystal ball, were used by mediums for curing disease. The crystal ball belonged to John Dee, philosopher, mathematician and astrologer, who lived between 1527 and the turn of the 17th century. Dee became an authority on 'angel magic' and beliefs that man had the potential for divine power. The thief also took the statement about the ball's use by the pharmacist Nicholas Culpeper, written on the reverse of ancient deed manuscripts in the mid-1600s. The theft happened on Thursday afternoon. Detectives are investigating whether the items were stolen to order.

Chapter 10

The next day Scott dragged me to the British Museum. Museums match bookshops in exposing one's sense of mortality. The surrounding glass cabinets mainly contained lumps of history requiring huge imaginative leaps to connect wood with ships, shrapnel to swords and teeth to mouths. They were all fighting ever-losing battles with the gift shop. In one cabinet with newly puttied-glass, we found a rounded case tapering towards the top. In faded ink the words read: 'Dr Dee's shew stone...' It wasn't a light sabre, but history rumbled. The other stands were vacant, presumably from the robbery. We crossed to the information desk, hoping it would fulfil its name. It did not, but pointed us to the archives downstairs.

"Thieves took the two wax discs," said a man looking too ruddy to be working in a basement. He had the bonhomie of a lollypop lady and was delighted by our interest. "Anything to get them back," he explained.

"Was it all the discs?"

"No, there used to be four. Our two were dug up at a crossroads in Poland. It's suspected that Dr Dee hid them there. The wax discs are engraved with magical symbols. They supported Dee's table of practice. They, well, they were filters, to stop too much from the other side." He sighed. "But our crystal ball, well-" he hesitated. "I'm not sure it was the original. It never *felt* right."

"A crystal ball?"

"By the aid of this magic stone," he said. "We can see

whatever persons we desire, no matter where they are, hidden in the most retired apartments, or even in the caverns in the bowels of the Earth."

"Pardon?" He'd lost us.

"Sorry, I was quoting, Dr. Dee." he explained.

"This was stuff needed to call angels?" Scott asked.

The man nodded. "Dee had a table, engraved with exact charts the angels used to communicate. The legs stood on the wax discs. And the crystal ball sat on the black obsidian mirror. All very neat," he smiled. "The tables were utterly precise. They were needed to decipher the angels' language. Without them no one got close."

"What did the police say?"

"You've already stayed longer than they did," he replied.

"Where did the discs come from?" Scott asked.

"From the Robert Cotton collection that founded this museum. Cotton dug most of them up. They tended to hide stuff in the ground in medieval times."

"And the other two discs?"

"They've been lost for years, since Dee's time probably. They're long gone, like his table."

"So, the angels were real?" Scott asked.

"People reaching high levels of spiritual development always sense presence of higher intelligence," he said. "Socrates called it his daemon, others God or Angels. Great insights bring empowerment, which people ascribe to other beings. It's probably just parts of our brain we don't normally use," he concluded. "But *if* anyone could do it, then Dee could – he *wanted* to."

My hand required redressing the following day. As I left the hospital, the new bandage underlining how loose the old had been, I decided to reinvestigate Marble Arch. I was passing and had no better plans. Besides, Foxe's disappearance was bothering me. If he hadn't crossed the road into Hyde Park where had he gone?

Marble Arch was deserted, and best seen from a distance. It was something even tourists instinctively understood. I circled it. The restoration work remained, a generator throbbed; builders remained absent. It was unclear what they were restoring. I peeped through the hoarding at the Arch. Tools and fluorescent jackets were lying around, but more interestingly there was a door into the arch. It was small and easily missed, but it led somewhere. About to shift the hoarding, I remembered the possibility of a tail, so walked on and rang Scott from the mayhem of Oxford Street.

Marble Arch looked surreal at night: floodlit elegance breaking the modern surface from a classical underworld. We sheltered in bushes alongside. Although wearing black, we appeared more *Beano* than SAS. We had lost the Society at Lancaster Gate by jumping tubes, or so we hoped. Scott found the crowbar from his bag. He'd sprayed it black, but mostly his hands. His directions were more precise:

"Go in. Make it count."

We were nervous, and I hoped my hunch that there were rooms inside the Marble Arch was right. We had barely discussed how to confront Mr Foxe, should we find him. We ran from the shrubbery and slipped through the hoarding. We found the door locked and apparently untouched. Scott positioned the crowbar at the doorframe alongside the lock. We exchanged glances like amateur skydivers, before he leaned on it. The iron slipped. I looked around and he tried again. This time, with a pistol-like crack, the wood around the lock splintered, and we opened it to damp cellar-like air.

We climbed a narrow wooden staircase creaking with

disuse. It led to a room occupying the top of the Arch. It was dark, with light leaking in from small porthole windows. There was no Mr. Foxe, but there was a small fireplace holding a fallen nest. On the wall, above a camp bed, sleeping bag and a duffle bag was a corkboard headed with gold flake reading: METROPOLITAN POLICE. A fork protruded from a half finished tin of baked beans. They were cold. Tennis balls hung from a part of lowered ceiling, doubling as planets. Streetlight from the portholes bathed the room in an orange glow. I reached for a book from the pile alongside the camp bed.

"*Don't move anything*," Scott snapped.

"And the broken door...?"

"Here's why he broke cover." Scott ignored my glaringly valid point. He held up a passport, and some black waxed paper. He continued to ignore his own advice by ripping off a strip and folding it into his pocket.

"We'll get our people onto it," he said, smiling. "And look, the pin board." He studied the pins with numbers written on tiny flags. There was another one reading S̶w̶i̶f̶t̶. He looked around. "I'm guessing Mrs Foxe doesn't know about this."

I suspected even the Met police had forgotten about their old station. It occurred to me that it might be a shag pad, but unless European renaissance maps and genealogy impresses women it was unlikely. I joined Scott at the family trees. Dr. John Dee and his wife Jane headed one, with their eight children fanning out below. Alongside it were Edward Kelley and his wife Joanna, but their lineage showed no children, other than a daughter from Joanna's previous marriage. However, a thick line was drawn from Dee's last child, Theodore, to Kelley's side.

Scott moved away. "What's this?" he held up a small key on a chain. I looked at it and hazarded a guess.

"The safe box behind the drawer?" I said, before hearing something. "What was that?" I whispered.

We froze, unclear what it was. If anyone came up the stairs we were trapped. Above us, a trapdoor was too high to reach. There was no further sound. Scott found his phone and took some photographs. He gave a final glance around, before creeping down the stairs. I was alone in the musty room. I thought of Mr Foxe, snuggling into his sleeping bag each night, eye to eye with a tin of baked beans. I imagined the sodium lights and flash of police cars spilling through the night. Why wasn't he at home? My eyes caught a flyer under the pillow.

PUBLIC AUCTION

WE ARE INSTRUCTED BY CUSTOMS & EXCISE BONDED
WAREHOUSE NUMBER 906976876
World class wine by the crate. Margaux, Paulillac, St. Emillion,
Chateauneuf, Pouilly Fuisse
NO RESERVE PRICES
WE ARE ALSO ENSTRUSTED WITH
Certified VS Jewellery, Solitaires, a section of rare watches all boxed and
papers, Rolex, Submariner, Omega, iMACS, iPads, iphones,
Brand new laptops. Persian Silk Rugs
French Impressionist Paintings: Gustav De'Breanski,
Joseph Mellor, Robert Fowler, James Snell, Walter Williams,
Alfred A Vickers, Geoffrey Chatten.
China, Porcelian, and Bronzes
And other rare and collectable valuables intercepted by
CUSTOMS & EXCISE

Auction to be held on Monday 12th
Radisson Blu Portman Hotel,
22 Portman Square, London, W1H 7BG

It was dated yesterday. A bidder card and receipt was paper-clipped to the flyer: Lot 764. Scott hissed from downstairs. I pocketed them, and left to find an uncharacteristically anxious Scott on the stairs.

"Quick!" he whispered, and I hurriedly joined him crouching by the door. Once we opened it we were unable to prevent ourselves from running the final yards, through the tools and clutter, to the bushes, where we squatted to catch our breath. No one had seen us.

My flat was unchanged, but I was not. Fred Perry-wearing Psychic Society agents now competed with Ronnie in my thoughts. In light of her being my friend's girlfriend I had been thinking about her far too much. Mind you, I suspected every man she had ever met was left thinking about her. I wondered what my father might have advised. He'd probably suggest I run.

I was pleased when Daisy rang, until she asked about the third week's paperback's sales.

"Not good," I replied.

"They're slow burners," she reassured me with consumer expertise that had never visited a shop. She was guiding German tourists around the rusting HMS Belfast at London Bridge, built to defend arctic convoys from their fathers. Daisy only mentioned that during her *first* tour.

"Don't panic," she reassured me, unaware that if you fail to make a splash in the first month then the ripples go nowhere.

I sighed, before telling her about 'the Society'. Inverted commas made them sound less real.

"Why're you whispering?" she asked.

It was a good question. If she knew, she'd also ask why I was standing away from the drawn curtains. I mentioned our run-in with the Society, who looked far more like agents than we did. And how *had* they known my name? Daisy swore to protect me, but retracted it once I pointed out Ayurvedic yoga was not yet classed a martial art.

The Life Assistance Agency.

Cases:	1
Clues:	0–6?
Staff:	2½
Business cards (Stock):	2998
Business cards ordered:	3000
Advertising placards:	1

Having g*oogled* to confirm that Marble Arch police station had closed in 1950, I phoned the auction house pretending to be Mr. Foxe. They confirmed that Lot 764, which had purchased yesterday, was now ready for collection in storage. I dared not ask what the item was. After all, I was the one who had supposedly won it. I remembered the Society mentioning an item held at customs on the Dictaphone at Mortlake.

I heard someone trip over downstairs. Scott was back. He entered the room like human cannonballs hit the net. I told him I had been looking at our stats.

'How're they looking?" he asked.

"Not good," I said, thinking of my book.

"Compared to what?"

"To a viable business."

He blinked, as though we were not competing with such organisations. It was time to tell him what I had found. The noise of bin-men slinging sacks into their truck meant he did not hear me the first time; I thought he had taken it well.

"You did *what*?" Scott asked.

I felt like someone still smoking beside a smouldering Portacabin.

"You stole an auction receipt from Marble Arch," he confirmed. "You'll be shoplifting next." I remained silent about my previous form in this area. "Christ – Cripps, what've you done?"

"Foxe hasn't picked it up yet."

"Presumably because you've got the receipt."

I told him it took a day for the stuff to clear. He went quiet, to think. There was no time for Springsteen.

"It must be important," he decided, "And we can't lead the Society to it. We were lucky last night." He leaned back, the rubbish cart rumbled towards Tottenham Court Road. "We'll have to pick it up."

"Disguised?"

"I doubt there's need for that," he said, and I regretted sounding so keen.

He stood up to think.

"We'll take a bag," he said "Then a taxi back to yours. The Society are on foot, and don't know where you live," he paused, "But they know your name. We'll have to go to Ronnie's."

"OK." I said, hoping he had also missed that enthusiasm, but he hadn't.

"Oh, I know," he smiled. "She'd pull in a monastery."

I wondered about the relevance of Dee's family tree in Marble Arch. My mother always refused to do ours. She knew where my father was coming from, and had no desire for genealogical diagrams to confirm it. I suspected that like me, she feared family characteristics survive, that you cannot run from them, not even further along the south coast. Our nature lies within us; we are simply the conduits. Beyond his eyes and grunts of indignation, I always wondered how much of my father she saw in me, if she did, she never told me. I took that as a bad sign.

The auction rooms smelled of furniture polish. Outside, traffic was muffled. It was a long way from an auction I once visited in Hastings to buy an air pistol. I'd shot at cans beneath the cliffs further along the beach, beyond the night fishermen. Despite it being missing from my CV, I found myself surprisingly skilled. The cracks pierced the night, leaving my ears ringing and my hands with a manly ache.

I clutched the bidder card. A man built like a pencil sat behind a desk that was empty, bar a ledger. He asked if he could help in a tone that considered it unlikely. I handed him the card and deposit receipt.

"Mr Foxe?" he asked, looking between us.

"Yes." Scott nodded without hesitation.

The man frowned. "Sorry about the delay. As you know, this item has caused issues in the past. We couldn't risk its presence in the auction room."

"Why's it so popular?" Scott asked.

"Because Mr Foxe, nothing gives something value like someone else wanting it. Now, let's get the paperwork, so we can retrieve it."

Scott pulled out his wallet. The man opened the ledger, scanning the pages with a ruler. He eyed Scott.

"You intending to pay?" he asked.

"Cash?"

"Paying twice?" the man asked, shutting the book. "You already paid."

Scott's knee pressed against mine. The man lay his fountain pen down as though to not wake it.

"It *is* customary to pay for your item following a successful bid. It *encourages* processing from the archives." He smiled, but I missed the joke. "And your ID..."

"We were told..." Scott started.

"That your passport was sufficient *yesterday,* Mr Foxe," he replied strangely. "I was away," he said sounding like a man leaving rats in charge of the ship, before stamping the card COLLECTED. He stood to straighten his jacket, and peered down the corridor to the entrance, where a security guard was in discussion with another visitor.

We followed him towards a wooden hatch further down the corridor. Behind us, the voices at the entrance were increasing in volume. He left us at the counter before disappearing through a side door. He opened the hatch, and found a muslin bag the size of a bowling ball. He laid it to rest beside another ledger, which he opened.

"Let's just recheck the documentation..." Scott shared zero resemblance to Foxe, even in a passport photo. I watched the turning pages, photocopies of customers' IDs flicking past, growing nearer to Foxe's. The man looked up, at the commotion at the entrance.

"Don't tell me this item will cause another scene," the man sighed. "There's always trouble. There was a fracas at its last auction." Our interest stopped him for a moment. "What *is* going on down there?" He leaned out, and Scott joined him looking down the corridor. I stared at the ID ledger holding the photocopy of Mr Foxe's passport photo. We were seconds away from being exposed. As the shouting increased, I feared I recognised Fred Perry's voice.

"Is there another way out?" Scott asked.

"To avoid another disturbance?" The man indicated farther along the corridor, "Smokers use it..."

I didn't hear him finish. I grabbed the muslin bag and ran. Scott quickly caught up. The man yelled through the hatch, but the security guard was busy with Fred.

We stopped running in a side street off the Pentonville Road. Scott was panting. He nodded me reassurance, but he needed to sit down. He was fitter than me, but his heart attack had closed the gap. We found a doorstep down an alley where he necked some tablets, before investigating our haul. In the bag was a round black mirror – I think it was volcanic rock. It was the size of a dinner plate, an inch thick and gleamed with promise. It weighed more than its size implied. We allowed it to sit in our hands, where it fractured the city skyline. A message bleeped from Scott's phone, breaking the spell. It was Mrs Foxe wanting to see us. We were finally in demand.

Chapter 12

We stashed the black mirror in a locker at Waterloo station, before the Society found us, and caught the first train to Mortlake. It was unclear why Scott wanted to see the house uninvited. I agreed, on terms including a riverside pint. Passengers fiddled with phones, boring Facebook friends with updates of their journey. No one was reading my book. Scott toyed with the small safe key hanging from its chain. I noticed we sat at the end of the carriage, so we could see who embarked. I asked what the beep was in Scott's bag. He pulled out the small box labelled *Stick'n'find*.

"The tracking device." He was so proud of it that I feared the Life Assistance Agency had been established as a result of its purchase.

"Magnetic, attaches to metal," he added, as the disc flew from his hand to limpet onto the fold-down table. He wrenched it off. "It's got a new battery."

Snuffling around people's gardens appealed to my voyeurism. After all, I remained a writer in spirit, if not practice. Mrs. Foxe's garden backed onto the Thames footpath, which was deserted. The river's current and tide contended for supremacy, searching for peace. The Budweiser brewery's chimneystack smouldered into the night. We crouched behind the floodwall, beside the Watergate Stairs where a moored boat bobbed gently. The only lights in the rear of Foxe's house were in the sitting room. We clambered over, landing beside a rusting compost bin. The unkempt flowerbeds served us well, as did the darkness. A 747 roared low overhead, QATAR floodlighting its belly. We looked up at passengers gazing down on the river.

We crept closer, peering into the rooms without curtains facing the overgrown lawn and shrubbery. There was nothing to see. I mean actually nothing. It was at odds with expectations. Clothes dried on a clotheshorse, and boxes lay about an unfurnished room. The ceiling was blackened, as though from a fire. I recalled the chipped cups. The Foxes were not as wealthy as their location and public rooms suggested. We withdrew back down the garden, to advance this time towards the sitting room. We crawled through the bushes to peer in through the French windows. Mrs. Foxe was sitting on the sofa, drinking from a glass tumbler.

"She's got company," Scott whispered, pointing out the table, "Two glasses."

My stomach lurched. We waited, but Mr. Foxe did not appear. She leaned forward to refill her glass from the decanter, and chinked the other glass before bringing hers to her lips, confirming my fears. She was drinking alone.

At the front door, Mrs Foxe greeted us with familiar reticence. She was drawn, and darker around the eyes. She clearly missed Mr Foxe. So had we, but Scott was able to reassure her that Mr Foxe was alive, even if he was unable to provide the details. We looked in the garage. An old 1970s jaguar lay beneath dustsheets. I was never much of a car nut, but Scott liked Springsteen. If you have time, these things add up to make a person.

I left Scott, and joined Mrs Foxe by the French windows overlooking the river. It was dusk. Swans floated self-importantly in the shallows, other birds kept their distance; I wondered if we could learn from them. Only a glint of light from a window on the opposite bank disturbed the serenity. I was about to mention it, when I remembered the black paper we'd found in Marble Arch.

"Does Mr Foxe ever use black paper?" I asked.

"Only for his brass rubbing. Why?"

"Nice car," Scott interrupted, returning from the garage. "Even nicer view," he added, looking over the water. I feared a flurry in labelling things nice.

"What's that?" he asked, noticing the flashing light across the river.

"He's at it again," Mrs Foxe tutted. "He *knows* Thomas is missing. It's our neighbour. Some experiment that's beyond me even if I did care. I'm unsure they understand it themselves. He flashes at five o'clock every day." She looked at us, "But enough of that. What do you have?"

Scott flipped open his notebook with a flourish that the contents ill deserved. Our findings were the sort of material cut from Indiana Jones films

"Well, he's not the first to have disappeared," Scott began, "There's been *others*."

"I know, I told you that."

Scott was unperturbed. "It might be related to Dr Dee."

"What *is* it with Dr Dee? He's been dead four hundred years, but you'd think it was yesterday," Mrs Foxe said. "Thomas is obsessed with him, an extension of his psycho-geography. Dee lived here, but..."

"Here?" blurted Scott.

"Not here, but in Mortlake. They named the flats next door after him. I think Thomas felt some connection."

The light from the opposite riverbank blinked for a final time.

"The flats are where Dee's house apparently stood," she continued. "He's an *influence* shall we say. Thomas used to dig the garden like a bloody mole. He's not found anything since the 1980s. Dee's stuff was ransacked years ago. Michael knows all about it. Our Rector." She explained. "I think Dee's buried there, with some chest, although Michael probably doesn't know much more than me." She smiled. "I was the one who spent my honeymoon sharing a car with a Dee fanatic. Thomas gave up calling angels after we married, and he severed ties with Oliver Turner. I think our tour of Europe was his farewell to places Dee knew. Thomas may even have been returning artefacts. I didn't ask too many questions-" She narrowed her eyes, "Then he read your book. He found your cynicism a challenge..."

"Where was your honeymoon?"

"Prague, France, Germany. I remember we stopped at a little church for an afternoon." She disappeared to fetch the honeymoon' photo album. "I still enjoyed photography then," she said, showing us a photo of the church. A huge boulder dwarfed the surrounding Yew trees. In the background a man was leaning over something on the ground of the churchyard.

"Leimbach," she said. "He thought Dee might have hidden his book of mysteries there. That's the secrets of the universe to you and me," she smiled, "But then isn't it always?"

Scott was scribbling furiously.

"A stack of Dee's papers were found in a secret desk drawer in the 1670's," she added.

Scott glanced at me. I realised the safe key we had found in Marble Arch was burning a hole in his pocket.

"They went to the Ashmolean collection," Mrs Foxe continued. "Thomas suspected there were more, and medieval paper was often reused. Thomas found pictures under Dee's writing, children's drawings of a church beside a huge boulder. That's how he guessed Dee had been to Leimbach. This was after Dee lost Kelley."

"Edward Kelley?"

She nodded, "They cast the same shadow for a while. They fell out, somewhere east. They didn't speak again. Thomas suspected Jane Dee gave birth to Kelley's son. Probably on their way back to England." She smiled, "I know far more about this than I should."

"We'll find him. Give us a week," Scott reassured her. We needed a year.

We looked in the study before leaving. As soon as Mrs. Foxe left, Scott knelt on the floor by the desk. He pulled out the safe key on its chain. I was about to say something, but he put a finger to his lips.

Pulling out the shortened drawer, he reached back to the safe. He motioned for me to stand by the door, as he reached in with the key. He grinned at the click, before pulling out a large sheaf of paper. We opened it, to find rolls of old parchment. It was cracked and dry, the ink faded. Its calligraphy looped and curled with medieval flourish. A thick pad of modern paper was attached to it. The front page was entitled. *The diary of Jane Dee: March 8th 1582 – March 1604*. He shoved it into his bag and replaced the drawer. I went to leave, but he had not finished, as he noticed indents on Foxe's leather bound desk, similar to his own back in Hanway Street.

"As Freud said, no mortal can keep a secret," he said. "If his lips are silent, he chatters with his fingertips."

He laid paper over it and found a pencil to scratch over it. The paper exposed patches of words overwriting others, and a doodle of what appeared to be a snowman with horns, alongside a lollipop:

P

There was also *every new line has a start*, and what looked like a grocery list. Scott took a photo with his phone.

We crossed the road into the church grounds. To the right ran the wall that Mrs Foxe thought had once bordered Dee's garden. Older stones remained visible beneath repairs. Alleyways ran behind the graveyard, dividing feudal plots. A stone arch stood peacefully amongst yews and gravestones. We entered the vestry, where a woman with a white collar was busy at a trestle table. The musk and notices for the ubiquitous spire appeals were all in place.

"Just didn't build them to last did they?" Scott addressed the five-hundred-year-old spire. "We're looking for Michael?"

"Michael?" She smiled, "You mean *Michelle*. You must know Mrs. Foxe, she calls me Michael."

"I'm Scott Wildblood and this," he announced meaningfully, "is Ben Ferguson-Cripps."

The Rector pulled a face of someone being told a name that should mean something, but doesn't. "We're helping Mrs. Foxe, and have some questions about John Dee," continued Scott.

"New attendees are only ever bloody occultists." She crossed herself. "Or arsonists." She put down the vase, and held up what amateurish font exposed as a self-published biography of Dee. "Perhaps you should buy this. It's by a local historian whom you might recognise. He knows his stuff."

Scott took it from her. "It's by Thomas Foxe. We'll certainly buy it."

She nodded like it was a good idea. The clergy unsettle me; they apparently know something I don't.

"Is any of Dee's stuff in the church?" Scott asked, after handing her the money.

She smiled at his optimism. "I doubt it. The medieval lot were like bloody rabbits." She crossed herself again. "Buried everything. Robert Cotton bought the land around Dee's house to dig it up."

"Robert Cotton, the founder of the British museum?"

"Yes, he was a private collector who bought the land about ten years after Dee died. I remember Foxe was excited discovering someone *else* had competed to buy the land. Someone called Talbot I think." She smiled again. "We're not talking recently; this was 1620 or something."

"Has anyone else been asking?"

She paused to weigh him up, "There's the usual enquiries from historians and hobbyists. We don't know where Dee's buried. But we know he's buried between two tombs that *have* been identified. I've looked into it. Dee was an extraordinary man, with a smeared name. The Victorians didn't like him. Nor James. King James lacked Elizabeth's tolerance."

"Dee's heart is buried at the altar?" Scott asked.

"Nonsense. There's no record of Dee's burial. It was 1608 or 1609, but it's no mystery, simply a gap in the parish records around that time. There was supposedly a trunk, but no reason why it should be Dee's. Much to the disappointment of our fantasists," she smiled at Scott. "Although his papers *did* go missing, they were found sixty years after he died, in a hidden drawer. But that was it." She hesitated, and looked to the door.

"Foxe gave me some things to look after. He told me not to tell anyone if they asked, but you haven't technically asked. Besides, the unpleasant visitors have already been. And he *is* missing after all." She squinted. "You're definitely not that Society crew?"

"You had unpleasant visitors?"

"Yes. If they'd found some manners, they might've got something." She paused, before leaving to find something from behind the altar.

It was a size-11 shoebox. Foxe was a big man. Inside were photocopies of what appeared to be rudimentary horoscopes.

I say rudimentary, they turned out to be far from it. Michelle recognised the top one.

"This is John Dee's," she said. "He did his own horoscope. It's amazing." She held it up. "Dee saw the light of day at 4:02 on 13th July 1527, at 51 degrees and 32 minutes north of the Equator. It puts his birthplace just north of the City Wall. Longitude's harder. There was no meridian at the time," she explained. It looked better than Mystic Meg. She handed them to Scott.

"I presume the others are his children. There's Arthur (b: 1579), Theodore (B: 1588) ..." she added.

"How many children did he have?"

"A few, but most were taken by the plague." She looked more closely at the horoscopes. These figures probably indicate their birthplaces," she said thoughtfully.

We looked at them, but they were impenetrable.

We thanked her and dodged rain all the way to the station. Once we boarded a train Scott looked around, before pulling out the notepad we'd found in the safe. Someone, presumably Mr Foxe, had transcribed Jane Dee's diary into contemporary (and readable) English.

"Now, we're really getting somewhere," Scott declared with the optimism of someone charging for a free newspaper. He read the first page, before handing it to me.

"I wonder what the Society would do to get hold of this."

"I'd rather not know," I replied, and started reading:

March 8th 1582, Mortlake

My handwriting is out of practice since I left the Queen's court. I am so busy with children that I have little use for written words. Even spoken words are little more than 'hold on a minute,' as they tug my skirts for attention. Despite this, I am determined to record something of my life as the wife of a man that others seek for knowledge, and even magik. All I need from him is to hear the dinner gong once in a while. Yet, how was I to know how precipitous my writing was to become? The acorns of today have little idea of the oaks they become tomorrow.

My husband has kept a diary since before we met. Nothing escapes his pages: every moon, every storm, the births of our children and even my menstrual bleeding. He knows more of my cycles than I do. If he is not writing, then he is reading. People are entitled to secrets, just so long as they have less than they do children. My husband has enough of both to forgive me for reading his diary pages. I started my journal before the 8th March in the year of our Lord 1582, but unless you are interested in the chatter of Mortlake's riverside wash steps I shall ignore those entries, and begin with the day that changed our lives forever.

The river Thames rippled like a lake, as it does at slack tide. Only where moonlight caught the surface could you see its current. An occasional branch passed, nature returning her skeletons to the distant coast. As I walked through the orchard to the front of the house, I looked up at the aging thatch of our dwellings. It was mouldy and as dark as the night sky. It needed repairing, but we lack funds. I heard local dogs barking. Heavy mist muffled the bickering as their keeper bedded them down. Before locking our front door for the night, I paused, to look into the lane, where I noticed some paper caught in a hawthorn bush. I stepped across and pulled it out. I tend not to read, John has that well-covered, but that is not to say I have forgotten how to.

'A necessary advertisement' Against the untrue and infamous

*reports of Dr John Dee, refuting slander and loose tongues
that claim he is a caller of devils and spirits. He is not, as some
have claimed, the arche conjurer of the kingdom...'*

The damp paper ripped and fluttered into the night. So, John
wishes to silence the naysayers of his mysterious experiments,
I thought to myself and smiled. If only he *were* the arche
conjuror of the kingdom, then we might have spare wealth for
a fresh thatch. I turned and bolted the door. The house was
quiet. John spends his evenings with alchemy, while we rely
too heavily upon Queen Elizabeth's generosity, a dependency
I could do without. But rebuilding the monasteries would be
easier than extinguishing John's spiritual ambitions.

An hour later, someone knocking at our front door set our own
dogs howling. The first stabs on the doorknocker were shy.
Those of a stranger, but with the offshore river wind buffeting
our windows, and presumably our visitor, the tapping grew
more insistent. The wolfhounds were keen I answered. With
there being no sign of John, I approached the door with
unease. After all, family, friends and tradesmen know to use
the parlour door.

The door was stiff with damp. It scraped the floor to reveal
a tall man stooped beneath the crumbling porch. A long cap,
beneath a hood, obscured his face and profile. He smiled, but I
wished he hadn't. I bid him 'good evening'. A heavy trunk lay
at his feet. I wondered how he had carried it.

"Good morrow," he said, pulling back his hood, revealing
black and unusually long hair over his ears. His eyes, even
in the gloom, were a piercing grey. A stretched face flowed
distinctly past a narrow nose. I was reminded of the men in the
royal court, all as shallow as their charm.

"Is the Doctor home?" he asked, flicking his hair with a

twitch of his head. It revealed a white streak running through its blackness. He appeared well enough and I wondered why he required a Doctor.

"Aye, my husband is home," I replied, already regretting admitting so. "But he's no physician."

"I stayed last night near the Brent-ford," he said. "I have travelled south. From Wales."

"Mortlake is a long way from Wales."

"Or from anywhere." He smiled.

Disliking his familiarity, I asked if my husband was expecting him.

"He does not yet know me," he replied in a tone suggesting he was worth knowing, something I instinctively contested. I peered past him into the darkness. A candle flickered weakly in the cottage opposite. Puddles scattered the lane. From a nearby copse an owl wooed the night.

"It's late…" I said, my implication clear.

"My journey was delayed at Worcester," he said meaningfully.

His manner annoyed me. His eyes were too quick and his mouth too tight. I recalled my own advice: never marry a man too welcoming of strangers. As with most experience it came too late. I already imagined John rubbing his hands with glee.

"May I enquire the reason?" I asked.

His eyes squinted. "I bring promise, hope and," he lowered his voice, "the *key* to Dr. John Dee's desire."

I had to laugh. "You're not his type."

The man smiled. He was no cook, but recognised he had overegged the pudding. I agreed to fetch John.

"Please inform him," he said before I departed, "That he may be interested in this." He delved into a pocket, and handed over a parchment roll. I recognised Latin in studied hand. I guessed it spelt trouble. "And if he seeks a scryer," he added, "then he need look no further."

I groaned. Scrying for angels was the nonsense John had pursued with Barnabas Saul and Bartholomew Hickman. Both had since left, but not without leaving a gap in John's life I struggled to fill. John followed so many paths it is impossible to establish where each begins. The smell of yeast from the nearby monastery's brewery was overbearing, unless it was coming from the stranger.

"And your name?" I asked.

"Mr Edward Talbot." He stopped. "I mean Kelley."

"Well, which is it? Kelley or Talbot?"

"Edward Kelley, m'lady," he insisted. "Talbot's an old name."

I frowned, and closed the door, to fetch John from his laboratory. It was a decision in every way bar one that I lived to regret.

It pains me to admit it, but the stature of our visitors' has declined since Queen Elizabeth's visit two years ago. She had stayed for long enough to admire Dee's mirrors and shew stones, and to cause a blockage of carts and passers-by in the lane. She had spoken with John where the wall divides our land with the church. Villagers still linger there, as though they are closer to God by walking in her footsteps. Perhaps they are. Now we have visitors who cannot even decide upon their own name.

I passed through the main hall with its shelves of books disappearing into the rafters, and followed the unpaved corridors to the laboratories. It was gloomy, but I hastened at the smell of smoke. The ill-fitting door swung into a thick green fog. I plunged in to find John. Amidst the smoke, behind a table piled high with books and manuscripts, I found him looking up from the floor. His eyes alert. A large black pebble balanced on his forehead.

"Angels," he murmured so as to not dislodge the stone.

"You see them?" I asked.

"I don't *see* them, Jane. I feel them. I *sense* them. But I don't *see* them."

I had heard all this before. His enthusiasm compensated for my mediocre interest. His last scryer, Barnabus Saul, had apparently compensated for my husband's inabilities.

"As you know, it is of great heartache to me that I fall short of Hickman's, or even Saul's skills." John said, as I helped him to his feet. "If the angels hear me, then they do not answer."

"How d'you know that?"

"They're God's servants, not mine, I need another scryer..."

I surveyed the mess of the laboratory. "You're in more need of a servant."

"No Jane, this space is sacred."

"*Sacred*?" I laughed. "If this is sacred then so's the piggery."

"The globes, the maps, and crystal balls are carefully strung in unison," he said. "*I* know where everything is Jane, and *that* is what matters."

He placed the pebble in a rack to join an impressive crystal ball, and circular black mirror the size of a dinner plate. I leaned on a large lump of stone on the table.

"Don't lean on that," he warned.

"Sorry." I moved away. "What is it?"

"Limestone. It's part of the London Stone, a powerful source that I've-" He coughed. "Borrowed." He stroked it, before turning his face to mine. He was tall and un-stooped by age. He smiled, and held my face. "Now for what can I do you for?"

"A visitor."

"I expect none."

"Well, he *is* unexpected. Shall I send him away?"

"Good Lord no, if the door knocks, then we must open it."

I had feared as much. "What's this?" I asked, stroking a ball of dirtied wax. It smelled of honey.

"It may be the key to my goal."

There have been so many keys to his goal over the years that I have lost count. His hand joined mine on the wax and our fingers entwined.

"It's a filter, for the table's feet. I intend to make wax discs," he said in a hushed voice. "Its secret must remain between us." He threw a cloth over it. "It's not for our guest's eyes."

"Guest? How do you know he intends to stay?"

"At this hour, no one knocks without expecting a bed," John brushed down his tunic. "Let us bring him in from the night, and discover what he wants." He looked around helplessly. "Now, where is my gown?"

I handed it across without a word. If clothes eluded him what hope did he have in finding angels?

I had felt Kelley's eyes upon me as I rekindled the study's fire, before I loitered outside to listen. John's voice was unmistakable. It holds enthusiasm as easily as our bed holds damp.

"Let us see why you travel such distance to visit..." John asked our visitor. "What are these packages?"

There was silence, interrupted by John again. "Ivory. Remarkable craftsmanship," he said.

"Yes, two ivory balls," Kelley replied. "Twist them, there's a-"

Even I heard the click.

"So, dark powder in the red sphere, and, in the other?" asked John.

Kelley allowed the silence to develop. I imagined him holding his breath.

"Red powder?" John sounded excited, "And a manuscript too." He laughed again, but less modestly. "Mr Kelley, thou may have discovered projection powder, the route to..."

"To gold?"

"Tether your horse," John said. "But we *can* experiment."

"To make more?" Kelley asked

"As I say, steady your hand, work needs doing." John paused. "This requires holy blessing."

"Your angels might help?"

"My angels?" John sounded cautious. He had printed the necessary advertisement at great cost to quell the rumours, not stoke them. "Word travels? How dost thou know?"

Kelley did not answer.

"My last scryer," John said. "Saul, he saw the spirits, but," his voice hushed. "They terrified him." He coughed. "You see them? They scare you?"

I heard scurrying in the thatch above as rats bedded down.

"No, Dr Dee, they fascinate," Kelley sighed. "But they *are* insistent."

"*Excellent.* John is my name. Friendships begin with trust. United we shall find spirits, alone we shalt not. They make it clear that it always takes two. Are you with me?"

I gathered my skirts.

"What is that noise?" John asked.

"I believe it's your wife at the door..."

"Earwig?"

I stepped away, annoyed that Kelley already knew John's pet name for me.

March 25th 1582, Mortlake

The two prisoners at the roadside wore little more than dirt, sweat and rags. Arthur held his nose at the stench, at their soiled clothes and rotten food flung at them. My son has his father's curious nature. The prisoners' legs had fanned the mud away behind them, while flies sat unreachable on their eyelids and cracked lips. We were pushing the handcart back from market. They were a miserable sight. We downed hands in respect. One of them wore a cloak, with bloodied stripes torn across its back. A flagellant. His nose and fingers were black with the plague he had once accepted money to banish. The other's body lay uselessly on the ground, lank braids hung past his face. His breath rattled in snorts. I noticed the man's ears. The bloodied stumps reminded me of a seashell John found in Norfolk while digging salt for experiments. I called Arthur away, but it was too late.

"Where are his ears?" Arthur asked.

"They're still growing," I lied, before kicking some bread within the vagrant's reach. He did not move. The new vagrancy laws coincided with my birth. The first offence attracted whipping, the second severing of ears. It was common shrift for a common crime. We moved on.

June 23rd 1582, Mortlake

Edward Talbot, or Kelley as he now insists, has not yet left. I wonder what man can remain without being missed elsewhere. He passes me too closely in the corridors connecting our rambling rooms, outhouses and laboratories. The smell of lavender oil traces his movements as hairs betray cats. Talking of his hair, it is hard not to notice that its blackness is becoming increasingly dominated by a white streak.

Today I showed the sweep boy into the study. He looked around in awe at the green silk Saracen, rugs and book piles, which strengthened John's insulation from the outside world. The celestial and terrestrial globes gifted by Mercator caught the late afternoon sun from the small window. This is how

John prefers the world, with opportunity to consider it. I nodded to the chimneystack rather obviously dominating the room, and watched the boy tie the goose's feet together to send up. I then noticed a drawing of a rounded man with horns beside the inkhorn on John's desk. I picked it up.

"Magpie, as well as earwig," John laughed, startling me.

"Where did you come from?" I asked, catching my breath.

"A good question Jane. And where do we go Jane? That's the important question." He picked up the drawing and put it on a shelf. "The monad represents my treatise, the Hieroglyphic Monad, I hope to present to the Queen."

"It looks like a horned snowman."

"It's symbolic of spiritual pursuit over that of gold. Man's spiritual transformation is the deepest element of chymical work, rather than mundane quests for wealth."

"I thought as much." I laughed. "After all, who would waste their time pursuing gold?" I feared he missed my sarcasm.

"Our guest is obsessed with the shiny stuff."

"Of course he is." He also showed interest in me that John had not noticed. I looked again at the drawing. "You expect our Queen's delight at this monad?" I asked. He nodded, and I warned him that alchemists occupy towers as easily as thieves, but dared not suggest the Queen might prefer gold to spiritual pursuits.

I have seen Kelley's manuscript and ivory balls supposedly found in a Worcestershire grave. They are underwhelming. Apparently, Kelley had purchased them from an innkeeper unaware that the red powder could turn base metals into gold. Either that or the proprietor recognised a wise punt when he saw one. God works in mysterious ways, but a glance at Kelley tells me not *that* mysteriously. However, he has rattled enough village tongues to require me to suppress the market rumours that he can raise the dead. All he wants to raise is his finances. I sense Kelley's history lies little further than a horse-stage away. He is a man born looking over his shoulder.

June 28th 1582, Mortlake

I was in the garden where our land meets the Watergate Stairs. The river had broken the banks of the inadequate north bank, and was spreading itself sullenly across the meadows. I was admiring the hovering Kites, when I heard approaching steps. Thankfully it was John, and not Kelley.

"Our pursuit's conflict," he said, looking tired and tugging his beard. "Kelley's left. He'd rather boast to tavern companions."

"He finds mystical affairs a bore?"

"No. He took offence at my request he deliver Rožmberk a note."

"Who?"

"A European lord visiting our Queen. He has interest in our endeavours. His offer of laboratories in Bohemia is generous, were it not on the condition of us producing him gold. It's always bloody gold. Why are men always so disappointing? So shallow in their desires?"

I remained silent this matter. Instead I asked about the letter.

"It was in Latin," he explained, "Kelley does not read it. Thus, he fears I plot against him."

"Do you?"

"Of course not. He's indispensible.

I was accustomed to John's rhetoric, so held my tongue. "Do you mistrust Kelley?" I asked.

"I beseech the Almighty God to guide him."

I was unsure that answered my question.

"The red powder succeeded in making gold," John continued. "And Kelley leaves, for the inn at Brent Ford.

Alchemy produces gold," he added, "Yet it also transforms men."

"Who're you warning here?" I smiled.

"Indeed, one *must* ask what is changing whom?"

I knew better than to answer that.

"We chase more than material wealth," he said, noticing buzzards hovering above us. "Like them, we must know when to dive." He looked back at me and smiled.

In light of his failure to re-secure a rectorship at Leadenham his reluctance to make gold is poor news.

If only John could find his angels as easily as I find his diary. It read:

Love is the spirit of God uniting and knitting things together in a laudable proportion. What dost thou hunt after? Speak, man, what doest though hunt after…?

July 4th 1582, Mortlake

Boats bobbed on loose moorings by the Water Gate Stairs. The lane and orchard were strewn with broken branches and twigs and the rotten Beech near the house has come down. The smell of torn earth filled the air. Kelley, clearly having just awoken, was leaning in the porch.

"How did you sleep through this?" I asked, surveying the chaos. I was collecting wood. The well was flooded, so hauling water that morning had been easy. I threw some branches to join the pile beneath the lean-to. Kelley looked pale as he left the shade of the porch.

"He's six today, is he?" Kelley asked looking at Arthur, who stuck his tongue out.

I nodded. "No children for you yet?" I asked, but he ignored me.

"Where's John? Still sleeping?"

"No, in London town. Were you both not up all night chasing spiritual creatures?"

"I sense you disapprove."

"I'd have to believe in them to disapprove."

"Your doubt is unimportant. They require no faith." He rubbed his head, and flicked his own tongue out at Arthur hiding beneath my skirt.

"So, how does this scrying work?" I asked.

"Like kissing while wearing a ruff."

"Oh?" I stepped behind a hanging sheet to hide my unexpected blush.

"It's all about being in the right place, at the right time."

He pulled his hair behind his ears and Arthur, who happened to look up, screamed. Kelley quickly shook his hair forward to cover the stumps.

"Still growing," Kelley grinned. Of course his ears aren't, but the white streak is definitely growing more pronounced. Arthur squealed and scampered away. Kelley looked back at me.

"We may need to travel." he said.

"We?"

"John and I. And his family, of course. Our spiritual creatures have plans in Europe."

"Or you do? I'm not going anywhere."

"Jane..."

"It's Mistress Dee."

"Mistress Dee, do not exhaust my patience."

I frowned, unaware that his patience was my concern.

"Your husband and I," Kelley continued. "We are yoked together. Darkness has replaced the light. Perhaps it were the storm, but bad weather brings bad ills."

His eyes held mine, before they blatantly dropped, scanning

my gown. I wished John would not leave Kelley behind alone in the house. He had the air of someone moving in.

"Where is John in London?"

"He's meeting Rožmberk at Muscovy House."

Kelley frowned. "Rožmberk?" he asked. "He seeks Dee's counsel?"

I shrugged, before gathering more wood that had escaped the standing flood surrounding the well. Kelley took some from me, our hands brushing as he did so. He moved closer. I sensed intention in his breath. The wind rustled the trees, and an apple landed with a thud.

"You're seven and twenty?" I asked. "You look much older."

He stepped closer. I was aware my breath had quickened to match his. We were interrupted by a howl from the riverbank. I blinked into action, gathering up my skirts, I ran along the wall to the Water Gate Stairs.

Arthur was crouched at the landing stone, having fallen down the steps. Clutching his head, he was screaming for me.

"Mama, it hurts, it hurts." I scooped him up.

"Let me see." I pulled his hand away, to where blood oozed from a cut above his right eye. Seeing the blood magnified his screams, and I carried him towards the house. Kelley stepped aside, to watch me pass.

"Bad ills," he whispered.

I remained in the garden. But reading John's diary told me what happened later in the house.

The crystal ball was in place, balanced on the black mirror. I recognised from their description that John had completed the wax discs for the table's legs. Kelley fell to his knees, while John left the room, for his small chapel next door. He faced west and also kneeled.

After an hour, a shout from next door disturbed him. John found Kelley in some kind of trance, his forehead rumpled in pain and eyes bulging manically; his eyelids completely disappeared. John was concerned, until Kelley mumbled.

"Uriel."

"*Uriel*?" John gasped. "The creature warning Noah of the Flood?" He squeezed Kelley's shoulder, "We have an *arch*angel?"

Kelley's face contorted with discomfort, but this was no time for compassion. John grabbed his quill, and sat to transcribe Kelley's mumbled words that were not his own.

"It is the will of God, thou should jointly have knowledge of the angels."

"You shall provide instructions?"

"Tablets must be drawn and perfect. From these all things shall be showed unto you. A table of sweet wood, two cubits square, each leg to stand upon pure wax, Siggillum sacred seals, as they are to be known. A divine seal, on which the stone shall sit."

Kelley's eyes rolled into his head, white strung with veins filled the sockets, but he remained on his knees. "A divine code, for the language to be dictated," he continued.

When the quill split, John searched for another.

Grid-like tables appeared from his quills: each cell, each strange letter, and every number drawn in detailed precision. John's heart thumped excitedly. The table would decode the secrets of the universe, of that he was sure. They were exhausted. Farm labourers stomped silently past the dewed-windows, when the final advice arrived.

10th July

The thin glass of the house shuddered in the gale. Tapestries flapped the walls in whip-like cracks. The furs, rugs and floor reeds I had stacked against the bedroom door made little difference. I scribbled what I had heard from outside the study.

"You knowest I cannot see nor skry without you," John had declared irritably.

"Then you must retain me. I am in demand Dr Dee, I cannot help that."

"I depend upon you to see them, but by the Lord himself I wish I didn't."

Their pursuits are ungodly. I have to tell someone. Tomorrow morning I will speak to our parish priest. Aldrich must know such dark events are occurring so near his churchyard.

11th July

The following morning, Mortlake's skies sprung with chattering birds. The Thames slid apologetically past banks it had ravaged hours before. I checked the stables to find the horses missing. Reassured, I waved Aldrich across from where he stood beneath the church porch. He marched across the lane littered with broken branches and standing water holding a large bible beneath his arm.

The priest had seen John's advertisement nailed up along the lanes, ...*refuting slander and loose tongues that claim he is a caller of devils and spirits*, and believed not a word of it.

"Your husband dost protest too much," he said. "Yet he believes the London Stone has powers. It's all flying frogs and peacock feathers..."

On that we agreed.

"So, you wish to eliminate these spirits?" he asked, looking to the clear sky. "It is a fine morning. We *shall* lay them," he reassured me.

I looked anxiously up the lane.

"I saw your husband leave," he smiled, "A poor rider.

Yet despite his denial, he *is* conjuror of wicked and damned spirits."

As I led him to the main laboratory, he admired the maze of corridors and rooms. "Crystallomancy," he tutted, observing crystals secure on their sunken shelf.

The room was gloomy. Cheap tallow candles encircling the holy man's feet, shimmering in bottles, smoked and spat. I watched, alert for the sound of horses.

"We must press on. It may take days," Aldrich reassured me.

"*Days?*" I almost laughed, "We must be rid of the spirits by the hour."

But it was too late. Wet ground must have blanketed Kelley and Dee's horses approach. I heard the two men already in house.

"Europe?" John was asking. "Why do they demand Europe?"

I had barely stepped aside to allow them into the room, before Dee registered the minister.

"Aldrich? Why do we find you here?" Stepping past the priest Dee spied the bottle and candles. "Laying of spirits?" he snorted, "You disappoint me, such archaic practice. These are *modern* times."

"Actions to save your soul John."

"My soul is my business."

"No Dr Dee, it is the Church's. Be warned. Life is short, and you must be careful," he shut the Bible. "With whom we associate," the priest finished, glaring at Kelley.

"Life *is* too short my good Aldrich." John agreed, "And each night I pray it might be longer." He levelled his voice, "But *I* choose whom to invite through my door."

"As does God."

John kicked over the candles. "Save your prayers for those requiring them."

13th July

A few days later, I knocked at his study door, to find John with bloodshot eyes over smoke pouring from a mortar bowl.

"Are you alright?" I asked.

"Leave the worrying to me, Earwig," he said.

"You master worrying, and my work here is done."

"Jane, our destiny lies in greater hands than our own," he grinned, rubbing his eyes.

We peered into the bowl, from which he lifted a lump with tongs.

"Only silver I'm afraid," he said. "Barely enough to cover the experiment. And the cost of an effective scryer is not cheap…"

"You're *paying* Kelley?" I asked.

"Skills such as his do not come cheap."

"His skills *are* cheap." I immediately regretted my words.

"Jane *Dee*. Do not besmirch the reputation of a man gifted such purity of spirit. He is assigned the crystal, there no doubt."

I braced myself for a moral lecture.

"Judge not according to appearance, but righteous character," he said, before seeing I was upset. "I'm sorry," he said with rare sensitivity.

"As am I."

"But, they direct us to Europe."

I paused. "Then I shall start packing."

Chapter 13

We had barely looked up from Jane Dee's diary since getting on the train at Mortlake. At my flat, Scott tidied up more takeaway boxes than I remembered ordering. I didn't know where Scott lived. I suspected he'd say something like 'everywhere', which put me off asking. I've always hated happy families, and always guessed Scott came from one; he was a one-man *Waltons*.

Daisy arrived, following a job interview, during which she couldn't hear the questions due to passing traffic. She'd answered, 'What did you want to be when you grew up?' with 'A fairy.' I was unsure interview de-briefing was a life assistance service, but she considered it so.

We found everything on the Internet, such as John Dee's Enochian magic supposedly intended to unleash violent occult forces to hurl us into another age. It sounded very Aleister Crowley, which was confirmed by the discovery that Crowley had claimed to contacted Dee's angels in the early 1920s.

Eating on our laps felt remarkably homely until Scott announced we should scry. I was unsure how this might help us find Mr. Foxe, but Scott felt it important and Daisy instantly agreed, before enquiring what it involved. She lit candles, while Scott revised Dee and Kelley's methods to contact angels. Dee had prayed, while Kelley prepared to receive, or fabricate, the other-worldly visitors.

Plenty had tried since Elizabethan times, mainly a bunch called the Golden Dawn, which is exactly what misguided groups contacting angels are invariably named. As with most esoteric practices it was important to empty our minds Scott explained, sounding like someone studying Bolshevism via Boney M's *Rasputin*.

It is only once you try to empty your mind that you realise you're invariably wondering how Arabic drivers reach the bejewelled tissue boxes on their rear parcel shelves, or why fifty pence pieces are seven-sided. Peering for something in the gloom, Scott was regretting the candlelight, when he changed his mind and instead pulled out the obsidian black mirror that Foxe had won at auction.

"What the fuck is that doing here?" I said, "That was stashed at Waterloo…"

Daisy gasped, instinctively realising that it had belonged to Dr Dee. It sat on the black cloth with royal grace. It was satisfyingly heavy. Like Scott, it knew its place in the world. Candles flickered seductively in its shimmering surface. It was clouded with age, and at risk of sounding over-poetic, gleamed magically. For a moment my cynicism melted. It was impossible to imagine where it had been, and what it had seen. But it showed us nothing. We stared at it for hours. It was eleven o'clock before I suggested we stop.

"Ouija board?" suggested Daisy. "It might open things up."

The 'things' she referred to went undefined, and Scott was predictably keener than me.

"What's wrong?" Daisy asked me, "If you don't believe, what's to fear?"

I mumbled something about Mum's end of pier tricks, but my reticence was hard enough for me to understand.

We leaned over a circle of letters I'd not seen since a brief experimentation at school. Our fingers rested lightly on an upturned glass, *Fairy liquid* bubbles were visible. How apt. Daisy stared skywards and cleared her throat, before asking if anyone was there. There was silence. Injured nerve endings meant I was unable to feel my finger on the glass when it twitched. We jerked in shock; the last person so terrified of an empty glass was my mother. Daisy shushed before asking.

"Who are you?"

The glass scratched across the table to E. I watched Scott and Daisy. Neither was moving the glass. I certainly wasn't. I reminded myself to breathe, as it edged towards the D. Ed? Who the fuck was Ed? It rested on the D, before shooting away with such force Daisy screamed, and tried to take her hand away, but Scott pressed her hand to keep it there. I must have looked as alarmed as Daisy.

"You OK?" she asked.

"Yes, I think so." I felt disorientated, like I'd been sedated and found myself on the floor staring at the ceiling. It was then I realised I actually was.

"What am I doing down here?"

"What were you saying?" Daisy asked, helping me up and back into the chair I didn't recall falling off. I felt chilled.

"Well, they're certainly awake," announced Scott.

"But we shouldn't be." Daisy was still looking at me with concern. She looked at her watch. "It's midnight, and I've got another interview in the morning."

Still light-headed, I walked her to the door. She stepped outside, her face catching a triangle of light.

"Sure you're OK?" she asked. "And what were you saying in there?"

"I don't know? What *was* I saying?"

"Never mind," she said, before giving me a hug, and I watched her walk away.

Back inside I found Scott staring at the crystal. He looked up.

"Ed? It's not Edward Kelley is it?"

"No," I rubbed my eyes. I felt nauseous.

Scott opened my laptop again. "Imagine shifting shapes, flames," he read aloud, allowing his shoulders to slump, "Let yourself get hypnotised."

"It's late."

"The best time. You see more in the dark."

His reply perfectly illustrates the idiocy I was faced with. The black crystal my mother would have sold her soul for, and probably mine too, sat between us. He started reading,

"Scrying is dreaming while awake," he started reading. His face lit by the screen. "Hold yourself in pure love," he said, "Remove harmful and mischievous energies." Sensing my mockery, he glared at me. "Intention *determines* us, Ben."

It sounded like conversations in Hastings' pubs: you get what you wish for.

"We want that hypnagogic state before we fall asleep," he said.

That I could manage. I yawned.

"We've all seen angels, if we think hard enough," he murmured. I thought of Ronnie. We stared into the crystal, losing focus in its depth. In *Mirrors and Lies* I had argued that the world *was* once more mysterious, a medieval world where less was explained than what was. It was a time of dark forests and dusty corners; a place without glass or reflections, in which a crystal *would* bewitch. Since then, however, we had invented fluorescent lighting.

It was easy to imagine how Dee and Kelley may have seen something; gloom and desire provokes a great deal. What does anyone ever see, but desire? However, by 2:00 the mirror shimmered brightly, as one of the candles flared before dying. Scott gripped my arm. A muted flash sparked the depths of my mind. I was stung by an unreachable snap of pain in my forehead.

"You see it?" he whispered. I felt a clutch of fear. In a millisecond of illumination, the world, the life I knew, lost colour. I saw sharp eyes and a furrowed brow once again. I was unsure from where. My head throbbed with possibility. Opening my eyes, I saw nothing but the room, and the lights of passing cars against the curtains.

"Oh my God..." Scott whispered, "Is it *there*?"

Something flickered. It was hard to explain *what* it was, somewhere between the mirror and us, or in it.

"It's staring...?" he whispered softly, but the shimmer disappeared. He sat back, and gripped my shoulder. I rubbed tiredness from my face.

"It's always two. *That's* how it works." He was thrilled. I looked at the fall of my heavy curtains on the floor. I was shattered. I shivered with cold and glanced back. The curtains rippled. With a shudder they morphed into feathers. I followed their plumage higher, tracing the scapular of a huge, folded wing, before encountering a face. It blinked, turning towards me, its wolf-like mouth frozen in a silent roar. My breath caught in my throat. From above cheekbones sharp as carved wood, its sunken eyes bore into mine. Its head flowed upwards to misshapen horns. I shook my head and looked away, cold with fear. But, turning back, there was nothing. I was mistaken – the curtains swayed from the open window. There was nothing there. I was imagining the very things Scott hoped to see. He murmured if I was OK? I nodded vaguely.

We went to bed. He slept on the sofa, his arm hugging the crystal. My eyes burned tightly. Something lingered, like the confusion between an anecdote and a dream. I shook my head, while if I closed my eyes I saw the outline of huge, folded wings and the scream. I rubbed my forehead. I was exhausted, but I slept fitfully, one ear to the wind outside.

Chapter 14

Scott disappeared after that. In the morning he and the black mirror were gone. All he left me with was a headache. His phone rang out, as did the LAA office. I tried not to worry, but was left haunted with what he claimed we had seen. I looked behind the curtains, but there was nothing there. However, crouching down, I found the floorboards gouged with three scratches. I'm glad Scott hadn't seen them; he'd claim they were from talons. The marks had probably always been there. There were curled wood shavings, but mixed with ancient dust. I opened the curtains to allow in light and reason. We had been wired and overtired, and around Scott it *was* easier to believe in things. Besides, it was not the first time I'd encountered flashbacks from youthful drug use.

Scott's absence stretched into three days. I told myself he had gone undercover, to protect the crystal, but I was worried. There's no good night for seeing angels, and I'm not referring to low cloud cover. I mean there is *no* night for seeing angels. People who'd baulk at chasing fairies happily claim to see angels, as though larger wingspan makes them more credible. And you can't change people's minds, believe me, I've tried. If you remove angels, what are they replaced with? Cheap booze in black plastic bags and 'sure-thing' betting slips. Yet perhaps there *are* strings in the air; invisible currents that tie events together as a result of that much maligned butterfly fluttering its wings to cause typhoons halfway around the world.

It was Saturday night and I was tucking into a second bottle of wine, while reading about King James' intolerance of the dark arts at the dawn of the 1600s. The mystics, alchemists and scryers were laid low, waiting for more enlightened days. The phone rang. It was Ronnie. She was in *the Dove* on Broadway market, a pub ruined by scenesters in well-practiced poses. Ronnie was drunk. I could hear media-chat and cocaine-sniffs in the background. She asked if Scott had turned up yet. She sounded irritated, before inviting me to join her. I was in the cab before I'd done my shoelaces up.

The taxi splashed through puddles, drunken whoops and yells at Old Street, as pubs turned out, and clubs pulled in.

I found Ronnie hanging off a bloke seemingly abandoned by his hairdresser half way through. He was so objectionable I understood why. With the hipsters' high-waist trousers, librarian shoes and braces, east London looked like a historical re-enactment of the Mayflower landing.

We did not stay. We had to leave while Ronnie remained standing. I remember paying the cab with disregard to cost. I recall the journey; the sway of the rumbling taxi, my body electrifying as she fell against me. It was too frequent to be accidental.

I helped her climb the stairs to the flat, heart pounding and breathless at her curves. I remember falling onto her sofa, our mouths meeting ravenously. Her eyelashes tickled my face like whispers. I remember her jeans, tight and black. She kicked off her heels in the bedroom. I followed her, needing water, but afraid to break the mood. Her fly came down an inch, revealing white lace, before she lay backwards to squirm off the trousers, pushing them down her legs with her back arched and stomach taut. I wanted our bodies joined. I needed her skin. Her jeans peeled off inside out and joined the shoes, revealing a tiny g-string. I was regretting my drunkenness, although without it I knew this should not been happening. I wanted to remember every smell and touch, her kisses, and the weight of her breasts; her body firm from the gym caught in the streetlight. It reminded me of taking ecstasy, when you come up, and the whole world exists to catch you. I grabbed her hair and twirled it in my fist, pulling her head back to kiss. I apologised.

"No, I like it."

I lay there afterwards, smiling in the dark, listening to her breath mingling with dwindling traffic outside.

Later still, as we swapped sides of the bed still-entwined, I heard the muffled bleep of my phone. I ignored it and she did not mention it. A bleep amongst the city roar and the squeal of brake pads, the cry of babies, gunshots and missing masonry. There was no turning back.

The next morning, I woke under a t-shirt. She was gone. Sunlight soaked the apartment, picking out colours like a stained glass window. But this was no church. I inhaled from her pillow in a manner scoffed at in films. I rolled onto her side, feeling for her warmth, where her tits and hips had laid, before guilt struck me in a hurricane. I wanted to look through the flat, to scratch into how she lived but didn't feel up to it. Fearful of missed calls I checked my phone. There was a text from Scott, but nine hours too late: 'Be careful. We're being watched' it read. I slunk down the stairs I had helped Ronnie up, eroticism surrendering to shame.

I walked along the alleyway alongside the warehouse, through a maelstrom of guilt. A car crunched over rubbish between graffiti. I pressed into a doorway to allow it past, but it drew alongside and the window slid down. It was Beard, my horror obviously pleasing him. I looked in. Fred was beside him, appearing as welcome as my hangover. Fear was slotting uneasily alongside my headache. I nodded, but before I knew it the door had swung open, and Beard was standing in my face. He smelled of Fred's Sobrani cigarettes.

"Where's the black mirror?"

"I don't know."

He pulled a face like Morrissey playing downwind from burgers. It was the wrong answer. I hoped my quivering jaw escaped their attention. He stared down his nose, and I felt something cold by my neck.

"Tell us what you 'ear, and we won't…"

I had no time to clarify what he meant, as I felt a hot slash by my ear. My hand instinctively pressed against it. It came back dripping with blood. He was back in the car.

I was left with a bleeding ear, and an epiphany of terror. I plummeted into childish fear. I was so vulnerable I wanted my mother. I wanted the light left on. I wanted to know who my absent father was. Beard and Fred allowed the window to slide cinematically up, before driving on.

Scott's text haunted my day. I resisted asking Mrs Foxe if she had seen him. It would take our incompetence to unsustainable levels. It was a few days later when Ronnie rang to suggest we meet. I was eating supper in my pants. I didn't say we'd have to stop meeting like this, it wouldn't have been funny even if it had made sense.

We agreed to meet in Shoreditch, and as I squeezed through another bar of hipsters apparently prepared for another Puritan-themed fancy dress party. I wondered what the hell I was doing.

She looked gorgeous, and I was about to tell her, when my phone rang. I ran outside in order to hear it. Thankfully it wasn't Scott, but Mrs. Foxe, asking why no one was picking up the LAA phone. I told her it should be diverting to mine, as Scott was 'investigating'. She sounded too upset, to ask what that vagary meant. I agreed to visit the next day, before returning inside. Ronnie was half way down a glass of wine, but I guessed correctly that she had no plans for a second.

"How's it going?" I asked, having bought a pint.

"Fine, I mean, well, you know. It can't happen again."

"Oh, I know," I said like it had been my idea. We sipped our drinks awkwardly, when I had a thought to breach the silence.

"Do you know much about paper?" I asked, hoping that as an artist she might.

"Paper?" She frowned.

I pulled a sheet of the parchment from Jane Dee's original diary that I had in my bag, and handed it across. Our fingers did not accidentally brush, despite my attempt. She looked at the paper.

"Where did you get this?" she asked.

I hesitated, "It's from our case. We're looking for the man who owns it."

"He's wealthy?"

"I think he *wants* to be."

"No, I mean this isn't cheap. It should be in a museum. It's flax linen cloth. It's delicate. It's not parchment, so needs to be preserved, not shoved in a bag." She smiled, "I can take it to someone. He's an expert in these things." She looked at me. "Is there more?"

"Loads more."

"Let me look after it."

I hesitated, selfishly thinking it might be safer for the Life Assistance Agency if she had it.

"Ok," I nodded, and handed over the envelope holding the original, and transcribed copies of Jane Dee's diary. I felt a little better with it off my hands. Meanwhile, ignoring our dalliance meant it had never happened.

The following day I took a train to Mortlake. I distracted myself from the guilt over Ronnie, by turning my mind to Dr Dee, and why a man of such intellectual standing, in such dangerous times, had been willing to risk everything by asserting that his crystal ball and black obsidian mirror was given to him by an angel. He was an Elizabethan intellectual in need of friends like my mother had needed customers, yet he persisted in alienating himself.

Scott had asked if I desired my mother's skills, but her skill was an unshakeable drunken belief that punters might turn up. Even if her other skills *did* exist, who'd want them? Seeing angels? Are you kidding? It creates more questions than answers. It'd make you too unique. Unlike my mother, I prefer to blend with the crowd. This obsession with being unique impotently battles the fact we *are* all far too similar. Kelley had clearly strung Dee along. With his barren marriage, Kelley probably wanted an heir, and envied Dee of his. Jane Dee apparently only needed to look at Dee to get pregnant. Or maybe Kelley simply fancied her. That was something I was familiar with.

Mrs Foxe no longer appeared like she dressed in Knightsbridge. Her hair needed washing and I could smell old food. I breathed shallowly, as she followed me through to the sitting room. We looked across the lawn. There were no flashing lights.

"I've been told to call you off," she said sadly.

I feigned ignorance that probably came across too well. "Who by?"

"By the Society." Her voice weakened, before she stared at my ear. "Your ear's bleeding." She looked away. I glanced at the pair of tumblers on the low table.

"My mum advised never drink alone," I said, my voice cracked unexpectedly. She looked at me oddly. My mother's funeral flashed through my head. Her friends looking at me as though I were responsible. Perhaps they saw my father. The congregation were the 'alternatives' she had distanced herself from. I knew they all thought I should have done more. A sniff alerted me to Mrs. Foxe wiping a tear away. I looked to the side.

"Ok. It doesn't matter *what* the Society said," she coughed respectability into her tone. "*Can* you find him?"

I struggled to maintain eye contact. "Yes," I replied, commitment ringing in my heart. "We'll find him." The promise clicked like I wished New Year resolutions always did.

She held my hand, squeezing it tightly. "Keep it quiet."

There was no turning back. It was a chance to make amends.

Chapter 15

The knock at my front door sent me under the duvet. I glared at the alarm clock like it had spilt my drink. Scott shouted through the letterbox, before bowling into my flat and demanding I pack like he had the car running outside, which it turned out he had. I grabbed clothes, and rehearsed my innocence. I was as relieved as I was terrified by his arrival.

"Foxe came back for his Jag," he said, sweeping through my flat switching off appliances. "I *knew* he would." I didn't have time to ask how.

"Grab your passport. I'll be downstairs," he said. "I've got Ronnie's car. We'll catch him up."

I'm rubbish at mornings. I've lost balance while taking pyjamas off more times than is acceptable. I found Scott downstairs, leaning on a Saab, in discussion with local kids awake inexplicably early. They had insolent swaggers and whispers of moustaches. Scott had taken them to task for dropping litter.

"Givin' the cleaner something, bruv," one argued, as I threw my bag in the boot.

"Drop twenties then," Scott suggested, as we lurched off to a fanfare of V-signs, before they super-glued my front door lock.

We joined the morning rush hour of flustered school mums and builder's vans flustered by mums. I glanced at Scott, hoping to read his face. Did he know about Ronnie? He hadn't killed me yet, so it was unlikely. I blanketed my guilt.

"Where're we going?" I asked.

"Foxe is following Dee's tracks through Europe. And we've got Jane Dee's diary to tell us where *he* went."

I froze.

"Erm. We don't."

"What d'you mean, we don't?"

I coughed awkwardly. "Ronnie's got it."

"Ronnie? How's she got it? You saw her?" He looked at me and frowned.

"Yes, to ask her about Dee's diary," I said too quickly. "To see if it's genuine, or not. I thought she might know about paper." I heard the distinct sound of a hole being dug, so stopped. "You were missing, and we were worried, about you." I added, but he went quiet. A bus pulled out, at which he sweared with unncessary venom.

"Fuck. Well, she'll have to transcribe it and email it. Damn it." He punched the steering wheel. "Text her, as you've got her number."

"Maybe it's better if the diary's not on us."

He had to slow behind the bus.

"Perhaps you're right. It is a liability. How was Ronnie?"

"Worried about you, but happy to help. Talking of which, d'you really think it's safe. This society. They *are* professionals-"

"And so are *we*, Ben."

I would have laughed had he not so narrowly missed a cyclist.

"Lunatic! Anyway, look," he continued, "Just remember, everything's subjective, tractor drivers are children's rock stars."

He thought some more. "But yes, perhaps it *is* better that we don't have the diary. Who knows what's in it." He went quiet for a moment, before his Iphone bleeped. He tapped it and handed it to me. A dot flashed in a map.

"I put the tracking device on Foxe's Jag, when we visited," he explained.

I was impressed at his initiative, if not his equipment. If it was to be trusted then Foxe was apparently already on the A2, heading south.

We hit the Old Kent Road. Ronnie's Saab was the old shape, a 900 turbo. The engine was sounder than its body, which was like saying the yacht was sinking but still had a mast. Scott was keen to underline the importance of looking after it, which would best be achieved by him not driving it. He was driving with equal attention on whom was behind, which for such a poor driver was inadvisable. I also soon discovered he considered yelling some variation of *'warapppt'* as fair substitute for braking.

"It even has central locking, from a remote," he explained, demonstrating profound lack of automotive development since the 80s.

We flew through Kent. The dot of Mr Foxe was flashing as it headed towards Dover.

"So, where were you?" I asked, attempting to sound nonchalant.

"Keeping an eye on things," he said, taking his eye off the road, which I wish he hadn't.

"I went to Leadenham, in Lincolnshire," he said. "Dee was Rector there for a while."

That Scott had not been in London was reassuring.

He looked at me strangely "You alright?"

I nodded vaguely.

"There's a stone over the Rectory's door," he continued, groping for his phone again, which he had somehow already lost. I helped him find it before he killed anyone. Flicking through the photos, he pointed at one of a door over which was inscribed:

IHVH, MISERICORDIAS DOMINI, IN ETERNV
CANABO, IOANNES DEE. 1565.

"Which translated by *our* people is?"

"I will sing the mercies of the Lord Forever. John Dee. 1565."

"And how's that relevant?" I asked.

"Who knows," he zoomed into the photo, "But there's also this." I leaned in, as he read out the second sentence engraved in the doorway.

"Every new line has a start / The present lives forever." he said. The same words we had found impressed upon Foxe's desk. They were followed by that bloody ♀ symbol.

Like trying to mate in zero gravity, Scott was desperate for connections, yet we still had no idea what any of it meant. My phone bleeped, with a text from Ronnie. She was agreeing to email Foxe's transcription of Jane Dee's diary for us, but not without a struggling artist's eye for a bargain. She proposed a higher fee than I would have agreed to, but Scott consented.

Tailbacks honked their way from the suburbs into London, while we started passing lay-bys and tractor turnings and signs to Hastings. My paperback had struck London's literati like a wet T-shirt at a dress ball and I was glad to leave it behind. Scott answered UK Customs' 'Did you pack your bag sir?' with the sort of uncertainty that officers would be fully entitled to arrest you for.

We had barely emerged into France from the Eurotunnel, before Scott registered surprise at having packed nothing but empty CD cases, and a letter from Hanway Street's landlord suggesting a need to worry for the safety of close family. The rent arrears was a rare subject that Scott preferred not to discuss. He also found a make-up compact that my leaping heart presumed was Ronnie's. If he was anticipating borrowing anything from me, he was to be disappointed. My bag contained jeans, dice and a copy of *Mirrors and Lies*.

The French sunshine felt stronger following forty minutes of darkness. We hoped that once we reached Europe the tracking device might work in time to reduce Foxe's lead. Scott tapped his phone but the app screen remained blank.

"It'll work again once we clear the interference."

I suggested he stopped interfering.

We stopped for petrol and studied the photo of the map from Marble Arch again. Psycho-geographers follow other people's journeys, hopeful they might step into a man's head as easily as his shoes. It seemed safe to presume Foxe was doing the same. Yet, he already had during his honeymoon, so it was unclear why he was repeating his own footsteps. We aimed for Paris. The French radio burbled incomprehensibly, as we found a honking traffic jam of Renaults and Peugeots transporting cigarette smoke through suburbs. I've never liked Paris, it's an anagram of pairs, and full of tourists looking lost, arguing and wondering why it's called the city of love. Thankfully, the tracking device finally blinked and bleeped. Foxe was already nearing west Germany, so we headed north.

The memory of Ronnie occupied my thoughts with the entitlement of a writer at their own launch party. France endeavoured to distract me by skimming past the window, while Scott did the same by slaughtering Bruce Springsteen songs. There was some reassurance in Scott no longer driving via the wing mirrors, although it failed to improve his road awareness. With the sort of cavalier attitude that completes a game of bowls before a Spanish sea invasion, Scott thought it unlikely that the Society were following, as we had struggled enough to buy a ticket for the Tunnel at short notice ourselves.

"Going like clockwork," Scott announced, like that was a good thing. There was nothing on the road but road-kill, and us.

"Reckon she'll come back?" asked Scott, implying I had been involved in his internal conversation. I thought he meant Ronnie.

"The angel we saw," he added, and I hoped he didn't notice my relief.

I was unsurprised that he had considered our mutual desperation – mine to sleep, and his to glimpse something – as a success at my flat. I had dismissed the horrifying hallucination as a result of sleep deprivation. Although the spelling of 'Ed' on the Ouija board was harder to explain, I wondered if Scott was leading me on. It reminded me of a Shakespeare quote I couldn't remember, involving the cloak of night and old England, the by magical ideas that I imagined had separated England from enlightened Europe by permanent sea fog. Later research found Edward Young fitting the bill: 'By night, an atheist half believes in God'.

Tiring of Scott blaming the steering for drifting us into incoming traffic, I took over. With as little idea about operating the tracking device as him, I was thankful for the change. I settled into a seat more accustomed to Ronnie. It was the closest we had been... I looked at Scott, but he was swearing at his phone. Ronnie's rejection stung. It denied our night together. We had left no cliché untouched: our bodies *needed* one another, at least mine had.

Scott dozed while I drove, until I was disturbed by a blast of latter-day Springsteen, *Tunnel of Love*, I think. It was getting late, so Scott suggested that we find a hotel. The first two hotels had no vacancies, while the third admitted to having several rooms, none of which were available without a telephone booking. Scott's suggestion that we phone from the car park slipped beneath their sarcasm radar.

We eventually found a roadside motel last decorated when brown was a good idea. It smelled of cigarette smoke. We dragged the beds apart and flipped the mattresses to discover they already had been. I was wondering what to email Mrs Foxe in the reports she had requested, when she rang Scott. He put the phone down following a brief chat. Foxe had apparently contacted her. He knew about us.

"*How* does he know?" Scott tutted. I shrugged, too tired to care. Scott picked up the tracking device that had not bleeped for hours. It was 'rebooting', apparently. He put it down. "Mr. Foxe apparently wants to meet *us*, but without leading the Society to him." he said. "We've got to ensure we've lost them."

Scott insisted on his 100 sit-ups/push ups to relax. I joined for the first five, before wandering into the bathroom to find a mirror flecked with a thousand flossings. A spider in the bath was climbing the sides, before slipping with as much understanding of its predicament as us. In the name of decorum I decided against using the toilet. The room was too small to tolerate the fallout of motorway fast food. There was a Gents by the reception, which I planned to use later. However, despite Dutch quiz shows as subtle as having lit petrol thrown in your face, we dozed off. Scott's alarm clock bleeped to inform us of the time, and the room temperature.

The next morning's daylight failed to flatter the bedroom. Leaving Scott to a breakfast consisting of more variations of pastry than I had imagined possible, I went to the loo near reception. A mirror stretched along sinks reflecting cubicles. Selecting a cubicle with toilet paper, I sat down. Having finished, I was about to leave when someone came in. I listened to the cistern refilling until they left. Finally, the door closed, and I emerged to wash my hands. I ran them under the tap, before looking up. Could I smell vanilla smoke? I wet my hair and looked in the mirror. I froze. On the mirror was writing. In lipstick, hurried letters read:

Does Scott know about Ronnie?

I leaned on the sink, while my heart flung itself around my ribcage. How the fuck? The thought of Scott knowing chilled my bones. I scrubbed the words away in frenzied rubs. The last disappeared as the door opened and I found myself staring at Scott. He looked as shocked as I did.

"Seen a ghost?" He asked.

"You're not dead yet," I replied in a voice I didn't recognise – I looked guiltier than a dog surrounded by chewed cushions. He walked to the mirror to rub his stubble. I looked away from my pale reflection and covertly wiped my hands on my trousers.

"Have I missed something?" Scott asked.

My ears throbbed; from elsewhere in the hotel there was a clatter. I froze.

"Have *we* missed something?" Scott asked again. "Like why does Foxe want to contact us? Since when did the fox greet the hunt?"

He appeared to be considering this, while smoothing down hair styled by motorway windows in the mirror.

"I'm guessing he wants his black mirror back." He mumbled, while I needed to draw attention away from the toilet mirror.

"Knorr? Know?" he asked.

"Eh?"

"There." He pointed at the mirror. The mirror remained smudged with **kno**. Blood rushed to my cheeks. My jaw numbed; my body paralyzed. Our reflections considered one another for a moment. I turned off the taps.

Sitting in the car, I looked fearfully around the car park. We all have private lives, but mine was shameful. Even Daisy would have withdrawn her support, which felt like the Samaritans refusing to pick up. Scott assured me that Ronnie was emailing Jane Dee's next diary entry for us. I hoped his timing was coincidentally.

He sat at the wheel, shirt open, silver cross dangling from his neck, dressed for a 60s road trip. The car leapt forward, before stalling, which he bluffed was intentional. He restarted and we pulled into the traffic. I looked in the glove compartment for an alternative to Bruce Springsteen, and found the shred of Turner's letter from when Mr. Foxe grabbed it from his wife. The Enochian read as mysteriously as ever. The tracking device then bleeped from behind my seat. Scott looked at me and grinned. The car lurched as he grabbed it.

"He's moving again." Scott straightened the car. "You ok? You look pale."

I blamed his driving, to which he took offence.

We headed eastwards. My hand throbbed. I looked behind for the Society. They had found us, or at least me. I was nagged by wondering how could I warn Scott.

I was unsure Scott noticed the blasts of car horns from other drivers, until he declared they matched the fading train whistles of The Springsteen's prairies. Did he know there was more between us than the device suggesting Foxe was in Germany and his badly sung lyrics? I was unsure how Scott had concluded Foxe was in Germany. Perhaps he understood longitude/latitude, but unless army training covered it during the first day, it was unlikely. I eyed the lipstick smudging my trousers and feared we were leading the Society to Foxe, yet I couldn't warn him. We sighed at the empty road for different reasons.

Apparently the absence of the Society in the rusting wing mirrors was sufficient to reassure Scott we'd lost them. It's hard listening to a friend's confidence in matters you know they're wrong to be. It reminded me of Daisy's well-intended literary encouragement. But what could I do? Scott based hope on pages not yet turned. Hope is dangerous. Hope was nights in Deptford, fantasising that the Council might terminate the neighbours' music, not because it was loud, but because it was shit. Ronnie had been a brief fulfilment of hope. I tasted my mother's ice cream dreams.

Ronnie's Saab drank petrol like sand, so we stopped at another petrol station. While Scott filled up, I found the toilets, which faced flat fields behind the forecourt. Once inside, I quickly rang Ronnie. There was no answer, so I tried again and she answered.

"It's me," I whispered.

"Who?"

I shrunk in size. "It's Ben. Please, never mention anything to Scott. I'm really sorry."

"It's ok," she reassured me. "Trust me, I'll never tell him."

I turned my phone off and cleared the corner to the forecourt, to find Scott talking on his phone leaning on the Saab. Seeing me, he nodded, and cut the call.

"Was that Mrs Foxe?" I asked.

"No, Ronnie," he said without missing a beat. I frowned at the lie, but said nothing.

We crossed the Franco-German border with an ease mocking two world wars. A customs booth laid on its side in disgust at lack of use. We drove on. Every car was German. Audis and BMWs powered past with a purpose the Saab had never experienced.

It was teatime; not that it exists in Europe. At 3 in the

afternoon Scott was invariably more interested in pots of tea than gold. Wincing at the takeaway from autobahn services, I suspected Europeans purposefully ignore Orwell's rules on making a good cup of tea. It's always bloody *Liptons*. Who drinks fucking *Liptons*? Can you even *buy* it in England? It's blended to end up in European hotel rooms, neither offending nor pleasing any one.

Chapter 16

We were closing in on Foxe, so I suggested driving. Scott operating the tracking device was the lesser of two evils. It gave him something to bang against his knee to make work, while driving provided me with distraction. A weather front dragged clouds overhead and we were in the sun. Scott declared this a promising sign.

"Ah. It's working," he said as the tracking device bleeped in confirmation. He frowned at the tiny map, before making a gargled scream. "It's this turning. *Here*," he pointed, and I swerved, sending us hurtling off the autobahn at shorter notice than the slow lane required. With horns ringing in our ears, we followed a B-road, before U-turning into a track, leading us to a village square full sleeping cats. We checked the device and Scott directed us down the narrowest road off the square. We followed a rutted track for a mile, wincing as potholes scraped the chassis. The device bleeped victoriously at a crossroads that had not seen as much action since the dark ages. The dot had stopped moving. A sign announced the village was Leimbach. It was where Foxe had stopped on his honeymoon to allow his wife to take photos.

"So where is he?" I asked.

The tracking device blinked confidently, but there was no sign of Foxe, or his Jaguar.

I recognised the impossibly huge boulder from Mrs Foxe's photograph marking the junction. Yew trees cast shadows across the small graveyard of an abandoned church.

Surrounding fields stood indifferent to its collapsed roof and broken door. There was no sign of Foxe. I killed the engine. *Greetings from Asbury Park* gave way to a silence. We sat back and through the windows birdsong filled the car, while Scott smoothed his hair down. I swear his hairline had *advanced* since we had met again. It was peaceful, like the world had stopped for a moment. Scott frowned at the tracking device's coordinates.

"D'you recognise these? Oh, Hold on..." He rummaged through his notes. "*Well*, fuck me with a boat hook."

He tapped the notepad's sketching of Dee's horoscopes, and looked at his tracker app on his phone.

"Dee's youngest son," he said. "Theodore was born here. It's the same latitude." He started flicking through photos in his phone – the one of Foxe's desk, and the rectory door in Lincolnshire.

"Look," he said. "Every new line has a start? *That's* it. A new line must've started here, with Theodore."

"And that lollipop?" I asked, studying the photo, of the inscription above the door. It was definitely the same ⸢ as on Foxe's desk. I stared at the largest yew tree. It lorded over the half-ruined church and its slumped headstones. The trunk was split in a dramatic Y. I frowned. The letter Y? It looked a *little* like a lollipop. Disregarding expensive roaming tariffs, I googled it on my phone, finding the Wikipedia page for the letter Y. I double-checked. I was correct; an unusual feeling.

"It's *not* a lollipop, it's a symbol." I showed Scott excitedly, "It's an early Semitic version of the letter Y..."

I pointed at the Y shaped tree. He followed my finger, before squeezing my arm urgently.

Birds hovered above the ploughed fields for grubs and worms. We walked around the tree, to find a deep gash in the centre of its split. Sap was bleeding from the large gouge.

The bark had been stripped away, and about a foot down, in the tender wood, was the indent of a shell, or a small tin. Whatever had been there was missing, replaced instead by our tracking device. Its light blinked.

"It's a joke without a punch line."

"Worse," he replied, "It's a punch line without a joke. *But*, we've turned a corner."

"In a maze, Scott, in a maze. He's lost us. I thought he wanted to meet us."

But he was not listening.

"What did he dig out of there?" Scott asked. "And how does he even know where to be looking?"

The sun was setting once we relocated the main road. We had also found an open tombstone in the churchyard. It was the one Mr Foxe had been crouching over in the background of Mrs. Foxe's photo. It was also impossible to know what had been stored there. To distract myself from Scott's driving, I started reading Foxe's Dee biography we'd bought from Mortlake church. A chapter opened with a Dr. Dee quote, suggesting secrets were 'hidden in the caverns in the bowels of the earth'. Where lies undisturbed for the longest? I guessed trees fitted this bill, as I presumed had Foxe, but how had he known that particular tree?

We drove without enthusiasm, like a bomber losing its fighter escort. It was unclear how Foxe had guessed we were following him, or why he had changed his mind about meeting us. We appeared to have all lost our tails, as there was no sign of the Society. Or maybe there were just no mirrors for them to write on.

We stopped overnight in Meissen. Scott arranged two rooms at a hotel near a small cathedral on the river. I was pleased with a separate room until he told me it was for the black crystal mirror. We were still sharing. I was gobsmacked that he'd been stupid enough to bring it with him.

"Of course I did," he said, like it was the most obvious thing in the world. "It's leverage for when we meet Foxe," he added.

"Leverage?"

"Yes, advantage or power gained by using a lever."

"No," I shook my head with disbelief. "I mean why do we need it?"

"Who knows? But always be prepared."

Scott had also once been a scout.

"So if the Society rock up," I asked, "they'll only search our room?" He nodded. There was little point in responding to this level of optimism.

We ate in a restaurant serving sausages. Chequered table-cloths covered the tables. Scott watched the door while toying with the useless tracking device and talking us through the case.

"If Oliver Turner replied in Enochian, then presumably Foxe wrote to *him* in Enochian, so no one else could read it. They've got to be after Dee's angels again. I wonder what changed? The Society clearly disapproves of such actions without permission."

"Cary Grant said it's impossible to contact angels without Dee's special tables."

"Cary Grant?"

I was reminded me that the legwork had been mainly mine, "Foxe's student at UCL," I prompted him.

"Oh, *him*. So who else came close?" Scott asked. "The Golden Dawn? Crowley? Foxe must have found something they didn't?"

It sounded far-fetched, and my sausage casserole held no answers.

We returned to our hotel, past houses, shuttered shops and quiet streets.

"I don't mean to alarm you," Scott whispered, instantly succeeding in doing exactly that. "But, I saw that Toyota earlier."

A car suited to mini-cabbing sat opposite the restaurant. Any hope that we'd lost the Society evaporated.

"German number plate. Rental," Scott whispered. We maintained our pace, but barely.

I was ashamed at feeling unsafe. I double-locked our door on that unmistakable loneliness lingering in hotel rooms. My ears tuned to the corridor outside, to clanking cisterns, the whirr of an aging lift and other guests' footsteps. It reminded me of doing magic mushrooms in Hastings; jumping at sticks morphing into snakes and grateful we had not brought the pistols. I tried to write, but with the imagination of a policeman, so gave up. They were following us.

Chapter 17

"We mustn't lead the Society to Foxe," said Scott, who actually looked worried. I was unaware he had it in his emotional repertoire. The recent phone call negotiating rent arrears with Hanway street's landlord had evidently dented his bonhomie.

"Well, in light of having lost him that won't be hard. How d'you suggest we don't, even if we do find him."

"Misdirection," he said in a tone implying he wanted to say it, as opposed to having any idea what it actually meant.

I tried to imagine what my father would do. It probably involved sleeping on the sofa after failing to negotiate the stairs. A single mother and lack of positive male role models had resulted in me finding my own, and I needed at least one of Denzel Washington's ten badass moments. I hoped the discomfort developing between Scott and I was my imagination. What *would* Denzel do?

We drove slower than Springsteen's hymns to the open road demanded. A regular glint of sun in a windscreen behind confirmed our worst fears. The Toyota followed our every turn. It was horrible, like Harry Dean Stanton in *Duel*, but without the comfort of it being a movie. Scott squirmed out of his shirt, the car twitching across the road as it mirrored his struggle. He looked younger in a T-shirt.

"That angel we saw at yours, I hope it didn't get in trouble," Scott said. "I'm not sure they're supposed to be seen. She looked ashamed."

"I hadn't noticed."

"I've had enough disciplinaries to know one with the big man wouldn't be easy." He glanced at me, which the car overtaking us wished he hadn't.

"Don't worry Ben, I know you're keeping an open mind, but trust me, you can choose to believe, so why not? What's the alternative?"

"The alternative is living in the real world and dealing with it."

By lunchtime we reached the small town of Chrzanow, and parked in the main square opposite a hotel engulfed by a blooming wisteria. A teenager was struggling to look cool while hanging napkins out to dry. Our tail was absent, but I feared not for long. Scott surreptitiously dumped the bag holding the dark mirror into the wisteria. Even I had to admit it was well hidden. The square and streets bustled with markets, which a brief explore revealed to be selling the same contents as Sussex boot sales. Shake humanity and chipped china, anonymous photos and military medals fall out. The only item of interest was a small revolver that Scott suggested I buy, despite it only being a starting pistol. I told him it wouldn't stop paper. All I saw it starting was trouble, but bought it anyway. As we returned to the Saab, Scott took a call, which dropped from poor signal.

"That was Ronnie," he explained. "She was passing lamas, and lost reception." He smiled and pocketed his phone. "There's bad news. Ronnie's been picking up phone messages from the office, and they've been sniffing around Hanway Street."

"The lamas?" I asked.

He laughed, but it wasn't funny. "They've ransacked it."

I was unsure how Ronnie would even notice it had been ransacked. I pocketed the pistol and we returned to the hotel.

Scott scribbled in the hotel ledger, as though making the pen work.

"*That's* your signature?" I asked. It was indecipherable. The hotel's interior was as English as it appeared outside. I half expected drunken RAF pilots to fall in the door. A board above the desk proclaimed tonight's special was homemade kartoffelpuffer, translated as potato pancakes. The hotelier asked if we were English.

"My son loves the English." She implied it was a blip. "Cricket," she added, like a game taking five days to complete was a disease. "His father's English. They visited when he was fifteen." She smiled, and spun the ledger with well-oiled motion.

"Is there a ground floor double?" Scott asked. I was unclear why this was relevant, but it was of sudden importance to him. She looked up from the ledger.

"It's booked."

Scott looked her in the eye. "Can it be unbooked? We are big fans of kartoffelpuffer," he added.

She laughed. "I suppose it can.

The single beds were keeping a distance of about six foot. I thought of Mr Foxe. Our room overlooked the square and its market dismantling itself with cheerful shouts and bragging of takings. Behind the other curtains was a dusty alleyway, which Scott studied carefully.

"Reminds me of travelling."

"A gap year spent finding yourself?"

"Losing myself actually."

"So, why the need for a ground floor room?"

"I'm not sure, yet..." he answered, trying to persuade froth from an invincible hotel soap. "But they're out there, so we need a plan."

The few cars parked alongside ours looked harmless.

"I can't see them," I said.

"Nor me, but it means nothing."

I was alarmed by Scott's uncharacteristic negativity. We had to lose them before meeting Foxe, and I wondered if that was why he'd aborted our rendezvous. The alarm clock informing us of room temperature interrupted my thoughts. He couldn't switch it off.

"Sealed batteries," he explained. There was a knock at the door, revealing the teenager from outside. He was wearing low-slung jeans that made me feel old. He probably made mix tapes too, as opposed to compilations. He offered us towels.

"I'm Scott Wildblood," he introduced himself, approaching like cavalry breaching a frontline.

"Erm, Luca…"

"Luca. I was wondering if you might help us with something."

"What?" he said noncommittally.

"Could you pretend to be him?"

He was pointing at me.

I later lay on the floor below the window, using my shaving mirror to watch them leave the hotel. Save an abandoned market stall having failed to compete with the allure of the bar in the corner, the town square was empty.

I was pleased Luca looked nothing like me, but with key-chains removed and wearing my jacket, he was not outside long enough to make much of an impression. Other endeavours were beginning to require two, like scrying. Mind you, it took two for Tina Turner and Rod Stewart's slobbering lump of *It Takes Two*. I stared at the curtains while they got in the car.

Scott revved the Saab, and spat gravel from the tyres as he accelerated towards an exit, miraculously without missing it. The moment their brake lights disappeared round the tight corner, a dirty Toyota emerged from its space in pursuit. It too passed from sight. I stayed where I was, keeping the mirror angled onto the square. With my hand's severed nerves, it was impossible to feel blood draining from my arm. Five minutes later our Saab re-entered the square, presumably thanks to Luca's local knowledge, not Scott's driving. He lurched back into the parking space as though he had dropped a cigarette on his lap. As the hotel door shut behind them, the Toyota reappeared to resume its position facing the hotel. I was still on the floor when they flew back into the room.

"Silver Toyota, by the fir," I declared, like an owner at Minicabs Anonymous.

We sat away from the window in a half empty dining room. I enjoyed the kartoffelpuffer more than I expected, but did not respond to Scott's plan; words failed me. Him slipping one of our dinner knives into his pocket suggested he had not been discouraged by my lack of enthusiasm. We returned to our room, and watched TV, until Scott announced it was time.

The streetlights bathed the square and cars in that orange European glow. I guided Scott's boots from my face and out through the window.

"If you're already in the fire, it can't burn you," he said before I told him to shut up. I was new to this life assistance lark, but feared we'd last as long as a pubic sector biro. Once outside, I checked the hotel knife in my back pocket. The plan was to slice into the Toyota's rear tyres, deeply enough to puncture them, so we could escape. The alleyway running from the square led into a small lane, just as Luca had described. We dashed down it, before circumnavigating the village, until I was on the far side, behind a tobacco stand. From across the square I could see the rear of the Toyota. Scott intended to approach from the street to my right, at which point I was to duck behind their car. It does not require previous experience in taking spoons to a knife fight to know you're doing it, even when carrying knives.

Sooner than expected, Scott broke his cover and strutted towards the Toyota. He was a few feet from the driver's window, as I arrived out of breath behind their car. I kneeled by the exhaust pipe. Any closer to the ground and I'd be digging. As my breathing slowed, I peeked round to see Scott by the driver's door. I watched, as he tapped the window with the starting pistol. Denzel Washington would have to watch his back. I'd not seen anything so cool since someone super-glued our teacher's ruler to a desk. The window wound down.

"Let's see your hands." Scott asked. There was a blur, as a hand grabbed Scott's starting gun and it disappeared into the car. Things were looking distinctly Star Wars prequels.

"I was too close?" Scott asked.

"Yes," said the voice from inside the car. "And I suggest your idiot colleague comes out too."

I froze.

"Associate," Scott corrected him, somehow without getting his head blown off.

My knees cracked as I emerged.

"*Don't* put your hands up," the driver demanded. "Let's not draw attention to ourselves."

I joined Scott, who was looking unfeasibly calm. A beady looking man, the sort who distrusted anything that moved, dared us to move. He held a significantly more menacing automatic pistol. It glinted dully, and pointed at Scott's midriff from below the car window. He had a ponytail that most people realise is a bad idea long before finishing university. Dougal from the *Magic Roundabout* had clearly made an impact on his fashion decisions. I peered past him, but could not make out his accomplice. If it was Fred, he was keeping quiet.

"Who're you?" asked Scott.

The agent expected to be asking the questions, and said so. Laughter spilled from the bar. A plane moaned overhead.

"What is this caper?" the driver asked. He sounded insulted at our under-estimating them. "*You're* not important to us."

"You can't scare us," Scott said.

There was silence, as the driver looked for split ends in his fringe.

"We're not here to *scare* you. We're here to hurt you."

"Can you 'ear me?" the passenger asked. I heard the click of a Zippo and my blood ran cold. His biceps flexed in a tight Fred Perry T-shirt, and he smiled like a TV presenter freezing their grin until the ad break.

"We've been doing this for longer than you," he explained. Our amateurism was joined by vanilla smoke. "Got places to be Cripps?" he asked. "People to see? Missing anyone?"

My feet embedded themselves in the gravel. The driver had not taken his eyes off Scott.

"We'll keep this." He said. The starting gun now looked like it shot *bang* flags. He slid the window up, as the Society seemed trained to do. Scott rolled his shoulders, and sighed heavily.

"Beer?" he asked. It was the best idea he'd had in living memory.

We stood outside the bar. Bees tickled passionflowers clambering a wall still warm from the sun. The chink of glasses accompanied the bargirl collecting empties. She would be elsewhere in a year's time. Scott looked as dashing as sailors with shore leave *think* they are. I suggested we call the gendarmes, but he dissuaded me. I feared he was hatching another idea. The bland lager blunted my nerves. I felt like a hangover on a carousel. I drained my glass.

"Not too much," Scott advised, as I had once my mother.

"Foxe can find us in Hanway Street if he need us. I've got things to get on with..." His face implied he knew I really didn't.

"Foxe will be in Europe until he's done. He's finishing what Dee started," Scott supped his beer, "He's obviously after angels. It's why he needs the black mirror." He paused. "It's why he needs us."

"What're you thinking?"

"Mainly about his testimonies for the Life Assistance Agency when we find him."

His positivity irritated like an itch in a wetsuit. Scott went inside for a menu. Fred had almost mentioned Ronnie. He had granted me a reprieve, but I was dangling on his strings. Even Scott returning with fresh beers, and a smile belying our circumstance, didn't loosen the knots in my stomach. When would he stop looking like he knew something I didn't?

Chapter 18

We returned to the hotel in a line less straight than the one we had left in. I felt the Society's eyes on us.

"Don't unpack," warned Scott. "Try to sleep."

Scott's advice made sense later, when he shook me awake. It was dark and he hissed not to turn the light on. He'd have been better advised asking me not to hit him.

"Can you drive?" he asked.

Even in this groggy state I could drive better than him. "Yes, better than you." That he let this go should have worried me. I'd already guessed Scott's plan B.

"They're probably awake," I warned.

"They have to sleep, they're not sharks."

I was too tired to contest this. Scott handed me my bag, which he'd packed, and I headed to the door.

"No," Scott snapped. "The window." He sounded nervous: a bad sign.

The village was sleeping off its market day. A pin dropped and a dog barked. Streetlights' shadows mingled. A bench stretched its shape across the square. I glanced at the Toyota. Its windows were dark. The bar was now deserted. Scott bleeped our central locking without the indicators flashing.

"Took the bulbs out," he whispered, handing me the keys.

We scampered across to the Saab, opened the doors and jumped in, throwing our bags in the backseat. I fumbled with the ignition. It missed and I tried again. The engine turned, revving as I let out the clutch and stabbed the accelerator. We darted forward. I hung onto the steering wheel, as we lurched in the direction Scott and Luca had earlier.

"*Shit, they're in the car*," I yelled, as their headlights sparked.

Scott's frat campus whoop was inappropriate. I clung to the wheel like a water skier. The consequences of being caught took indefinite shape. We sped past the village limits, their headlamps gaining as we swept through the night, catching shuttered houses and parked cars.

Outside the village, the road sank between hedgerows that lashed at the wing mirrors and sides of the Saab in furious whips. Our headlights caught feral eyes shining from bushes as we charged through clouds of insects. Already, only feet from our rear bumper, our pursers' full beam was blinding. We hurtled over a bridge, and I swerved, with only faith keeping us from colliding with traffic cones of sudden road works. My mouth flushed with metal from my fillings, adrenaline shrunk my tongue, and my feet lost strength on the pedals. Only my hand remained oblivious to the chemicals tightening their way through my body. Eastwards the sky was lightening.

"Faster!" Scott shouted, but their Toyota was outperforming its specification – a Sussex boy racer spelling souped-up trouble. As the road widened, they swerved hard left and right, swooping and veering, angling for a way past. I threw the Saab into their way. They flashed their lights, while I suppressed the urge for safer speed. Hedgerows gave way to fields of wheat, before we skirted the edge of a town, catching wheelie bins and foxes in our lights. Our engine screamed; the revs in the red. I was scared. The road widened into a dual carriageway. There was no traffic, but there soon would be. The dog-whistle whine of our turbo kicked in as the suburbs dropped back. Our ears popped, as we climbed a hill, its incline something else to help lose our narrow lead. As I followed a long curve upwards, their Toyota found extra torque and pulled alongside; furious faces caught in the lights. Fred, brandishing the gun, lowered his window.

"*Fuck*," I dropped into third, stamping my body weight onto the accelerator. The revs jumped beyond the dial. I turned to Scott, whose face flickered with worry.

"What?" I glared at him, but he began smiling.

"At last. *Look*," he laughed, smacking the dashboard victoriously. They were falling behind, suddenly lagging as the road climbed, towards a now definitely lightening sky. What had happened? We were losing them, somehow without the Saab bursting into flames.

"Phew…" Scott sighed, like he knew what was happening.

Their headlamps shrunk to circular glowing eyes in the rear distance, and we charged into the remaining night.

A few miles later, Scott allowed us to pull over. He failed to see that my hands needed prising from the wheel. They lay shaking in my lap. His own enthusiasm had crumpled. I looked at him, alarmed at his face contorting from glory to pain.

"You OK?" I asked.

I could smell the engine burning. He grunted, thumbing for his pills from the back seat. With my still-trembling hands, I traced pharmaceutical jangle to the bottom of his bag and handed them over. He fumbled the tablets before necking them. I didn't know where to look.The sky was already blue, mocking our tiredness, as dawns love to. I got out and circled the car. The front mudguard was crumpled, not enough to flay the tyre, but certainly Ronnie's wrath. Scott relaxed, and although remaining pale, finally opened his eyes, to tell me what had happened.

"After they called you out from behind their car, Luca stuffed damp napkins into the exhaust."

Their engine had lasted longer than Scot had expected. Any

longer and we'd have been stopped, permanently.

"Why didn't you tell me Luca went behind the car?" I asked.

"Because you're a bad liar."

Blood rushed to my face in defence.

"No I'm not."

"Really?" His face became hard to read. "You're transparent."

I'm unsure at what time in the evening we arrived in Krakow. My phone died and I was afraid to look at the Saab's clock once our adrenaline subsided. We booked into the first hotel we found on St Stephen's Street, secreting the car behind a pillar in its underground car park.

Scott fell asleep clutching the black mirror, while I enjoyed the most comfortable beds so far. However, like finding a late tent pitch at Glastonbury and waking up on the main stage, I awoke in yet *another* room with carpet smelling of damp. The Life Assistance Agency's *Where not to stay in Europe* was gathering chapters.

"You're late," Scott said, with the smugness of someone having seen a hotel breakfast. "Lateness implies you've got better things to do," he added.

I could have listed those, but needed to intercept the trolley disappearing into the kitchen. I made tea from a used teabag, and stirred sugar into the pitiful restorative.

"We'll stay somewhere better," he said.

I looked up at the collapsing polystyrene ceiling. "Like that'll be hard." I sipped my tea. "I thought we'd lost them…"

"It's precautionary." He pushed his chair away from the table. I noticed the bag holding the obsidian mirror at his feet. "Mrs. Foxe texted, Foxe is here in Krakow. I told her where we're staying," he said, smiling like a plan had come together.

Before we checked out, we found an email from Ronnie. I rather wished she wasn't sending us emails of Jane's diary, which she was studiously transcribing into emails. I presume Scott had promised her compensation that she'd have to join the queue to collect. I could have done without being reminded of her existence. Her email was business-like. It confirmed that the medieval paper was genuine, and had even dated the diary's contemporary translation to 40 or 50 years ago. We found an Internet café to print it off, and sat in a square to read it:

WEST

21st September 1583
The two ships scraped the quayside of the Gravesend docks. We eyed the storm gathering offshore, but John agreed with the captain that it posed little threat, like he actually understood coastal weather patterns. It's hard to know where his knowledge stops and his pretending starts. A crayer was running in, its sodden sailors grinning as they collapsed its salt-caked sails. Our ship was one of the older square-rigged caravels creaking on the rising tide. John watched the loading.

We had left Mortlake three days ago, leaving my brother as temporary caretaker. He already disappeared into the house before our wherry sculled the Thames' bend. I knew John feared he might never see his carefully catalogued books and equipment again.

Our party now includes Edward Kelley's new wife, Joanna. She is bewildered by everything, particularly the sea, which she has never seen before. I'm unsure anyone had even *told* her about it.

Kelley's marriage took everyone by surprise, including, it appears, Kelley. Joanna is a solid looking girl, years younger than her frown suggests. Her hair is blonde and thin, with grey eyes. She is rather underwhelming, and despite the wherry's bow tapping the Mortlake riverbank to invite her on board, she needed both its oarsmen to assist her boarding. We conversed during the ride from London, about her fears of travelling through Europe. I guessed the angels had demanded the union, but if so Joanna knew nothing about it. What would they request next?

"Why are we going?" she had asked, and I struggled with an adequate reply.

At the quayside, gulls quarrelled overhead, as Kelley watched John searching for something. He was panicking like a pardoned man mislaying the paperwork.

"Have you seen it?" he asked a sailor impatiently.

"What?" the sailor grunted, not unreasonably.

"My holdall... where *is* it?"

John stared to where his book trunks were being unloaded. The sailor gave a cursory glance around, while Kelley, from the short foredeck, held up a leather holdall. John looked up, and despite a flash of anger, looked relieved. He stepped up the gangplank and took the bag from his so-called scryer. Both Kelley and I noticed John had not allowed it from of his sight during the journey past London's jetties and docksides.

"Personals," John explained hastily.

Kelley nodded, acknowledging the bag's importance. "Rather spacious for your comb," he said.

"I won't be swimming with it," John agreed, as Arthur ran into his legs. "Careful," Dee warned his son. "May God be with us," he addressed the sky, before disappearing below deck, 'though not before hitting his head on a low beam. "*Sard* it."

I laughed. Swim with it? John couldn't swim *without* it.

I stood below deck, clinging to the reassuring solidity of the narrow bunks. I needed to find my sea legs and quickly. As we passed a Long Ferry from Gravesend, the Thames' slack tide gave way to the swelling currents of the English Channel. If the ship sank, we would plummet with it. I mumbled prayers for our safety. Salt ran white along the boarding, and sailors' footsteps clattered across the deck above. The Continent lay somewhere ahead, as blank as our purpose.

The sailors reassured us of a calm crossing, but it was not the motion that sickened me, it was the dark depths below. I sensed the Unknown creeping through the dampness sloshing about the hull, desperate to drag us under. It is a powerful pull. All that kept us afloat was the wind, propelling us quicker than we could sink. I prayed for the wind to prevail. Sweet wine, sticky on our feet, betrayed previous homeward passengers' impatience to drink continental souvenirs.

The boat lurched to the side, as John stepped up from the cramped mess in which we sat. He ducked his head beneath the braces framing the brief corridor, but still struck his forehead. I would have liked some reassurance from him, but he reached past me for his astrolabe and sextant.

"I wish to check the ship's latitude," he explained, before leaving with his copy of William Bourne's *A Regiment for the Sea* under his arm. He nodded as he passed Kelley and Joanne in the low chairs of the cramped mess. Kelley smiled to me along the narrow aisle: providing the reassurance John had neglected to give. I soon followed him, and put my head out of the hatch into the sea spray. John was on deck, standing in the bowsprit, watching the pilot haul in the logline to note their speed. He mapped out the stars slowly in his journal. As the ship idled at dusk, the crew studied the foraging gulls that were never far from shore, and our boat followed them home, towards the black coast of Northern France at the starboard. I joined John as he packed his equipment away. I smiled at the signal lights of a passing ferry. I felt part of something:

the wind of change, of potential, momentarily filled my own sails.

Having docked, we lodged at the Three Golden Keys. It overhung a dirty street strewn with old hay. The next day, with horses arranged and arrangements for stabling in Bremen confirmed, we left Emden's filthy streets and piers collapsing into the estuary. Scaffolding announcing new buildings stood at its outskirts, before the countryside opened beneath moody skies. The wagon's canvas flapped in the wind, and the children braced themselves against the boxes of books. We would learn to anticipate ruts of the road. Finding room on the lead bench, I overheard John and Kelley as they rode in front.

"You enjoy marriage?" asked Kelley.

"It's a stake in the ground. It prevents wandering," John replied, wisely in light of my listening.

"As if that stops you."

I was reminded of first seeing John Dee in 1575. I was not writing my diary then, but I remembered seeing his tall frame. His wife had passed only the previous night, yet despite his grief he had helped our Queen ashore. I was to meet John again, during his visit to Hampton Court, before the House moved for sweetening. Despite his height, he had a serious smile that was not entirely without playfulness. He had chosen an auspicious date for her Coronation, and it was his expertise in cartography that resulted in frequent invites, leading to our introduction.

I shook my head back to reality. The Forests here are thicker here than in England and the men were still talking. Dee laughed his equine laugh.

"We must ask the angelica again. You're sure they demand Krakow?" he asked.

"Indeed, they do." Kelley nodded.

I recognised John's frustration at seeing nothing in the crystal since Mortlake, while Kelley apparently so effortlessly succeeded. I watched Kelley's long hair fall forward, exposing its increasingly noticeable white streak, and the missing tops of his ears. I feared for how long their motives would remain mutual.

I was drifting asleep. I fear I am pregnant again. Not that it stops Kelley from casting his eyes over me like a horse trader.

"How old was Catherine, when she passed?" Kelley asked John.

"She was thirty." John sighed, "Death's cloak is one I wish not to wear."

"And rob yourself of your heavenly destination?"

"Catherine died the night Queen Elizabeth visited." Dee's voice went quiet. "I was lucky, I found another, but to outlive a wife is a curse I'd wish upon no one."

"The Queen's visit?"

"Aye. We spoke by the church, a pleasant conversation. I pitched the idea of a national library. She said best teach them to read first," John chuckled. "She has treated us favourably."

"She's treated *you* well."

"Perhaps," John agreed. "But royals have poor records in holding back tides. They die as easily as anyone." He sounded sad. "Prepared for this evening?" he asked,

"As always." Kelley's sarcasm was lost on John.

They moved into the adjoining room and I heard them billowing the hearth back to life. They worked silently, setting up equipment and breathing shallowly.

"*Convinced* of a good night for an action?" Kelley ventured tiredly.

"A night *not* scrying is a night wasted," John smiled.

"As I was afraid you'd say."

"You know their insistence."

"Far better than you."

11th February 1584

We traced a river running through a forest, and halted at foundations marking out a future church. It lay at a crossroads marked by a large boulder. A freshly painted sign read *Leimbach*. Despite not being built yet it was a fine place for worship. While we stretched our legs, John stepped into the trees. A notice warning of wolves was pinned to the trunk of a Yew. Dee put his ear to the bark.

"What're you doing?" Kelley asked.

"Trees are where God wrote his plans," Dee explained.

"Aren't *we* his plans?"

"We're where he panicked," John chuckled.

"That *is* blasphemous."

"In a few years that nail will be a part of the tree, as you shall be of the earth," John laughed. He patted the tree again. "Trees know the world, yet never travel. They'll be here long after we've gone."

Our going is slow. It is cold. Steam rises ghost-like from the horses' flanks. Horses are not changed as frequently on this part of the Continent. Our party is exhausted, yet John still uses his books for pillows, hoping the words might embed themselves into his dreams.

To ease the horses, we dismounted for a steep hill. As Kelley walked ahead, I nudged John beside me.

"Your coat's dragging the mud."

He gathered it up, before tightening his belt.

"What happened last night?" I asked, but he did not answer. "John, for Christ's sake," I said. "D'you even know what you're messing with? These are daemons, pure and simple."

"They're angels, Jane, not daemons," he said. "And are men's business…"

"Because women aren't stupid enough to look for trouble?" I looked ahead at Kelley. "He's an interesting mouthpiece to God. What's he promised you?"

John paused, before stopping to hold my face. It felt good. He had not touched me for weeks.

"God's greatest gift," he said with a smile.

We continued, and I slipped on the mud. He offered his arm. Villagers passing from outlying fields avoided eye contact.

"That cloak don't help," I said, flicking his sleeves. "Makes you look like the sorcerer your advertisement claimed you aren't."

The fields surrounding Krakow teemed with cows and pigs. Farmers were fattening them for market. Birds carved the sky in chattering arcs, competing for food scraps from kitchens, sewers and markets of the streets below. We passed through Krakow's North gate in patchily repaired city walls. The busy thoroughfare was deeply rutted with gullies from the rain.

"We'll find friends here," Kelley announced, fired by their return to civilisation. "No more mud and peasants for now."

"Whom do we seek?" John asked.

Kelley hesitated, "Rožmberk, a man keen on our pursuits."

"Rožmberk? You and I fell out when I requested that you deliver that letter to him in Southwark, yet we seek him now?"

"He has several laboratories in Bohemia province," Kelley tugged hair over his wretched ears. "He needs help to muster gold."

15th February 1584

I found John tonight reading a letter that he failed to hide as I entered.

"Bit slow," I smiled, "What is it?" I crouched by the fire to add a log.

John hesitated. "Correspondence, from the Papal Nuncio. We must be careful; the Catholic Church tightens its sails." He smiled. "King Rudolph enjoys alchemy, but it's unclear for how much longer."

I heard the Royal Court in Prague embraced mystics and lunatics, strange animals and magik fumes. Krakow was where Kings were buried, not born. He handed me the letter:

You have summoned spirits, with the aid of certain magical characters, and we beseech that you stop. Your endeavour is immoral, impossible, and unsanctioned by the Church.

"A warning, from the Papal Nuncio."

"You fear it?" I asked.

"No, but perhaps insurances must be made. We cannot depend upon lasting tolerance or understanding."

"Made?"

"Yes. Or cast." He winked.

Krakow's windows gleamed with rain and its streets were strewn with straw from loose thatch and leaves. I heard the street door to our rented house slam. The side window was tiny, but overhung the street, so I glimpsed John hurrying down the street. I checked the children were still sleeping, before shrugging on my jacket, and following him. I soon glimpsed him, as he failed to duck in time beneath the overhanging houses running to the river. He swore quietly to himself as he rubbed his forehead.

Clanking echoed down a narrow lane, blows fell with satisfying rhythm. I could smell burning. Two horses waited outside to be shoed, stamping old straw. Dawn men shovelled droppings into sacks to sell for manure. The building was the sole stone establishment in the street. Thin clouds of hot air trailed in steady streams from its windows. Storks fought for space on the warm roof. Realising the futility of knocking, John opened the door, and disappeared inside. I waited momentarily, before sneaking in after him. The heat struck me like a wall.

In the middle of the room, a boy prodded a forge, while another manned huge billows stoking the flames. The blacksmith was hammering a horseshoe on a high table without care to the sparks falling around him. I crouched behind a worktop.

"Prawdziwy popludnowy?" The blacksmith asked. I saw him taking in John's long coat and sleeves. Perhaps it sometimes pays to look like an alchemist, even at this early hour.

"Undertaking commissions?" John replied in Polish. The Smithy put down the hammer and nodded. I noticed copper and zinc labelled on depository cupboards. "You work with brass?"

"If it's strong enough." The Smithy nodded to the boy, who laid the billows aside. The fire calmed. He peeled off his heavy leather gloves.

"For you?" asked the Smith.

Dee shook his head, "Partly. It's a gift." He pulled back his cowl. "For the Emperor."

"The Emperor?" The Smithy's eyes widened with the prospect of a royal commission. He stepped away from his work, and found a stool. He sat down, to find some paper, inviting John to describe what he wanted –

"Two 12-inch brass discs..." John did not hesitate. "They

need to impress."

"12 pouce? No problem."

"You are a skilled engraver?" John asked.

The man nodded, "Good enough for the King."

The man's interest had significantly improved. John asked for charcoal, to draw the round-bodied shape of his horned monad.

"I need this engraved on both," he explained, "And on the other side…" He unrolled parchment, on which were drawn intricate tables, "This *exact* pattern. It must be precise. But only on one disc."

The blacksmith frowned, but made no comment. He folded away the order and showed John back through the workshop. I quickly slipped out of the front door in time to crouch behind a horse trough. From the darkness of the workshop the forge glowed like the underworld. John paused at the door.

"Add some calamine," he smiled. "It's not gold, but it's the nearest we'll get."

I recognised the Smithy making a mental note not to take John as a fool. "I'll require a deposit," he said.

John smiled, and delved into his pockets to produce gold coins.

"I trust these will suffice."

"They won't turn to slate?" The blacksmith asked, taking them.

"Not these. Trust me."

The blacksmith bit the coins, and nodded. He had worked with enough gold to know this was the real thing.

Krakow. March 7th 1584

Despite the warning, we remain in Krakow. John called for me from their room in the eaves. The alchemists were struggling to light the hearth.

"Perhaps the tinder is damp," John said, rubbing his forearm aching from striking the flint on the steel. I took it from him. It sparked, yet the tinder would not take.

"Sparks, but no fire," John said. "Like before your arrival Edward." He looked to Kelley, who nodded modestly. Kelley looked pale and overworked. The white streak dissected his hair like lightening.

I continued to rub the flint, while John unwrapped the circular black-mirrored stone. I watched as he placed it upon the silk cloth atop the larger wax disc facing Kelley. He then laid out the intricately carved tables that translated their communications. John moved away, as Kelley took a deep breath and closed his eyes.

"Why not ask your angels to light it?" I joked, but John did not laugh. I looked back to Kelley, who was staring into the crystal ball on top of the black mirror. He was mumbling words I did not understand.

"The charcoal's dry…" I explained to John, handing him the scrunch of wood shavings. He took them and kneeled, when Kelley called out as though in pain. His hand clutched his forehead, as his eyes rolled back into his head.

"You should leave," John said, but before I could move, a flame sprung from the fireplace, catching the wood in John's hand. He yelped, dropping it to the floor. I stamped out the fire, while looking at the fireplace that had so resolutely refused to light.

Krakow 28th March 1584

"Where's Kelley?" John asked me.

I was sitting with Joanna. We were sewing repairs into our clothes torn by the roads. Kelley had been absent from St Stephen's Street since leaving for a tavern last night. I was about to answer, when Joanna interrupted.

"Visiting Rožmberk," she answered, to which John spluttered in disbelief.

"Rožmberk is here in Krakow? Does Kelley seek new patronage?" John asked. He sounded worried.

Joanna looked confused. "I'm afraid I have no idea."

She really is not the prettiest of women, nor is she the brightest, or she would have noticed Kelley's interest in me. Seemingly unbeknown to her, and indeed John, I feel his eyes burning into me wherever I go. His leering has grown less subtle the further we've travelled. I am uncertain if John is turning a blind eye, or is too distracted by his angels.

I heard Kelley return much later on. I feared John had been waiting for him downstairs, and I was right.

"I hear you seek Rožmberk?" I heard him ask.

Kelley was too shattered for denials. "Rožmberk has left, for Prague," he answered.

"And how is that your business?" John asked. Kelley did not answer.

"So," Dee asked. "The angels. They wish us to remain in Krakow? Or leave for Prague?"

Kelley groaned, "Who cares?"

"It would appear only one of us."

At this point Ronnie interjected in the email. 'I'm not putting it all in', she wrote, 'They go to Krakow, then Prague and then to some windswept, out of season castle that wouldn't last a month on Air B&B. And there's loads of stuff about Arthur, and Dee's other kids. It's hard to know what's important, but some of it reads like a 6th form project on 'living in medieval times.' I guess it'll all make sense?' Ronnie was right. We were following random trails in the hope that scent always leads to prey. We continued to read.

Krakow 29th March 1584

It was in the morning that I crept into their room beneath the eaves. The morning rain chased down the windowpane; water gathering in the rotten sills. It was deserted. John's *Monas Hieroglyphica* lay on the table. I glanced at it, but understood not a word. Linen hung over the windows to filter dust from the street below. The table, covered with its cloth, stood upon its seals, and in prime position was the crystal ball. Kelley's black cap hung over his chair from where he stared into the ball. I looked at the last thing John had written:

Were you not commanded to be gone? The message is clear: Go to the Emperor in Prague.

Horses arriving outside disturbed me. I went down to find John greeting a man dressed in finery that has no place in daylight.

"Dr John Dee?" he asked.

"It is I. You are from the Church?"

"An affiliate." The man nodded. His red tunic was adorned with badges engraved with angels and seals of the Catholic Church.

"We hear of your endeavours, and the Papal Nuncio disapproves," he said, wielding a letter like a whip.

"We are a society," he added. "Necessary to ensure that God's Will remains at the centre of everything."

"His will?" Dee was sharp. "Or yours? Last time I looked, God granted us all free will."

"Indeed he did, which brings the need for responsibility. Our society shall endure Dr Dee. You shall not. It would pay you to remember that." He handed John the envelope.

"Is that a threat?"

"No. It's a suggestion that you leave Krakow."

"Then we shall," John smiled, as though already having made the decision.

Our visitor appeared shocked at his submission. Disappointed at lack of fight, he left to re-embark the running boards of his carriage.

"Excellent. Then we wish you safe passage," he declared, taking the credit. "We wish you well, Dr John Dee."

16th April 1584

Our party has reached the far-flung village of Chrzanow. The sun filtering through trees illuminated the curling mist. John inhaled the cool air. The children giggled at the edge of the clearing.

"Farthing for 'em?" I asked, sitting beside John on a felled tree. "The usual spirit creatures?"

The children skipped away, melting into the grass.

"The sprites enquire of our desires. They ask what we *want*," Dee explained. "Kelley's desire is obvious to a blind man, but he fails to see that wealth without longevity is worthless."

"John, you're the oldest man I know."

"Flattery will get you everywhere, Jane," he laughed, putting his arm around me. I moved closer into the uncharacteristic affection. The sun was breaking the trees, the light catching bursts of midges amidst the rising pollen.

"When do we get to see our lord?" I asked.

"At death." He grew solemn. "But death is cheating. I wish to prevail, until I meet his eyes here on earth."

"Then pr'haps your desire is as obvious as Kelley's."

There you go boys. Seems even a Life Assistance Agency needs help, Ronnie. x

Chapter 19

Ronnie's send-off kiss drilled deeper than I dared admit. However, she was doing a great job and there was something thrilling about Jane Dee writing about the church foundations at Leimbach. The presumption of everlasting religion abandoned by time.

We found a new hotel, which *was* an improvement. The towels were heavy before they got wet and the soap frothed. Guests were diving into a swimming pool and inclusive bar with equal relish. Krakow beeped and honked for attention beyond the hotel walls, but the guests were enjoying a holiday that could be anywhere. Even I doubted that the Society would be looking for us in an all-inclusive tourist hotel. Scott went for a swim.

It is good to see new places alone. You can make up your own mind. I wandered around Krakow, looking for shades of what John Dee might have seen. I even spent an hour in a cafe drafting a new blog entry, although it was too early for *Memoirs of a Life Assistance Agency*. Our exploits were too distant from office hours for anyone to believe. To know the beginning, you must know the end, and my 500 words acutely demonstrated how little I understood.

I had started writing to escape Hastings, to bring the Alps, or the Bahamas or at least the North Downs, closer to home. The smell of dead fish and boat diesel can be as an effective muse as mermaids. During school, I fantasised about teachers leading classes to the Ferguson-Cripps sports hall, having parked in the Ferguson-Cripps staff car park.

I watched the impossible-chic young women of Krakow, as they ignored the black-dressed widows of their destiny shuffle past. Paris promotes itself well, but I knew less about Krakow. I enjoyed that afternoon, reading guidebooks and enjoying the aimlessness. The city's future and past hung perfectly poised in the summer air. For a few seconds the consequences of my behaviour lifted. I even vaguely enjoyed a limp European tea served in the typical soup bowl, but my relief mainly consisted of not being followed by a sinister organisation; you know, the simple pleasures.

I closed the guide about Krakow having been Poland's capital until 1596, when King Sigismund moved the capital to Warsaw, following an alchemical accident that burnt down the Wavel castle. Women trotted past my cafe, clutching dogs turning their nose up at anything not being carried. Krakow, like many European cities, is a city of closed doors. There is the underlying sense that stuff *is* happening; it's just that you aren't invited.

I was chewing my pen when I spotted Scott across the street. The café was too quiet to shout from. I was about to leap up, when Scott stopped. No passersby noticed as he clutched his chest. I paused, unsure what to do. He staggered, finding a lamppost for support. He wiped his face, which following a visibly deep breath, rearranged into a more familiar expression. I was poised to do something when he started looking for something in his pocket. I stood, but he saw me and waved. I felt foolish, like sunbathing when the sun goes in. I stayed put, as he recovered his medal-winning swagger, and made his way across.

"Memoirs of the Agency?" he asked, arriving at my table with sweat still on his forehead.

I closed my notepad, and he sat down like he needed to. He tapped the air for the waiter and ordered a coffee, before his phone rang. It was Mrs. Foxe. He told her where we were, and she put the phone down. Ten minutes later, Mrs Foxe rang back to suggest we visit 'the café in the square by five o'clock', for a rendezvous with Mr Foxe. Scott was more delighted by this than someone already sitting in a café should be. His coffee arrived and he stirred in enough sugar to define living dangerously.

"We're getting somewhere," he said, but swapping one café for another did not feel like it.

I feared someone was following us, but Scott reassured me otherwise. Back at the all-inclusive hotel, the poolside bonhomie had moved to the Reception, where guests indulged in watered-down booze and raucous inability to hear conversations. As we collected our room key, I looked around the foyer. The niggling sensation of eyes upon us burned my back, but the only people nearby were busily enjoying their retirement.

While congratulating ourselves on finally finding the first beds fit for purpose in Europe, we watched afternoon quiz shows awarding kettles as prizes. We left in good time for our five o'clock meeting. Scott waited in Reception to watch for potential tails. As I left the room, an elderly man was holding a stack of towels at the adjoining room's door.

"Mój szkieletowy klucz nie pracuje," he started, before seeing my alarm. "My key, key not work," he translated. I nodded, showing him into our room with a smile, again admiring the towels that could double as rugs, before joining Scott downstairs.

We reached the designated café with half an hour to spare. I was nervous about finally meeting Foxe, although Scott appeared as sanguine as ever. Across the square, the sun glinted in the windows of an impressive apartment block. Through mouthfuls of local cake, Scott contemplated our chase coming to an end. He was convinced that we would soon get paid to settle Hanway street's rent arrears; having an office to return to depended upon it. I was enjoying the idea of going home, when Scott got a text.

"Shit, he wants to meet tomorrow," Scott said, reading it. We finished our drinks, and joined the pedestrian rush hour. It was the first time since leaving England that the evening yawned emptily ahead.

As we neared our hotel, the guests weren't dancing on tables twirling shirts above their heads, but it was close. I was still envying their pleasure when we opened our door.

I was stunned. Someone had trashed our room. The contents of our bags were scattered across the room in a manner I had always been *accused* of unpacking in, but this was not laziness, it was systematic.

"Lost them have we?" I muttered, while Scott stalked through the room.

I held up the muslin bag, "The mirror's gone." I felt strangely hollow. Scott emerged from the ransacked bathroom, shaking his head.

"How did they get in?" he asked.

"And know we were here?" I asked, "We only told Mrs. Foxe." I paused. I could see even Scott's positivity was dented.

"It must've been after room service...Ah," I said. "The old chambermaid." My realisation arrived like the thump of luxury hotel towels hitting carpet.

We tidied the room more easily than my head. The Society appeared to have lost patience. But, how *had* they found us? We felt too weak to compete for the free buffet downstairs, so ordered room service. There seemed little point in asking reception if they employed male chambermaids. The devastation of our room adequately answered that.

We went to bed. Scott helped me drag the dressing table across to block the door. Soon afterwards, people above us began fucking as though for one-night only. It pummelled with everything I wanted to do with Ronnie. Scott lay across from me. I was unsure if he was asleep. We were like prison inmates. Each night we endeavoured to stay awake the longest, before one admitted defeat and lay hoping to fall asleep first, before the other started twitching the sheets.

I was too nervous to enjoy breakfast. We had brought napkins to a towel fight. The hotel felt like a station after the last train. The previous night's reverie was now nursing a headache. Scott collided with a 'Caution' cone. I double-took at a smiling cleaner, but he was shorter than the one last night.

Scott's phone bleeped. Inexplicably, it was Mrs Foxe suggested the same café *again* at 5:00. Her cautionary text confirmed that the Society *was* watching, although we had no idea from where. We sat by the river and I wrote Daisy a postcard. By 2:00, we stoically accepted the inevitability of three hours drinking tea. Someone once suggested I seize life by the horns, as though minting the phrase. I warned them about stampeding, but it went over their head. We ordered more tea. Scott leafed through his scrawling notes, while I watched a pigeon battling with a discarded sandwich.

"Others," he read, struggling with his own writing. "Who're these others that have disappeared that Mrs Foxe mentioned? Scryers? I'm guessing Oliver Turner kept scrying after he left Foxe. He seems to think he's the talent."

"Just like Edward Kelley did."

I told him about King Rudolph 2nd, who had pursued Kelley's alchemy skills.

"King Rudolph who lived up there?" Scott pointed at the Wavel, an austere, squat castle atop a steep hill. "Let's have a look. It's not like we've got plans."

At the summit, Inter-Railers scratched their names into the

parapet overlooking the river. We followed a driveway curving into a square fronting the cathedral. School children poured from a coach like marbles across a polished floor; enthusiasm that history was about to quash. Scott quickened his pace to overtake them, and we bought tickets from a booth before the children arrived. The monk tore off tickets without eye contact, and indicated a marble entrance carved with intricacy only future Godly blessings motivates. Angels blew trumpets to the Holy Spirit and Jesus, who gazed towards God himself. The gold glinted historically, but left me cold.

A sign indicated the tombs to the left. Another monk stood by the door leading to the catacombs. His pure white rope-belt clashed dramatically with his black cassock. We descended stone steps into crypts of freestanding tombs. We walked round twice. The smaller coffins of royal children were particularly chilling.

"Got through their kings didn't they," observed Scott. Noticing a flower on a coffin. He slipped under the rope, "Rudolph 2nd," he announced. "That's the one you mentioned, the one Dee and Kelley met. Seems alchemy and the search for immortality got him to the same place as everyone else." He ducked under the rope, and found a brass plaque. Hearing footsteps, he froze.

"Keep watch," he hissed.

His phone camera flashed, and I loitered back towards the entrance. Our ransacked hotel room had ruptured something. The Society knew what they were doing. Police states and dictatorships use similar tactics. The steps were deserted, and hearing the approaching school party, I returned to the crypt, calling Scott's name, but my voice echoed without response.

"He's not here," said a voice, as Fred Perry and his longhaired Dougal chum joined me. I grabbed my heart in shock. How had they found me?

"Where is he?" Dougal asked me with Stasi like efficiency. He had the face of a man struggling to read a newspaper in the wind.

Meanwhile, Fred appeared to have attended the gym recently, using his ego as weights, and was wearing a t-shirt far tighter than necessary. He opened a door I had not noticed, and pushed me into a white washed office.

"Nice escapade back there," he said, and I thanked him, before Dougal suggested I refrain from speaking. The temperature plummeted. They pushed me onto a chair.

"Where's the black mirror?" they asked.

I frowned. If they hadn't ransacked our room, then who had? "You've not got it?"

They looked at each other, somehow aware I was not bluffing.

"What d'you mean?" Fred asked.

"We don't have it anymore. But, if you don't." I frowned. "Who has? Maybe it was Foxe?" It wasn't the best time to be thinking aloud.

"Foxe? What're you talking about Cripps? What's Foxe up to?"

"We don't know. Who knows? He's probably chasing gold and immortality like every other fool." I said, as unexpected petulance joined the fear filling my body like a fever. Having exhausted all I could tell them I hoped they could not see my leg trembling. "Sorry you didn't find it," I said.

"Find what?"

Our hotel room hadn't been the Society. Clearly taking a personal dislike to me, Dougal stepped forward. I concentrated on his cowboy boots; they made him harder to take seriously, until he pulled a pistol from his jacket.

"We can't kill him," Fred warned. "Not here."

I stuttered in agreement.

His companion returned the gun to his pocket. He bent down. Garlic was on his breath.

"What do writers value most?" he asked me.

The answer was a decent Wi-Fi connection, Facebook Likes and short story competitions, but it was not time for honesty. Dougal studied my hand, and picked up the letter knife. In a flash, he wrenched my left hand to the table and pinned it down. I gasped. His free hand flicked the knife into the air, catching it by the handle. He grunted at his own dexterity. Fred stood aside, but Dougal paused to listen. I had also heard a metallic clang. Was it Scott?

"What was that?" Dougal listened, but heard nothing more. He stared at me. "Mr Foxe is practising without authority." He brushed fluff from his Harrington Jacket. "It's unsanctioned."

"He's in Krakow…" I managed. My hand was hurting from his pressure.

"Where?"

"I don't know." I felt a rush of panic. I wanted to tell them something, but had nothing.

Fred noticed the watch, which I'd never moved from my left hand.

"Right hand," he whispered. Dougal threw my left hand aside, and grabbed my right, instead pinning that to the table. My numb right hand couldn't even feel his grip.

"Why's Foxe looking to meet you?" Fred's tone suggested he would not be asking twice. "*Where's* he meeting you?"

"I don't know."

The knife plunged through my hand with almost comic violence. I recoiled in shock, but not pain. I gagged. My hand, pinned to the table, appeared as though someone else's. Dougal, apparently unhappy with my reaction, pulled the blade out. My hand followed, before detaching with a sucking noise and flopping to the table with a splatter of blood. My good hand instinctively covered it, to stem the wound. The knife rose again, poised. Blood was spilling from my palm. I felt faint.

"Where is he?" they asked again, but a shape behind them distracted me. Something shimmered on the whitewashed wall. It was part of it and yet not. It blinked. I could not discern its sex, but its narrow head blended with the whiteness. Its grey eyes looked at me, not unkindly. The lines on the wall formed a lupine face. My eyes widened, as I swear the spread of wide feathered wings stretched open behind it.

Dougal's eyes bored into mine. "What're you looking at?"

I'd lost focus, finally understanding how possible it is to freeze with fear. There was confusion, before a knock at the door disturbed them.

"Scott," I shouted with a bravado that surprised us all.

Dougal slapped my face, whipping my head to the side. It stung like barbed wire. Blood dripped from his cygnet ring. He was poised to strike again, when the door opened. I could not see who it was, but they spoke in Polish. I caught the glimpse of a black cassock. Dougal looked even less happy, when he made me stand, and his upper cut to my stomach winded me with an ease demonstrating how few sit-ups I did.

"We'll be watching," he said, pushing me back into the vaults. A monk stood there, refusing to meet my eye, but handed me a cloth. I heard children somewhere, as I stumbled away, wrapping my hand as blood fell in dark stains on the stone cladding. I climbed some steps and found Scott outside, pacing anxiously on the grass. He actually gasped when he saw the gash on my cheek, and reddening cloth bandaging my hand.

"Nothing I can't handle," I lied. I had never felt less like Denzel Washington. I started running, "Let's get out of here."

He looked back at the entrance, and for once consented, joining my retreat.

Chapter 20

Krakow's A&E bandaged my hand with an expertise honed by stag-do injuries and the velvet revolution. I told them a club bouncer had done it. I wish it had been, bouncers tend to draw a line under such matters. The painkillers were welcome. They dulled my memory, although made my angelic hallucination even less sensical.

We made our way to the café with an hour to spare. It seemed pointless to check if we were being followed. I feared the sedation was wearing off, but the bandage remained reassuringly tight.

We chose a table by the window.

"It might surprise you," Scott said, "But our trip to the crypt was well spent." He handed me his phone and I scrolled through various photos of a manhole cover.

"Oh, yes. Well worth a stabbing."

"Behind the coffins," he continued, too excited for sympathy. "*Look*."

The metal disc was engraved with a horned snowman.

"It's the desk doodle from Mortlake." He said. "It's Dee's Monad engraved on the brass plaque. So, I lifted it up."

I recalled the clang from the crypts. "To find what?" I asked, interested despite myself.

"This."

The first photo showed an empty sewer, but the next caught the brass plaque's underside. Scott zoomed in.

"They're detailed tables," he said. "I think it's the angel

charts preserved for posterity, but there was wax residue from a recent brass rubbing."

"Foxe has copied the table? But how did he know it was engraved on the back of a manhole cover?"

Scott's phone bleeped a text: To the right of my nickname at 5 o'clock.

"What the fuck does that mean?" I asked. It was 4:40. Foxe was being cautious enough to have encrypted his message, but so effectively as to elude us too. And why did he even want to still meet us if he had got the black mirror. I looked around the square, but saw no sign of the Society, despite this my heart raced. What *did* Foxe mean? I recalled the distance between NHS beds.

"Six Foot," I said, "Foxe's nickname is Six Foot. He means six foot to the right of something."

"At five o'clock?"

I recalled the light flashing across the Thames at Mortlake.

"Perhaps, where the sun hits at 5:00? Like his experiment," I said.

It was 4:50. Shadow was pursuing sunlight up the façade of the private looking building across the square. Windows glinted as it passed. At 5:00 precisely, two floors below the roof, the sun flashed in a window. The neighbouring window appeared exactly six feet to the right. We looked up and saw someone wave. We had found him. Now we had to meet him without leading the Society to him.

Before returning to our hotel, we skirted the apartment block. There was no entrance. We guessed access was gained from the street running behind it. We needed to lose the Society again.

In our hotel foyer, a man was chalking up a jazz tour. No one took interest in us as we took the lift. Our room no longer felt our own. Scott lay on the bed to consider the ceiling, analysing how people lost tails in films, before finally deciding that we disguise ourselves. This time I was less enthusiastic, but even that was better than the plan he suggested. It was as tight as a sponge, yet I had no better suggestions.

An hour later the jazz bar excursion was gathering downstairs. The minibus driver stood outside smoking. From the hotel shop, Scott bought an *I Love Krakow* cap. He looked like an actor playing a lorry driver. My Tyrolean hat made me look like a twat. We boarded, returning smiles, while looking outside for the Society. We found a seat halfway along the aisle by the fire exit, and peered out. That was a mistake. Staring at me from a car was Dougal. Our eyes met. His car lights ignited, as the bus's door hissed closed and it began to move.

I froze. "Fuck."

Scott frowned. "We should just leg it."

It seemed a poor time to be lifting advice from my father's rulebook. He saw my disappointment, and his voice softened.

"I know you've had enough," he said.

If 'legging it' was the best we had then we were fucked. The bus drove on, our companions gaping at the city, or their reflections. I was weak with fear.

We stopped at traffic lights. My heart was thundering. Scott tensed as I recognised Krakow's main thoroughfare from yesterday. Without hesitation, he stepped down the fire escape, bracing himself as the bus jerked forward. When we stopped again, before I could coordinate our location, there was *crack*, as Scott's brogue kicked open the fire door. Passengers looked up in confusion. We landed in the cobbled road as though wearing roller-skates. We scrambled up, to run alongside the bus and across the junction into the square from earlier. We heard honking, but didn't look back. Following Scott's lead, I dashed over the cobbles. We crossed tram-tracks framing the square, before ducking down the alleyway behind the apartments. I bloody hoped Foxe was expecting us.

We ran past narrow unnumbered doorways, before reaching one apparently in use. We were panting. It required an entry card. Scott prodded at the buzzer, as I looked back down the street. At the end, 50 yards away, Fred and Dougal skidded to a standstill. Seeing us, they yelled, before sprinting down the alley, hands fumbling for pistols in their pockets. Scott jabbed the buzzer again.

They were charging towards us, jackets flapping, guns drawn. I tugged at the door, when with a Swiss click, the door swung inwards. We jumped through, and closed it with a heavy vault-like clunk. We found ourselves in a tiled corridor containing nothing but a lift. Scott punched the controls without success. Eventually, with another watch-like click, the lift arrived and its doors opened. We stepped in, before the lift flew upwards. We whooshed into velvety darkness. After an amount of time that made it impossible to work out how high we were, there was the gentlest of jolts, and the doors parted onto a richly carpeted corridor. There were no windows. Other than lighting subtly running along the corridor, it was dark. We passed doors as secure and impersonal as airport lockers. Reaching the far end, we looked back, to see a triangle of light spilling neatly into the corridor from the lift. The carpet cushioned our footsteps, until we arrived at the final door. There seemed little else to do but ring the bell. The door opened immediately.

Chapter 21

The room was impressive. Its mirrored glass windows overlooked Krakow's square and rooftops. It was an apartment in which fitted kitchens look as good as they do in showrooms. Large, leather bound books filled an entire wall. I felt strangely safe. Mr Foxe had the posture of someone unafraid to be tall. I was expecting him to be doddery, and easier to read. His eyes appeared accustomed to worry, but glinted at our arrival. He wore a blazer and shaving foam on his chin. He looked younger than he should, almost glossy, as though his head sat on the wrong shoulders. Allowing us into the room, his eyes lingered on me for longer than was comfortable. From the intercom's screen, we saw Dougal and Fred stamp silently about the alleyway.

"The Life Assistance Agency. Congratulations." Mr. Foxe made our arrival sound like completing a computer game level. I studied him. Meeting someone *actually* six feet tall meant I needed to revise my dating profile.

"At your assistance," Scott said. He offered a hand while the other delved for a business card. Foxe shook it, taking in Scott's hair and ironed shirt. Scott looked the part, but Foxe was more interested in me.

"So this is Ben," he looked at me intently. "Ben Ferguson-Cripps. At last." His smile was serious, like it had heard every punchline. He shook my good hand as though we were already acquainted. His skin was rough, like a gardener's.

"*Mirrors and Lies* was an *invigorating* read," he said,

before Scott finally located a crumpled LAA card in his pocket and handed it across.

"Life assistance, people lost and found…?" Foxe read, "How *very* opportune." He looked at me. "But, you don't appear to believe in providence?"

He smiled and put the card in his pocket. The embossed printing was clearly paying off.

The room was dark, with strangely arranged furniture and a scorched table. The bags and holdalls stacked by the door, along with a folded table, discouraged lingering. With a flash, I recognised him. I had seen him before.

"*You* were the towel guy. You searched our room."

"I'm sorry about that. But not as sorry as I was at not finding the obsidian mirror."

"If you'd found it, then we'd have no bargaining power." Scott smiled.

It was my turn to freeze with realisation. "You've still *got* it?" I asked, staring at Scott. "You've actually still got it?" I held up my injured hand. "Well cheers for telling me."

"It was for your safety," Scott replied,

"My *safety?* I'm scarred for life, and I don't just mean my hand. If that's you looking out for me, then stop. I can look after myself."

"Can you? He looked at me like there was something he wasn't telling me. And I was reminded of his phone call at the petrol station, apparently to Ronnie. Who *had* he been talking to? Foxe registered my torn cheek and re-bandaged hand.

"It'll heal. Now, the mirror, it's with you is it?" he asked Scott, his eyes burning dangerously.

"It's here." Scott patted his satchel.

Foxe put his hand out. "May I?"

"Not yet…"

"Scott, one must be careful. Roller-coasters are less fun without straps."

His concern was laced with threat. We watched the Society still stomping around on the small screen.

"But, we should probably leave..." Foxe said, tapping the bags with his foot. "My car's downstairs. We'll leave together."

Mr Foxe unzipped the holdall, to pass Scott an automatic pistol, a Browning 8mm I think. Scott returned it, explaining he had only been in the military for three days and would miss the ground. Foxe frowned, before handing it to me. My teenage self grinned at its weight, while my adult self expected the worst.

"It's loaded," he warned, showing me the safety catch.

"I'm not sure I could use this, with my hand." I added, suddenly aware of the level of shit we were clearly in.

"Well keep it just in case." He looked to the bags. "Now give me a hand. The good one," he smiled.

Scott was already holding a Gladstone bag. "Do we have to do *everything*?"

"Find some respect," Foxe replied.

I put the gun in my pocket, but it was too heavy, so stuck it in my belt. It felt like a brick. We took the lift, to the basement. The car park was gloomy.

"Is he always so *ready*?" Foxe asked, watching Scott walking out of the lift with the bags.

"Try sharing a car with it." I laughed.

"Well, as the Chinese proverb says, be careful what you wish for," Foxe said, reaching the Jaguar. Scott looked interested in our conversation, but Foxe quickly opened the boot. I lifted the kit bag, to hoist in. It was heavy as though carrying scaffolding.

"On top," Foxe advised. "We may need it."

The Jaguar's leather interior improved upon the Saab's, although Foxe's driving was no better than Scott's. An arpeggio of car horns and internationally recognised hand signals accompanied our arrival onto Krakow's streets. Evening sunlight provided a genteel filter, which offset Foxe's erratic driving. It served us well; there was no sign of the Society.

As Krakow's suburbs thinned out, the roads emptied. We avoided major routes. Foxe knew where he was going, even if we didn't. Scott sat beside Foxe, presumably looking for an opportune moment to find Springsteen on the radio. I later calculated the distance between Krakow and Prague as 250 miles, but it could have been twice that distance. We winced from the low-sun and thunder of overtaking trucks. We were driving overnight, so stopped for supplies.

Any BHP the Jaguar once delivered had been lost, and we eased through Poland at speeds more accustomed to delivering milk, yet needing to visit every petrol station we passed. It made our Saab look like a Prius. We searched for change at toll roads, and all kept an eye on the mirrors when we thought the others weren't.

I drove for a while. The Jag had the responsiveness of a hovercraft. I handed back, now understanding the reason for the erratic driving. I listened to them while I tried to sleep on the backseat, my head jammed between the window handle, desperate to stretch my legs out through the window. Even Scott could barely get a word in and I wondered if Foxe was hard of hearing, or simply lost interest in what people were saying.

"The Society dislike unauthorised research," Foxe said. "They're not heavies, most of them live in libraries, but don't let that fool you. They *employ* heavies. They protect esoteric knowledge. They consider it theirs, and I've found something new."

"Have you?" asked Scott.

A lorry powered past. "D'you believe in angels?" Foxe asked.

"I do."

"And Ben?"

"Lapsed atheist," Scott told him. I wanted to interrupt, but despite Soviet-era roads jarring my head against the door with agonising regularity, I hovered above sleep.

"Isn't it a bit late for following Dee?" Scott asked, giving up on the radio.

"Possibly. No one really knows what he was up to, I'm unsure even he did. He may've been a spy for Queen Elizabeth. But he *was* a cartographer, thinker, and astrologer. The angels ruined his reputation. But if anyone *has* ever spoken to God's angels, it's Dee. I believe the start of Dee and Kelley's success coincided with a comet in 1583, which was Haley's comet before he saw it." He smiled. "The next isn't until 2061, but there's another…"

"Didn't Aleister Crowley succeed too?" Scott asked.

"South coast fantasist," Foxe tutted. "Crowley believed himself to be the reincarnation of Edward Kelley. "That is *very* unlikely indeed."

"Well, he did marry Rose Kelly in 1903," I recalled my own research. The connection only now made sense.

"Ah, he awakes," said Foxe. "Yes, Crowley found some of Dee's hidden belongings, and even claims to have seen their angels."

I sensed a competitive streak, before abandoning sleep and sitting up.

"But no one's been closer then Dee and Kelley," Foxe continued, "And mankind's ancient enough for *someone* to have succeeded. Dee was intellectually prepared. He was *committed.*"

Loose change shifted in the door pockets as the car lolled through corners.

"Crowley understood Enochian?" I asked.

"I'm less sure about that, but he understood Dee. He guessed Dee preserved his angelic tables. Crowley isn't the type Dee wanted involved in magik, but it's the risk he took in preserving the knowledge. You can't control who finds it."

I couldn't help but think my cynicism of *Mirrors and Lies* had been wasted.

"But you and your banker friend, Oliver Turner?" Scott asked. "You had the tables in the 1970s. But you stopped, when you met Mrs Foxe? So what's new now?"

"I had to choose, between my pursuits and her. So I returned everything to where Dee hid them, but there's been..." Foxe hesitated, "...Developments." The word hung there, demanding elaboration that failed to materialise.

The wheels on the road droned, and Foxe took a deep breath.

"Ben, it sounds far fetched, but Enochian's *authentic*. It has grammar and syntax. It was phonetic, *before* the Rosetta stone discovered the existence of such a thing. Sudden clusters of vowels and consonants aren't found in natural languages. Enochian bears no relation to any known language. The angels weren't all harps and trumpets. It was dark and confusing. The angels mistrusted Kelley." He sighed. "It was complicated."

"It always is," I grumbled

"You want to work with Oliver Turner again?" Scott asked with all the sensitivity of a Soviet condom. "Is that why you've stolen the London Stone?"

"Borrowing, not stolen." Foxe looked awkward. "*It's temporary*." He sighed, "It's imperative. It's the only bit surviving. If Dee used it, then so must we."

"Why's it so important to speak to the angels?" I asked.

"Perhaps that's what we'll discover."

"Or not," I said. "So where did Dr Dee go after Prague?" I asked.

"They spent two years in Prague, without much success. Kelley moaned of lacking jewellery, while Dee began to suspect his scryer had ambitions other than seeking the knowledge of angels. They fell out over a gift Dee presented to King Rudolph. It was the bronze plaque that Kelley presented at one of the Habsburg's balls. Kelley failed to understand why it was not gold, and Dee wasn't going to tell him the gift's importance beyond its monetary value. They were eventually accused of being spies and thrown from Prague."

"Were they?"

"Who cares? Anyway, they were accused of being unqualified to mediate between God and Man. They were told the Church should undertake that communion, not mavericks. An envoy called Sendivogius and the Catholic Church demanded their practices stop. Our heroes were reassured they had refuge. It just wasn't Prague. It was at this meeting that Dee was told that his gift, the bronze plaque, had been installed in Krakow where it belonged. It was meant as an insult, but actually served Dee very well."

"Where?"

"In the Wavel's crypt. Where you found it shortly after my own visit."

We started looking for motorway services. We were hungry.

"So," Foxe continued, "Dee had nowhere else to go."

"How about back home to Mortlake?" I suggested, hoping we might pick up on the hint, but Foxe laughed.

"God no. Dee wasn't finished. He wanted more, he wanted, well. I think he wanted immortality."

"He'd have known what to do with it?" Scott asked.

"Indeed, I think most men seeking it fail to ask themselves

that important question Scott, but John Dee wasn't one of them. He had enough interests to fill two lifetimes, although, even he may have struggled to fill eternity. He accepted the only invite left open to him. They wrote to Rožmberk, a threadbare Lord at the edge of Europe, and prepared for their last journey to the East."

"Is that where we're heading?"

"Off the map?" he smiled. "Yes, I guess so. Now, is that a motorway services?"

After another questionable meal that failed to provide any of the five recommended portions a day, we found another email from Ronnie. As Foxe insisted on driving I read it in the back, before passing the phone to Scott.

FURTHER East
July

Approaching Prague, we were joined by better-groomed horses and properly shod wagons. It was about time. I noticed Joanna tighten her hair ribbons at the whiff of tanneries, not that Kelley noticed.

John tells me Prague is the centre of Europe, or at least of Johanne Putsch's continental map. I've been assured that the hilly city is home to King Rudolph, the Emperor, who collects anything intellectually twinkling, although I suspect that like most royalty he will be a bore.

"Prague is a radical place, it'll welcome visionaries and seekers of the truth," John declared, like he'd overheard my doubts.

"Know some visionaries do you? I asked.

"Please desist from such cheap humour Jane." He looked ahead, at Kelley swaying on his horse. "Can you keep him busy?"

"Why?" I asked.

"I need to send a messenger back to a forge in Krakow. They need to know we'll be staying at the house of Tadeáš Hajek in Prague."

I nodded, and spurred my horse ahead. Kelley looked back, and grinned as my horse rubbed alongside his.

Prague. 15th August 1584

I swayed through the Emperor's court. It teemed with so many colours it was hard to focus, with perfumes, cologne and spices locked in aerial combat. I recognised some cartographers from their visit to Mortlake some years before. Ignoring one another's company, they stared disappointedly from a corner. Rudolph was apparently more interested in astrologers this week, and sometimes kept visitors, even diplomats, waiting for months. I stopped beside a squat bird with big eyes sitting on a low wall. It nodded, so I fed it a strawberry from a nearby bowl. Its red beak indicated I was not the first.

I looked across the busy staterooms to where Kelley was speaking to a dark skinned man with long white hair: the same colour as Kelley's own streak. They were deep in conversation, which surprised me, since the darker man did not appear wealthy. When Kelley looked across, I feigned great interest in the bird's wing. When I looked back, the two men had gone. I patted the dodo farewell and moved through the cheerful crowd. I was standing by a window, admiring the spires of Prague below the castle, when there was a presence at my shoulder.

"Enjoying the view?" Kelley asked, as I caught him staring at my breasts. He glanced away.

"Who's that man?" I asked.

"Oh, yes, fascinating man," he said. "He's never cut his hair." He pointed across to where the dark man was now inspecting hanging tapestries. "The Hindu sect never cut their hair."

"They've not invented scissors?"

He laughed. "It falls out every couple of yards, but they save it, to be buried with, so they're reincarnated whole. That's if they don't achieve immortality, which is their goal." His eyes lingered upon my body. "That's thirty years' growth, probably five rods…"

"You could stuff an elephant with that."

"You've heard of them?" Kelley chuckled, "Hindus consider elephants sacred."

"So they can be buried with them?" I laughed at my own joke. "You plan to keep your hair and nails to be buried with?" I asked. "To become immortal?"

"It pays to keep options open."

"Dangerous words in a world of faith Mr Kelley," I replied, "Be careful whom you tell."

"You sound like John." He looked around. "And where is our esteemed Dr Dee?"

"I understood Tadeáš was showing him the tower."

"Ah, the alchemy laboratory? The Emperor's inordinately proud of it." I felt his hand on the bone pins of my dress, at least I think I did, as he guided me from the window. People thronged around, bustling to justify their presence.

"You appear to have your own agenda here?" I asked.

His hand tightened on my waist. He was about to reply, when a man approached, his cloaks sweeping expensively along the floor. He wore a hat, which I guessed someone had once said suited him. People stooped beneath its peacock feathers as he passed. Royal rooms are cold, but it was unnecessarily flamboyant.

"Mrs. Dee, let me introduce Vilém Rožmberk."

The man bowed elegantly in reply. "Of Trebon," he explained, through too much saliva. The man's wooden teeth needed refitting.

"A beautiful place," he added. "But if I've been talking

for longer than five seconds I'll have already mentioned that."
He smiled. "It's peripheral. The Empire's lights shine dimly
from our mountains." He sighed without acknowledging it,
as though no longer noticing the troubles weighing upon him.
"We anticipate your visit," he added with a toothy grin.

I frowned, remembering him from London.

"Rožmberk has invited us to stay at Trebon," Kelley hastily
interjected.

"I thought you'd accepted?" Rožmberk sounded confused,
oblivious to Kelley's staring at him to change the subject.

"Yes, yes, a generous offer." Kelley mumbled.
Rožmberk looked between us. He appeared to have understood.
I said nothing, but instead admired the ornate ceiling.

Prague's carriages passed our door so frequently that only
heavy knocking alerted us to a visitor. Kelley did not move
from the table. He sat in the parlour with Joanna and I, where
we stitched her farthingale's whalebone. The road had torn us
all of weight. Luckily Prague appeared to be influenced by the
modern Venetian styles. The dress hung on me like a slack sail.
With the bedrooms full of sleeping children, public tailoring
was unavoidable. I ignored Kelley watching me like dogs eye
a butcher. John was in the laboratory tower on the far side of
the castle.

The knocking continued, and I took the needle, as the maid
answered. The sun was setting along the street, catching the
houses' grimy glass in a golden glow. Kelley watched the door
open.

"Beware of strangers at the door," I whispered.

"I was a stranger once," retorted Kelley, leaning back his
chair and wiped plum juice from his mouth before flinging the
stone to join others in the corner.

"Exactly."

Our guest, unlike John, did not need to duck his head as he stepped in from the street. For someone better suited to rolling, he walked across to the table. I swallowed back a giggle. He was short, round and red in the face like a robin. Tugging down his tunic and puffing out his chest, he looked to me,

"Madam Dee?"

"It is I."

"I am Michael Sendivogius. I study at the University," he announced proudly, as the feet of Kelley's chair found the floor

"I know who you are," said Kelley, standing to invite the man to sit, "One of the King's finest alchemists."

"Meets another." Sendivogius sat down. "Thank you. It's an honour."

I guessed he had mistaken Kelley for my husband. I was about to correct him, but changed my mind. The lavender oil was making me choke, so I excused myself, holding my breath as I passed through the room. The chairs scraped the floor and the men began to talk.

I notice guests of the King's court enjoyed introductions as brief as the friendships; they all know *of* one another. Kelley had heard of Sendivogius, and was hiding his enthusiasm poorly. Upstairs, I stripped off the dress and rearranged my hair best I could, before returning downstairs to see a jug of cider had reached the table. The mood had changed.

"Seton has the powder's formula?" Kelley was asking, "Alexander Seton?"

"Yes, he was imprisoned." Sendivogius watched Kelley's face, "For a red powder." It sat somewhere between a question and statement. "He refused to divulge its secret. And I understand you too have a red powder?"

"I do." Kelley nodded, as though revealing one of his magic tricks.

"Which makes two of us. On his death, Seton bestowed

me with the powder's keeping." Sendivogius puffed his chest.

Kelley leaned forward, before thinking better of it. "Then it failed to provide him with what he hoped?"

"Immortality?" Sendivogius laughed thinly. "No. Imprisonment killed him *before* he explained his method." He glanced at me, before looking back to Kelley. "And for you? How does it respond to quicksilver?" Seeing Kelley hesitate, Sendivogius pressed. "The King will be interested."

"Its mysteries remain sealed to us," Kelley replied.

"Where did you come upon it?"

As I reached to pour a small cider, I recognised decision in Kelley's voice as he told the story of the innkeeper in Wales.

"And you wish these spirits to conjure you more?" The visitor asked.

There was a commotion outside, the yell and crash of someone dismounting a horse with their foot caught in its stirrups. Undeterred, Sendivogius pressed on.

"Yet, the powder's secrets remain intact, even to you Dr Dee?" he asked.

I spluttered and Sendivogius frowned. Kelley hesitated, realising the visitor's mistake.

"But I am Edward Kelley."

"Oh."

Our visitor's disappointment even reached me at the window.

"Your master is not here?" Sendivogius asked.

"My *master*?"

The kerfuffle outside was enough to distract me from their collapsing camaraderie, and I opened the door to find John, who was brushing himself down.

"It's not my horse," he was explaining to the stable boy, as though this might explain his falling from it. "Curse'd storks," he added, but the boy was busy tethering the horse to the house loop and trying not to laugh. I looked up to see the pencil-like birds squawking at one another on a nearby rooftop.

"We have a guest," I whispered, holding John's shoulder. "Wanting a red powder?" I added and John stared at me, as though wondering what else I knew.

"Sendivo something?" I said.

"Sendivogius," Dee announced, before cursing as his head collided with the rotting lintel above the door. "What brings you here?" he asked, rubbing his forehead and looking at the beam like it was newly installed. Sendivogius stood, his face red and unsure who this tall visitor was.

"And whom, may I ask, are you?"

"I am Dr John Dee."

Sendivogius choked in surprise. John sat down with a groan, and pulled the buskins from his feet before throwing them across the room.

Kelley stood eagerly to explain. "He was asking of our red powder."

"*Your* red powder, Edward." John looked around. "Been here a while I see."

Sendivogius appeared confused at John's insight.

"Your drinks are nearly finished," John explained, oblivious to the straw in his hair. "I hear naught but this red powder," he said. "We press to the shoulders of angelica, yet all Kelley asks for is secrets of gold." John poured from the jug. "No good will come of this powder," he warned. "Foolishly bragging around Prague only attracts the wrong friends."

"Pardon me?" Sendivogius appeared insulted, something I realised he specialised in.

"Our reputation may already have preceded us," Kelley intervened.

"Through fault only of your own, Edward."

Sendivogius looked uncertain, unsure to whom he should be

addressing. "Apologies Doctor Dee, but I too am in possession of a similar substance," he said.

John's eyes flickered with interest, but dimmer than Kelley's.

"I would look into it," John hesitated. "But, your pardon please. Our current pursuits demand our fullest intentions."

The silence suggested a deadlock.

"I have clearly taken too much of your evening." Sendivogius stood at this second rebuke. "Time is as valuable as the gold we seek Mr Kelley, perhaps your *angels* offer something greater." He stopped by the door; his neck crimson. "I will sleep upon this offence," he announced, "God be wi' ye."

Kelley accompanied him outside for muffled words. The horse whinnied, and I feared the worst.

Chapter. May 1586

Rain, feet, hooves and paws had chewed up the fayre ground. Prague's city guards walking the walls overlooking the Sunday celebrations did their best to remain aloof.

"Ma, what *is* that?" Arthur asked, as I pulled him away from a bear chained to a stake. It appeared as unimpressed by the outskirts of Prague as I was. Chestnut shells were scattered around its feet.

"A bear," I explained.

"A *what*?" He could not tear his eyes from it, "In chains?"

I thought of the miserable creatures in the Southwark pits, mouldy fur torn to shreds, surrounded by dead mastiffs. This one was lucky to be in chains. The fayre trip had been my idea, following John and Kelley falling out the previous night. Their argument had awoken us all.

"Good thing you don't ail from whooping cough," Kelley interrupted.

"Why?" Arthur asked.

"Old England cured whooping cough by riding on a bear's

back," Kelley continued, and I forgot not to smile.

"How did they stay on?" Arthur asked.

"By forgetting they had whooping cough." His laugh faded as John joined us.

"Superstition I fear," John corrected what had delighted Arthur. "The root of all superstition is men observe when a thing hits, not when it misses."

"Yours?"

John shook his head. "Francis Bacon."

Beyond the smoking pork stall, men were clambering from barrels. Kelley turned, to plait the white streak in his black hair into a ponytail, so it hung past his face like white rope. He kneeled beside Arthur.

"Tug it," he ordered. Arthur yanked it.

"Not that hard!" Kelley smiled. The boy did so again more gently.

"Now, what's in your ear?" Kelley asked, before reaching past the boy's ear. "How did that get there?" he asked, withdrawing his hand to reveal a yellow fruit.

"What is it?" Arthur exclaimed, holding it tightly, his eyes wide. Kelley reached for it, but the boy gripped it.

"Where did you get that?" I asked, as Arthur hid behind my dress. "Lemons are a week's wage."

Kelley shrugged. "'Tis a shame magicians are the only ones not believing in magic," he answered.

"Some are easier to fool."

We looked ahead to where John was counting pennies to buy a tankard. He stepped away, staring at the sky, as oblivious to the rolling drunkards around him as they were of him.

"He works me hard, Jane," Kelley's arm brushed mine. "The daemons scheme."

"I heard you forgot the angel's alphabet," Arthur said, missing the irritation in Kelley's eyes.

"The Enochian alphabet," Kelley nodded. "It's complicated, like naught we've seen before."

We held our noses as we passed stocks. The prisoners smelled worse than the rotting vegetables.

"The *language*." Kelley paused. "It requires a filter, a sigillum. John's memorised all the signs and letters that they dictate, through me." He winced as the sun came out from behind the clouds. "Heaven remains a high fence even for men as tall as John Dee."

"Perhaps intentionally?" I suggested. "So, you cannot speak the language, but John can?"

"Yes. I hear it without understanding," Kelley bristled. "As John forever reminds me. I see them point to coordinates in the tabled grid. John translates." He quietened as dignitaries passed. "And we're closer than ever."

"To angels, or gold?" I asked, but he ignored me.

Our hands brushed as we rummaged in a seller's box of apples. Arthur remained absorbed by his lemon. I studied Kelley's long face. His eyes lingered too long on my mouth and chest, yet my heart quickened. He released his white streak from its ponytail and I glimpsed the missing ear as he returned it into his cowl. He handed pennies over for the apples. He remained an unlikely mouthpiece for anyone but himself.

"So," I smiled, "You dictate what you don't *understand*? They could be saying anything. A risky business."

"Talent can be a curse."

"So can arrogance." I bit an apple. "So, why the argument?"

"My head was afire. I requested simpler methods, but the daemon parted. I hear more than John knows. Besides, he doesn't *always* understand what he scrawls." He pushed loose hair from my face, which I surprised myself by allowing.

John approached, having been in conversation with the Emperor's astronomer. "Good man that Brahe," he announced.

I stepped away from Kelley. "What's wrong with his nose?" I asked.

"Lost it in a duel, it's half electrum."

We followed saplings lining a corpse track back to the city. I stroked Arthur's head, tracing the scar from Mortlake's Watergate Stairs. The love of a son can be hard to bear. A red-faced man nearby tutted, and I recognised Sendivogius, who ignored our party entirely.

Chapter. May 6th 1586

We were preparing for the Royal Ball when I found an exhausted messenger on the front step. His horse looked equally as tired. After offering the poor animal some water, I invited the boy in. John was delighted that his message had reached Krakow's blacksmith. While the boy drank ale, John pulled the brass discs from the messenger's saddlebag. They hit the table with a satisfying clunk, both engraved with his Monad symbol. Flipping one, John nodded appreciatively at the detailed grids and tables used to translate the angels conversations. The flip of the other was blank. John found some coins in his jerkin by the door, enough for the eight days' lodgings back to Krakow. The boy's grin implied he'd sleep in fields and pocket the money. John carefully wrapped the one-sided disc, leaving it on the table. Hearing Kelley ducking down the narrow staircase, he quickly concealed the double-sided disc at his feet. I said nothing. He looked up at the arrival of Kelley and tapped the package.

"A gift for our King," he explained.

"It's *our* King now is it?" Kelley said, tying his hair back, though his ears remained concealed. "You're not joining us at this evening's ball?" he asked, but his invite sounded disingenuous.

"My present shall replace my presence."

Kelley tapped the parcel on the bench beside him. "But, we already have a gift."

"A fur coat?" John laughed. "Rudolph never leaves his castle. I am unsure he even leaves Vladislav Hall."

"So, what's that then?" Kelley said, touching Dee's cylindrical parcel. "The alchemical secrets he wants?"

"Surely that's what you're taking?"

John's sarcasm was hard to call.

He smiled. "But do ensure you give him this." John opened the parcel so Kelley could see. "It's a brass plaque. Engraved with my horned Monad. It comes with the offer of my treatise, the Hieroglyphic Monad, should he wish me to present it. You will inform him?"

"If I find his ear."

Kelley was a man in much need for ears. John rewrapped the plaque and held it tightly, before mumbling a prayer and handing it to Kelley.

"Very well, I shall ensure he receives it," Kelley said, and we left John for the ball.

My bodice was tighter than I intended. With chandeliers floating amidst a heady cloud of musk and sweat from the guests, the ballroom was everything I had imagined. I had eagerly accepted the invitation that John had turned down. I had little interest in returning to Mortlake without at least having attended a Habsburg royal ball. I was unsure if my breathlessness resulted from the dress or the excitement.

"Not dancing?" Kelley asked, seeing me seated. He leaned in. "You dance like smoke," he whispered. "John misses out."

I felt an unbidden flush of pleasure. "He's too busy dancing with angels…"

"Not without me he isn't," he smiled. "May I? With a true angel…"

The strings picked up and we joined the chain. My stomach fluttered. He pressed me needlessly close, before swinging me away, though not before a squeeze of my arse. He was a better dancer than I expected, his hair a flicker of black and white. Looking around for Joanna, I flitted to my next partner, but she had disappeared.

"Hello again."

Through my fluster I barely recognised Rožmberk, who had invited us to Trebon. He was wearing an advisably smaller hat and a wooden smile broader than his dancing, which was in the old-fashioned style. My feet barely touched the marble floor as we seemingly flew around the room, but Kelley's eyes were harder to shake than my changing partners.

The sun had set, with a cooler breeze finally having picked up from the nearby mountains. I was drunk. There was no other excuse to be leaning so heavily on Kelley. We were walking down the hill. Joanna had fallen someway behind. Prague's rooftops were dark below us, with only the occasional signal light flickering in distant hills. The stars were bright.

"We'll wait for Joanna here," Kelley said, leaning on the wall overlooking the city. He gazed up at the sky. "It's a good night for it."

I agreed without knowing to what he referred.

"Angels," he clarified, after two watchmen passed.

"Don't sell me what my husband's already buying."

"You don't want to see them?" The wine had magnified his cockiness.

"Doesn't it take two? And crystals? And rivers running uphill, peacock feathers and stewed frogs?"

"Yes, it *does* take two."

We leaned on the parapet of the winding road, overlooking darkness.

"But, now the talent's unlocked who knows? Perhaps it can be done alone," he continued, taking a deep breath. "The more natural it becomes, the harder it is to control." His mouth sounded dry. "Here, I'll show you. Hold my hand tighter."

I hadn't realised I already was. I ignored the tremor of excitement, as Kelley murmured strange words, I guessed Enochian. I stared into the thick blackness. No one passed, and I grew more interested in the pulse between our palms, when something flickered in the night. Kelley gripped my hand firmly. The stars disappeared with a blur, as a shape blacker than the sky obscured them. I went cold with fear.

The silhouette drifted, and a gust of wind ruffled our hair. Suddenly, two eyes sprung open in front of us. I glimpsed cheekbones, sunken like a winter wolf. A scream caught in my throat. I heard the beating of impossibly large wings. Yet still more stars disappeared behind their thin canvas, as it reared away. I shook my head. It was so unclear. And then there was nothing. My hand dropped away, as my breathing recovered. I sighed, loudly, before being overcome by a fierce dizziness. I remained leaning against Kelley, as Joanna caught us up.

"There you are," she said.

I detached from Kelley, grateful for the darkness saving my blushes. I had forgotten about Joanna. We walked on together in silence.

John was washing cobwebs and dirt from his hands in the kitchen bucket when we entered the house. I saw he had been reading, and also that he was disappointed to see Kelley in too high spirits to commune with the real thing.

"A good evening?" he asked without interest.

"For dancing," declared Kelley, as he watched Joanna pass upstairs without interest. "We all need distraction." Kelley slumped down across from Dee. "I have Turkish Delight." He pulled the delicacy from his pocket and poured himself a short wine.

"Enjoy the delight while it lasts, Edward. Permissive times never last."

"Good parties never do."

Both John and Kelley had returned from buying green glass and vials to find we had a visitor.

"What's this pomp?" John had asked. Horses adorned in purple tack and heavy saddles stood outside our lodgings. A soldier held their harnesses. John frowned. "Isn't that Sendivogius' horse?"

Indeed, it was. We stepped into the house, to find a room full of people.

"To what do we owe such regal company?" John asked no one in particular.

"I am Envoy from Rome," interrupted an undernourished looking man attempting to appear unaffected by his journey and failing. Mud from the road remained splattered across his purple robes and garish hat. Sendivogius, with crimson self-importance, stood behind the Envoy. I went upstairs to put an ear to the floor.

"Your practices are to stop," the Envoy declared.

"These are private communications,' John argued.

"You are unqualified to mediate between God and Man. Any communion should be undertaken by the Church, not mavericks."

"I answer to God."

"And that Sir, is why I advise you to leave while we remain smiling."

"Is this the Emperor's demand?"

"As we know, the Emperor ..." the Envoy implied they all knew too well, "...struggles to focus on affairs of the State.

His mystical investigations and curiosity may distract, but he remains embedded in the orthodoxy. Your sorcery serves Queen Elizabeth more greatly than his own interests."

"I am no spy."

"Would an Englishman claim otherwise?" The Envoy coughed. "I declare that your hereto patron, Rudolf II, Holy Roman Emperor, King of Bohemia and Hungary, Lord of Austria, banishes you from the Czech lands."

"The Enlightenment ends so soon?"

"Do not catastrophise Dr Dee, there are always places for men such as you. Just not Prague." He turned on his delicate heels, before pausing at the door, "Oh, and your gift. Your brass Monad, it is installed in Krakow where it belongs."

"Krakow?" Dee sounded worried. "For smelting?"

"No. It lies in the Wavel's crypt to an audience of dead kings. It has found its audience." His laugh suggested he had made a joke. "Such bribery may be common to Englande, but not here. God be wi' ye."

I heard the door and the horses depart.

When I returned downstairs, the mood was reminiscent of the South Bank following a bear baiting, the atmosphere was torn to shreds.

"We're leaving?" I asked, strangely sad not to see the dodo again.

"Earwig, we shall confer with our angels to confirm this course of action."

Kelley was astounded – they had just been commanded to cease angelic actions.

"They need to be consulted?" he asked.

"If we leave, then we may have to accept Rožmberk's invitation," Dee said.

"Then perhaps I *shall* join you," Kelley replied.

The man has no shame.

Chapter 22

We stopped briefly at what had once been a coaching inn. I stashed Foxe's pistol under the car seat. We parked beneath a branchless Scotch pine looking as shattered as we felt. We ate without appetite, and soon left. Scott insisted upon driving. Foxe directed him, with one eye in his own wing mirror. He knew the back roads like a driving instructor. I looked back and saw nothing, but pulled out the pistol anyway. It lay heavily in my lap; a safety catch away from anarchy. We passed the next tollgate. Foxe spoke fluently to the gatekeeper in Polish, before typing the man's mobile number into his own phone. We drove on. Five minutes later Foxe made a phone call in Polish.

"Keeping an eye on our tail," he explained, finishing the call. "Toll booth says we have company."

"We *have* a tail?" My anger surprised me. The tenacity of the Society was terrifying.

Foxe turned in his seat, "We'll lose them."

Scott punched the steering wheel, skitting the Jag to the left. "We can't outrun them in this duvet." He eased off the accelerator.

"Don't fucking slow down," I suggested.

"It might be for the best," said Foxe looking ahead.

We passed through forest, and onto farmland glowing in the moonlight. The road descended.

"Stop here," Foxe demanded.

"Give me that gun," said Scott.

I handed it to him, already missing it. Scott pulled up, tyres skidding slightly on loose gravel, and cut the engine. I hurried out after them, not wanting to be left alone. The car was slewed across the incoming lane of the road, which gleamed in the moonlight.

Other than my heavy breathing, the countryside was silent. Thunder rolled in the distance like an approaching train. Copses of silver birch huddled in the fields like ghosts and from somewhere an owl hooted. Leaves rustled across the road.

"Cross wind, Easterly. Six miles per hour," Foxe announced.

An approaching car displaced the quiet. Scott held the gun like a non-smoker holds a cigarette. He knelt down beside me, behind the car, to stretch the gun across the bonnet. The clouds were beginning to obscure the moon. The white road markings glowed like minus signs. His wrist wasn't straight. I reached to correct it. Foxe rummaged in the Jag's boot. It slammed shut. They would not be long, and I was right, but as headlights of our tail flashed through the trees and broke the brow of the hill, I realised another error on Scott's part. I grabbed the pistol.

"Safety catch," I barked.

Before I could return it, headlamps bore down upon us. I pushed Scott away to position myself, stretching my own arm across the bonnet to stabilise the gun. Once again I was grateful my natural left hand had been spared.

The gun was heavy with purpose. I had no time to think. A pistol's sight is more rudimentary than a rifle's, there's less margin for error. The Toyota charged over the rise, driving faster than I expected, headlamps burning the night. I opened fire into the car's path, like targeting clay pigeons, allowing the moving target to do the work. The noise of the gun was shattering, and the recoil throbbed in my arm. I fired again,

aware of the delivery being far more rapid and noisy than I
expected. The bullets flashed into the front of the car, stopping
its nose dead. A headlight exploded, and it swerved, with only
one eye. The windscreen shattered, and the roof sparked with
bullets, as the front tyres exploded beyond my expectations. I
kept squeezing the trigger and bullets *kept* coming. The Toyota
hit the verge, and jolted; the bonnet sprang open, smashing
backwards into the remains of the windscreen.

My gun clicked; I had emptied the magazine. My stomach
was tight and I'm unsure I blinked. The car halted, half-burying
itself into a squat hedge running alongside the field. It let out
a puff of steam and started blaring its horn. I remembered to
breathe. However, as I looked from the damage, to my gun and
back. It did not add up. The damage wreaked by the pistol was
impossible. I looked around, to where Mr Foxe had stepped
out from behind the Jaguar's boot, and stood with his feet
planted in the middle of the road. Hanging on a strap at his
hip was the unmistakable flared muzzle and curved magazine
of a Bren machine gun. It was smoking from lack of use, but
was evidently not rusty, and nor was he. Oblivious to any
returning fire, he squeezed off a final short burst. The Toyota's
horn mourned across the empty countryside. Foxe snapped off
the Bren's magazine before laying it in the car's boot.

"Do *I* have to do everything?" he smiled.

Scott looked as astounded as I did. Foxe clapped me on the
back.

"Ben! You *are* alive."

"Shouldn't we call an ambulance?"

Foxe dismissed it. "People are harder to kill than you
think."

The smell of burning suggested otherwise. He walked
across and opened the driver's door. The horn stopped. The
sudden silence was deafening.

Foxe returned. "Ready?" He nodded on our behalf. "The next passing car can call an ambulance," he added.

I sat in the back, as Foxe packed away the Bren. We drove away, leaving behind the burning car, scorched rubber and unrepentant decisions. Mr Foxe had an unexpected steely look.

Chapter 23

I couldn't stop thinking of the Bren gun and asked Foxe where he bought ammunition.

"It's the same calibre as Lee Enfields," he explained, which told me nothing. Remembering the photograph of the Bren gunner, I presumed it was an heirloom. As silhouettes of trees and telegraph poles grew defined against a lightening sky, Scott took his turn in the backseat. He dozed off with an ease familiar to the recently sedated, while I considered the countryside.

Industrialised fields stretched to the horizon. I wasn't ready to give up London in lieu of shooting badgers yet, but recognised rural calm I was old enough to at least start considering. Poland appeared as lost as we were. The ghosts of Soviet occupation remained evident. I supposed tucked away in the hillsides were quaint gingerbread houses and villages of folklore, but from the main roads, the countryside was scattered with derelict buildings and abandoned farm machinery. Place names were apparently picked from Scrabble sets with only high scoring letters remaining.

I looked out at the flat landscape, wondering what the hell we were doing. Haystacks passed by, or rather we passed them, like it was a film. At least I think we did. I was tired, and aware that since leaving London I was following career advice from someone who's main life skill was miming guitar solos to Whitesnake's *Is this love?* But, like someone waiting at a pedestrian crossing and wondering why cars are stopping,

I knew I was responsible for my own predicament.

The car climbed a hill between impenetrable Hawthorne hedges. Reaching a junction where the road split, Foxe pulled over and got out the car. He looked around as though to confirm he was at the correct spot, before taking a stick to the verge undergrowth. It was like he knew where to look. He had soon beaten back enough to find an old stone cross half buried beneath brambles and dirt. Its left arm was damaged, and engravings worn smooth by rain. He reached behind it, but found nothing except the remains of a bedraggled feather. We watched from the car as Foxe stood admiring it, before looking to the sky. He stood there for ten minutes, before getting back in. He pulled his seatbelt across without explanation. It was the first time I'd noticed him wear one. He also looked sad.

Prague unfurled over the hills like a medieval quilt. We passed a road curling and winding up the hill towards a castle ruling over city rooftops. We drove amongst vehicles squeezing through streets more suited to horses. My mouth tasted raw: of hotel tea and exhausted chewing gum.

"They'll know we're here, but not where," explained Foxe.

"I thought we'd lost them," I said, but he ignored me.

With Scott snoring on the backseat, we found a break of green traffic lights, and good fortune swept us to a hotel. It lay down a narrow street. Its lack of promotion suggested a business plan depending upon all its competitors being full. The receptionist, looking like he had a crushed velvet jacket at home, glanced up from his bookings. A horseshoe hung above the desk.

"Hope it stays upright," observed Scott.

"The root of superstition," said Foxe, "is men observing when a thing hits, not when it misses."

"Yours?" Scott asked.

"Francis Bacon," replied Foxe, before paying for our rooms.

I had my own room. From next door I heard Scott swear at his alarm clock.

I found them both downstairs in the morning, enjoying croissants and a companionable silence. It was disconcerting. Foxe's immaculately pressed suit matched Scott's ironing. I joined them and poured a tea. I had to wonder what the hell we were doing. After all, we were facing a man who should have been replaced by grateful thanks from Mrs. Foxe and a bank transfer to the Life Assistance Agency. I had got too caught up to even inform Mrs. Foxe that her husband was safe.

"Here's the comet that's best seen from Prague," Foxe halved the paper and tapped the page as he passed it over.

"It appeared during Dee's time." He said. "Coinciding with when Kelley first appeared at his door."

"Is that why we're in Prague?" I asked. I had always intended to visit Prague for a romantic break, not with a life assistance agent and medieval hobbyist.

"Indeed it is Ben. It's a meteorite. The Perseid meteorite shower is a stream of debris stretching along the Swift-Tuttle comet."

"Swift! From the corkboard pin," Scott said.

Foxe stared at him, but it was too late. "The pin from my desk drawer at Mortlake?" Foxe asked, folding his napkin with the sort of precision suggesting repressed anger. "What else did you find there?" His eyes narrowed into Scott's.

"Not much. And that only makes sense now." Scott paused. "And I'm using the phrase 'makes sense' loosely."

"Well, it appears we're quits over privacy." Foxe took back the newspaper.

"So Dee and Kelley scryed under this meteorite shower?" Scott asked, changing the subject.

"They did. It lasts for a month between July and August. There is nothing, which so much beautifies and adorns the soul and mind of man as does knowledge of the good arts and sciences."

"Francis Bacon?"

"No, Dr Dee. Alchemists believe planets are important. They coordinated alchemical experiments with comets, eclipses, and so on." Foxe strode across to the window, to peer through the blinds into the street.

"A drink later?" He asked, and I noticed light catching his well-worn shoes. I suspected the Bren gun wasn't the only family heirloom. We watched him walk across the breakfast room.

"We should follow him? We can't lose him now," Scott said.

"I've seen how he responds to people following him."

"Good idea. Maybe it *would* be better if only you did."

Chapter 24

Mr. Foxe was sightseeing. Heading towards the river, he peered at every corner and eave. I lost him on the main thoroughfare of a New Town last living up to its name in the 1560s, but spotted him by a newsstand buying another newspaper. He looked around, and I ducked behind a performing street statue, swiftly paying him to remain still. Watching Foxe stroll away, I caught up and grabbed a copy of the same local newspaper. I required no Czech for the cover story and picture. It was a burnt-out Toyota. It was impossible to discern if the occupants had survived.

Crossing Charles Bridge, Foxe greeted the real statues with a subtle nod. I almost lost him in the crowds, but found him admiring a house in the corner of a square lined with trees and unwashed gravel. The eaves of the house were carved with books open to the sky, their wood peeled by weather. I was hiding behind a kiosk opposite, when I felt someone watching me. I looked round to see Scott loitering in another gift shop twenty feet away. He looked embarrassed. How long had he been following me? I thought of Ronnie. I walked back, ignoring his urging that I stay with Mr Foxe. I asked him what he was doing. He put down an *I LOVE Prague* mug.

"Keeping an eye on things."

"For how long have you been doing that?" I asked, immediately regretting it.

"A few days in London..." His voice was strangely blunt. It was during his days missing that I had slept with Ronnie. The familiar tsunami of guilt arrived, but he looked past me.

"You've lost him," he said.

There was little point in searching for him, so we returned to our hotel, to relax in the lobby. Midday was announced by the dull toll of bells. We checked that Foxe's Jaguar remained in the hotel's backstreet garage. It was still there, so Scott reattached the homing device as precaution.

We lay alone for a few hours, alone with exclusive use of a TV remote, though not before Scott unsuccessfully tried to break into Mr. Foxe's room. Czech TV had taken the lowest denominator of Holland's schedules, and halved it. Instead, I emailed Mrs. Foxe the good news that we had found her husband and that he was at least safe. She immediately asked when we were coming home. Another email from Ronnie also arrived, with more of Jane Dee's diary.

Ronnie started the email apologising for paraphrasing. Apparently, unless we wanted the intricate details of negotiating potato prices with peasants and how to dry linen while on the road, then we weren't missing much. She reported that the Dee party had left Prague by this point and travelled eight days to Trebon. Here they were to stay with the nobleman Rožmberk. It was obvious that the social standing of their hosts was diminishing. At this rate they'd be going for drinks with the sailors eventually taking them home. Dee had been alarmed by a vision in Prague's library before they left, and was now afraid that 'Perhaps daemons *do* ride angels' tails', but Jane Dee had not expanded. However, Jane *was* now certain that the angels had commanded Kelley to marry Joanna, and feared what else they may demand. As the forests of their journey grew thicker, it was hard not to sense that their journey was coming to an end.

Even I had to admit that the most amazing thing about their endeavours was Jane's description of Kelley's talents when he and Dr Dee were scrying. The tables from which the angels apparently dictated their missives were four grids of 2,401 Enochian letters. Surely no man was able to recall the location and corresponding coordinates of 2,401 letters in an alien language?

Having read Ronnie's email, and grown tired of interpreting the potential meaning in her single, lower case kiss, I lay there savoring the noise of traffic and overhead roars of flight paths home. I feared we had lost Mr. Foxe, when there was a knock at the door. It was Foxe, inviting us for the drink I'd been pretending I didn't need.

We found the basement bar well-suited to heroic regrets. A mahogany bar curved pleasingly into the darkness.

"Losing me again was rather careless." Foxe laughed, before gulping his beer like he had five minutes' shore leave.

"Where were you?" asked Scott. "Grave digging, brass rubbing?"

Foxe looked at Scott. "You're better than you look."

"That probably isn't hard," I admitted.

We ordered more beers and I told Foxe I had emailed his wife.

"I know, thank you. And we *will* pay you," he replied, successfully reading between the lines.

"I didn't mention the Krakow pied-à-terre."

"There's probably no need," he agreed. "Mrs Foxe trusts me, but more importantly, I trust myself. Men think they can live with their actions, but most consequences are hard to imagine." He looked at me, as though picking up on my guilt. "It's easier with no family. Got much Ben?"

"I never met my father," I admitted, the beer providing an unexpected crash mat for an untold story. "He was a truck driver. He delivered sugar for Tate and Lyle, but was always miserable. Mum said he was in the loony bin; in the 60s I think. Apparently he constantly moaned about not enjoying anything. He's dead now. I think it was driving sugar around, without seeing the sweetness of life. The irony killed him."

Foxe actually laughed. It was an old joke, but I appreciated it.

"Your book described it well," Foxe agreed. "I can't think who he reminds me of."

Girls looking like they had escaped from the Hanway Street modelling agency giggled into the bar. As with most pretty girls I couldn't speak their language.

"Are you as elusive as your father?" Foxe asked.

I shrugged, before Scott brought the conversation to the tomb.

"So King Sigismund was an alchemist?"

"Yes, but not a particularly talented one."

"How about you? You seem expert in the methods of Dee and Kelley."

Foxe waved for more beers. "Who isn't?" he asked, sliding notes to the barman. It was inappropriate to start listing names. Scott's shining eyes spoke for themselves.

"Yes, they made gold," Foxe continued. "Well, Kelley didn't, only Dee could."

"So, it's gold you're after?

"Well, who wouldn't be? *However*, Dee and Kelley were offered something far better..."

Scott's interest was going to topple him off the barstool before the beer did.

Foxe took his change. "They were offered something they weren't entirely aware they'd asked for. The greatest gift of all."

"Whitney Houston?" I joked.

"Wasn't that the greatest *love* of all?" Foxe grew serious. "Look, all this," he gazed around. "We lose *everything*. You know that? We know life, yet Death wins. We live, ignoring, denying and drowning the inescapable fact of our death." He hesitated, as though allowing in hope. "Angels change that. They change *everything*. They conquer death."

"So, you intend to scry under a comet with Oliver Turner?" Scott asked, "To finally see Dee's angels?"

"It's actually a meteorite shower, but..."

"Whatever. So what's changed?"

"I've recovered what was missing."

"The angelic tables from the bronze disc?" Scott asked.

"They help, but no, something else."

"The crystal ball Oliver Turner nicked?" I asked.

"No, although it is required." Foxe sounded irritated. "Oliver Turner is skilled, although not as highly as he thinks. But he *is* obsessed, which helps. He was obsessed with City money, before he turned his mind to writing and spiritual matters. You can afford to once you've topped Maslow's hierarchy of needs. Turner, like Kelley, is always looking for scrying companions. And scrying always takes two." He sighed. "Kelley abandoned Dee after they swapped wives. If I'm honest, a little like I did Turner. And like your father did you." He looked at me.

"Friends have fallen out over lesser things than swapping wives," Scott said, glancing at me. I drained my beer.

"Dee wrote to Kelley for thirty years without reply," Foxe continued. "It broke his heart. But Kelley broke his neck, by falling out of a tower he'd been imprisoned in."

"Why was he imprisoned?"

"For failing to live up to expectations." It was his turn to look at me and I also wished he hadn't.

"Dee trained his son Arthur to scry," Foxe continued, "But nothing came of it. However, family traits *do* survive. We are only custodians of our genes. Descendents of Dee or Kelley are likely to have the same skills."

"To contact angels?" Scott asked.

"Yes."

"Are there descendants?"

Foxe hesitated, "Only Arthur survived Dr Dee."

"But didn't someone try to buy Dee's land in Mortlake?"

Foxe stared at Scott. "Michelle again?" He smiled. "Bloody Protestant rectors, can't keep confessions to themselves. It's hard to know. Robert Cotton bought the land, but records show a Talbot also tried. It's the name Kelley used as a pseudonym. As did his son, Theodore Talbot."

"Theodore survived?"

"It wasn't only family heirlooms or family members that were buried. It probably suited some to change identities too. King James was intolerant of spiritual explorers. So, Dee was careful. He buried his possessions near or under landmarks that would survive, so they could be found again in the future if needed. It's what sent me on a fool's mission in the 70s, and I don't mean marriage. At that time Turner and I almost found someone to help us. I'm unsure if he knew who he was, but he disappeared-" He stopped. "He's probably dead by now."

"But Turner's still pursuing him?"

"He won't give up on finding a partner. It's dangerous. He's destroying lives to enrich his own." Meek academia gave way to Bren gun confidence.

"After I left him," Foxe continued, "the Society supplied him with alchemists, so long as he kept them informed, but now he's stopped telling them anything." He lit a cigar. "He's a tricky fish. Let's say old ways screw you as easily as the new."

"He knows you're coming?"

"Well, I'm confident he'll be interested in *your* endeavours. You saw an angel didn't you?"

"You implying we didn't?" Scott asked looking hurt. "I can assure you we did."

"Assure me? Or *show* me?" Foxe's eyes glinted with hope or booze. "You took liberties with my black mirror?"

"It was too tempting."

Foxe paused, "Well, it's good to be curious. It bodes well."

"Is Oliver Turner worth disappearing for?" I asked, "Worth stealing the London Stone for?" I added. "Worth chopping down trees, digging through catacombs and upsetting the Society, not to mention worrying your wife and almost killing us?"

Foxe drained his bottle. "Times are tough. Lecturing doesn't earn what it once did." He smiled. "Desires drag us by their whims." He said, before ordering yet more beers.

"How about the Society?" I asked, "They seem unhappy."

He laughed. "They're like the Catholic Church, or a yoga franchise, everything goes through them. They're never happy. They stopped tolerating mavericks in favour of the status quo some time ago."

"They don't look like academics."

"It's hired guns for this sort of thing. Who did you have?"

"A muscle Mary in a Fred Perry."

"Oh, him. You've gotten off lightly then."

My bandage suggested otherwise. I stood and excused myself to the toilet.

Unlike Scott, I avoid waters I cannot swim in. I caught my father's face in those toilet mirrors, and if I hadn't been so drunk I might have seen what I was running from. Since the UK's smoking ban I'd forgotten how smoky bars could get. It was a night when the first beer chooses the rest. I needed fresh air, so left the others in the bar, to sit by myself on a bench in the street. A TV blasted from a balcony above. An unfamiliar feeling overcame me, until I realised I was relaxed, or drunk.

We had found Foxe, lost the Society, and it was only a short time before we returned to Mortlake and we could put this behind us. We could pay the rent and find punters needing life assistance not involving Elizabethan chancers. I picked at my bandaged hand. There was a blast of laughter as someone left the bar, and footsteps, before Mr Foxe plonked himself beside me like loose change on a counter.

"*That's* better. It was getting hard to breathe in there." He relit his cigar. "Scott's *really* seen them?"

"He's believed in fairies since I met him," I replied.

Foxe tutted. "Trust me, they're not fairies. Ten years of Internet has displaced 16,000 years of myth, legend and belief Ben. But I know who'd win the fight." He tapped ash gently from the cigar. "The more that's explained, the less we enquire. Perhaps *you* spend too much of your life discrediting stuff." Midges swarmed around lamps amongst the coppiced trees.

"You're another Kelley," he added.

"Hardly. He *contacted* them-"

"They tore his head apart. All talent, but no vision." He smiled, "You know how King Ethelred defeated the Danes? His brother Alfred fighting, while Ethelred prayed?"

"Of course." It seemed churlish to say no.

"Well, Kelley argued he was Alfred."

I nodded. I was filling a cup from a waterfall; stuff was going in as quickly as it was spilling out. Smoke billowed luxuriously from Foxe's mouth.

"Dee *was* dependent upon Kelley," Foxe said. "A mistake I intend to avoid with Turner." He looked at me, "Enochian's spectacular stuff Ben. Dee's angelic writings are unique. It's reminiscent of Tibetan mandalas, *full* of phonetic patterning, repetition, rhyme and alliteration. This verbal patterning is characteristic of glossolalia." He clocked my confusion. "Speaking in tongues." A fox scuffled in a nearby bin. "The words echo Sanskrit and Egyptian, languages unknown to medieval Europe."

"You seriously think it's an angelic language?" I argued.

"They exist Ben. Get used to it."

"Whatever happened to getting cynical with age?"

"'*The soul is born young and grows old, that is life's tragedy*'- Oscar Wilde. Alchemy isn't *that* far-fetched. It is creation sped up. Alchemists believe inert substances are filled with spirits, that like mankind, all matter is on the move." He rubbed his grey stubble. "This is alchemy."

"Stubble?"

"Your body transforms consumption into fingernails, toenails and hair. Mother's milk builds a child. *That's* alchemy, Trees convert carbon dioxide into timber and foliage-"

I stopped listening. A breeze had picked up, and stars shot above us.

Chapter 25

I awoke with a head that had mistaken cigars, opening a mini bar and purchasing hotel porn as sensible ideas. We'd soon be discovering Foxe's tolerance to expenses. The evening had concluded with vodka, and Foxe quizzing Scott on his heart attack. I guess men of his age want to know how to survive.

I lay there reconstructing the evening like a prosecuting counsel who hadn't been properly listening. I knew little about Foxe beyond his reluctance to die whilst staring at the sea. Scott knocked, to ask if I wanted to join him swimming. He was wearing the tightest trunks I had ever seen, and I told him so.

"You don't hang around getting in the water wearing these." He smiled like a man who had not been drunk seven hours ago. "Leave 'em wanting less," he chuckled. "Last rule of show-business," he added, strutting away, before returning to hand me his notebook. "See if there's anything we've missed."

The notebook made as much sense as lipstick on wet tissue. Scott soon returned to wake me up, smelling smugly of chlorine and saying, 'That's better' as irritatingly as I had expected. I'm no swimmer. I get more exercise climbing out of the pool than anything I do in it. Besides, that morning I would have drowned.

It was inexplicable how Foxe looked half his age at lunchtime. I appeared to be carrying his hangover for him. Also claiming to be a poor swimmer, he had been for a walk, and he now suggested we visit the castle. Scott was predictably keen, and their enthusiasm carried me to the summit where we had lost

Foxe the previous day. I was too hungover to care if we had a tail. I should have tried it sooner.

The Powder Tower, renamed for storing gunpowder once the Emperor's taste for alchemists passed, was now a museum. I had no idea why Foxe had taken us there, although he may have explained it. There was little to learn in its tight circular rooms, other than observing the view Dee and Kelley had once enjoyed over Prague and distant mountains. Foxe pointed out the painted ceiling.

"Alchemical colours."

We looked up, at the faded black, white, yellow and red paint. My head hurt. Foxe leaned on the windowsill

"I wasn't *entirely* honest last night," he admitted. "Dee stayed nearby, at the Faust House, which used to be Tadeáš Hajek's, Rudolf's physician. The one with eaves carved like books." We peered across the tiled rooftops and church spires.

"Oliver Turner," Foxe hesitated. "He wanted us to carry on. But, it was getting dangerous. Using Enochian can bring about spiritual disintegration. It *can* burn, or worse..."

"Worse than spiritual disintegration?" I said. My hangover was already telling me all I needed to know about spiritual disintegration.

"The angels don't like being contacted?" Scott interrupted.

"Atheism lapsing again, Ben?" Foxe smiled, before raising his hand to silence me. "I'm uninterested in theological debate, *if* you have any." He recognised my mood was unlikely to provide much beyond buying junk food.

"This is science, theology and faith. A new start for mankind," he continued. "Dee and Kelley brushed something grand. No one's ever been closer. But, Oliver Turner and I got close. He was good, although not the special one I thought he was." He stared at me, "So, in answer to your question. No, the angels don't like being contacted. They live in shadows.

They move at night. They're not *supposed* to be seen."

I must have made that indignant sound of my father's.

"Familiar with those seconds of magic in each day Ben?" he asked, "Those dots of joy, where things make *sense*?"

"Not for a while."

He ignored me. "Well, they're the fleeting specks, dots impossible to grasp, *but*," he smiled, "If you join them, they draw God."

"God, or gold?" I asked, which made me feel clever.

"Gold is perfection of terrestrial substances. All minerals eventually evolve into it. It's perfection, like God is, so in a sense, yes. It was a goal."

"You think alchemists speed up evolution?" I asked. "That's bollocks isn't it?"

"Dee didn't think so. He applied the theory to man himself, suggesting spiritual evolution of man eventually results in him becoming closer to God. As above, as below. Alchemists pure enough to be closer to God were more adept at alchemy."

'Kelley was pure?"

"Kelley was ahead of his time," Foxe replied, which didn't answer my question. "They wouldn't have met," he added. "But he'd have enjoyed Thomas Hobbes' dismissal of kindness inherent in Christianity. Kelley believed human self-interest was at the heart of being. He saw kindness as sentimental and weak. How he was able to scry effectively is as mysterious as scrying itself."

"A narcissist," Scott said. "And how about Dee?"

Foxe blushed. "He might agree with Rousseau. That kindness is what makes us human. That lack of imagination inherent in unkindness threatens happiness and probably sanity."

We left the tower. Medieval Prague had nowhere to hide. Caught in the summer, she was flirting brazenly with tourists.

Her darker winter self would be mortified.

"So how did the angels communicate?" Scott asked.

"The tables of 12 x 13 letters contained all human knowledge," Foxe explained like we needed to know. "They gave Kelley co-ordinates from the shew-stone, the crystal, that sat upon the obsidian black mirror," he added. "The calls were given one square at a time. Dee found the corresponding letter in the square and wrote it down."

"Dee trusted Kelley wasn't making it up?"

"Four grids of 12 x 13 letters?" He looked at me. "*If* Kelley was hoaxing Dee, he'd have to memorise the exact position of 2,401 letters. Kelley couldn't *see* the squares. Dee blocked them from him, *and* Kelley had his back to Dee. The angels directed Kelley to call. Dee found the appropriate letter. If Kelley had been a fraudster he'd have had to create a unique language." He paused. "Which is impossible by the way."

"Not really. Tolkien did it. And what about Game of Thrones?"

He glared at me. "Well, *incredibly* difficult then. Particularly in the so-called dark ages."

Scott was predictably convinced.

Foxe continued. "The carefully charted tables worked like a TV remote, and were lost until I found the plaque that Dee gifted the King."

"So why was Kelley so inept without Dee?" Scott asked.

"Isaac Newton, a great alchemist himself, suggested the natural and supernatural worlds can't be separated. The skill in judgement, the blend of chemicals, the instinct and exact distillation, all depend upon the alchemist and precise circumstances. Without purity of spirit the alchemist is only a chemist."

"So Kelley's goal of alchemy, to make gold, was impure…"

"He would never succeed, at least not alone. It always takes two. He needed Dee's purity."

Chapter 26

We ate at the hotel. The owner weaved the tables expertly. I was relieved we remained unimportant enough for his velvet jacket.

"History neglected them," Foxe was saying. "Dee wouldn't have cared, but Kelley would have. He worked hard for favour." He laughed. "He was the sort of cat that'd survive terminal velocity. Anyway, Dee believed his Abrahamic system was used by the first man, Adam, to talk with God and the angels. The tables contained all earthly knowledge-"

Scott's phone rang. It was Ronnie and he left us for some privacy.

"Enjoying this?" Foxe asked me, as I chewed the veal.

"Bit tough."

"I meant chasing Dr Dee."

"It'll end in tears-"

"Like it did for Kelley." Foxe said. "A messy end to a messy life. He disappeared as mysteriously as he appeared. No false names this time. Dee heard in 1595 that Kelley had been 'slain', although there were reports of him practising alchemy in Russia in 1597."

Foxe watched as Scott returned to spread copious butter on bread.

"You're *really* not scared of death are you?" Foxe smiled. "Anyway," he turned to neglected business. "The obsidian mirror. I'll be wanting it." His tone was final; negotiation was over.

"What if we say no?"

"Scott," Foxe said, "I know it's under the table. I can take it, or you can give it to me. And I know how to use it. To you it's a paperweight. So, unless you have alternative ideas?"

For once, Scott did not, so used his foot to slide it beneath the table.

Foxe nodded. "I'm impressed you found Marble Arch. I was on the roof."

"The trapdoor?" I remembered.

"You purloined the auction ticket, but how about the key?"

"The key?"

I had to smile. Scott's innocence had chocolate around its mouth.

"Yes, the small key, hanging on the chain? What did you do with it?"

"It's in our Hanway Street office."

Foxe stared at Scott, possibly before accepting we had not found the key's use. It was a tough call.

"Ok. So, we're working together," he said. "And I *do* work better with people, and you both seem intelligent enough."

Scott looked surprisingly pleased at being patronised.

"You'll have to come with me though," Foxe continued, "To Oliver Turner's house. You know too much, at least until it's over. It'll be safer to stay together."

"Safer? Aren't the Society dealt with?"

"The Bren's an accurate weapon Ben, but not destructive enough to undo an entire organisation."

"But, isn't this the point when we invoice you and wait too long to be paid?" I asked. "We're done here."

Scott frowned, but someone had to put a stop to this.

"You'll be reimbursed for coming with me," Foxe added.

"We'll do it," Scott agreed. "Let the rainbow come to you Ben."

"Excellent." Foxe grinned. "You might even come in useful." He made us sound like an impulse purchase in Duty Free. "We'll find Turner tomorrow," he said, wiping his mouth.

Scott looked like he'd got the last seat on a train, but I was less sure.

"You'll find him that easily?" Scott asked, and Foxe nodded.

"I know where he lives. He's too pleased with himself to hide away entirely."

That night, once I'd packed, and double locked the door, I read the latest email from Ronnie. It was the penultimate transcript of Jane Dee's diary.

EAST

Arrival in Trebon

The horses struggled with the mud and sunken cobbles of older roads. Kelley rode ahead, eager to arrive. That night we found another hovel masquerading as lodgings.

Kelley argued a low profile was advisable on the road, and refused to scry. Instead, John bought wine. If only this were a more regular alternative to angel business. Kelley warned of pouring left handed bringing bad luck. John sighed like a man finally losing patience with idiots surrounding him.

"I'm left handed," he paused. "And don't," he held up his hand, stalling Kelley's words on his lips, "Suggest the Devil is left handed. The sly fox is probably ambidextrous."

The chill at the table was not only the mountain mist billowing down the hillside outside.

By the following morning, sleep had strengthened something. In the distance, we admired the snowy peaks of central Europe. The storm-front had passed, dragging behind it a change in the weather. There was a frost and the animals' breath steamed into the wintery air. Their fodder intended to last eight days, was now stretched to ten by poor roads and crosswinds. It was not only the horses I feared growing weak. We had lost a food casket, and my children were already hungry.

"Where is it?" I asked the coachman, who shrugged.

John overheard me. "We've lost a book trunk?" he asked, stepping forward in panic.

"No, John, *food*. We've lost pickles, and bread."

"Praise be, they are replaceable."

"We can't eat books, John."

"Without books there's no nourishment."

I stared at his slender frame as though the horse had spoken, "But it's the children, John." I shook my head, "It's *us*."

Arthur, on the lead horse, shouted, and pointed ahead. Smoke curled from chimneys of Trebon's public baths outside the town. The mood lifted as our horses were led to troughs, and the wagons washed down. We bathed and applied large doses of lavender water. Our faces were raw from wind and the sun. Beyond the baths, yews encircled a burial ground. Flies bothered fresh mounds of earth. We kept our distance. The Black Death was stalking Europe with an alarming confidence.

John stepped away to speak with a gravedigger. Leaning on his shovel, he reassured John that the Plague had not yet reached these parts. John returned to us, patting children's heads as he passed, possibly counting them. I was unsure he knew how many we had. For Kelley it was easier, Joanna had not yet borne him any offspring. I think it bothers him. I wonder if that explains his lecherous looks at me. His glances are unmistakable, and an opportunity to squeeze me in private is never passed. Obviously I push him away, but it does not stop him.

I stood at the edge of the clearing. A logger's path

disappeared into the dark forest. I wet a twig and dipped it in the rosemary salt to brush my teeth. Kelley's sudden proximity startled me. He stood, watching me.

"What are you waiting for?" I spat bits of food, as well as blood. "You don't want my twig?" I laughed, "You're standing on hundreds."

"That's a fine 'un." He stared at mine.

I shook my head, gave my teeth another scratch, before scooping water from the pail to rinse my mouth and handing him the stick. I walked away, unable to resist glancing back, as the twig disappeared into his mouth.

Trebon castle was small and dominated by a narrow tower. Like much of the property it had fallen subtly into disrepair. Crumbling parapets had crows nesting in arrow slits and the main gate had a rusted portcullis. I smiled; the standard of our destinations was diminishing rapidly. The castle held no prisoners. Presumably it was too easy to escape from. There was only the disused west tower that might serve such purpose.

Rožmberk was pleased to see us. He twitched incessantly, with the air of a dying man desperate to find peace. I saw rot in his furs and, up close, noticed his thinning wig was patched with string. If anyone needed alchemists amongst his guests, it was Rožmberk. His wooden teeth looked as uncomfortable as ever, accentuated by his shaven face. Shaving is apparently the latest fashion, and I only wish John took a little more interest in such shallow matters. A guard patrolled the parapets, although I suspect there is none at night.

It is Rožmberk's delight at our arrival, which concerns me most. What has Kelley promised? Our rooms and their laboratories have been prepared, and I guess Rožmberk expects imminent results. With the sun setting and our party slumbering, felled by full stomachs, John prayed. I know we are on the run, although he has admitted nothing. Political tides are turning; shadows are passing over the enlightenment.

I was pleased to have been more successful than Arthur at ignoring the sewer below our window. He had thrown off his bedclothes in disgust and left the room earlier. Overnight rain had overflowed the cesspits across the central courtyard. I stood, stretched and wrapped my furs close, before crouching to look out the window. I recognised Arthur in the distance, talking with workmen. Wood smoke drifted over the freshly dug meadowlands. John was elsewhere. I was hungry, and decided to look for the kitchens.

I dressed and crossed the courtyard. Despite the rain, the rising sun beaming through the main gate could be Heaven sent. Water glistened on the cobbles, and from somewhere a cockerel compensated for its unpunctual start.

I nodded good morning to the farrier leading a nag from the stable. Its hooves stamped, irritated at being awoken. I recognised it was one of ours and hoped we had not looked so knackered on arrival two days ago. There was little sign of our host, which did not surprise me. Last night's wine consumption should floor him for a week. Rožmberk had been tucking in before we joined him in the Great Hall that only justified describing itself as such in the absence of any local competition.

This morning was crisp, with the smell of a new wind. Avoiding a large puddle in the courtyard, I joined a gossiping huddle of servants below the west tower. Its door was ajar, beyond which steps led upwards. Through a fortunate twist of acoustics, I heard voices from above.

"They are not from God."

"Then from *where* Edward?"

It was John. Had they not yet gone to bed? I peered up a rotting spiral staircase. I could not see them, yet heard them clearly enough. I climbed a few steps and paused by an arrow slit. The sky framed in a cross.

"They don't burn your mind John, not like mine. I beseech you, it is time to rest." Kelley sounded shattered.

"*And* this new demand?" John asked. "Do not blush my good man."

"I am tired."

"We both are, Edward." Then more softly, "What disturbs you?"

"They demand that we must share..."

"Share what my good man? Tell me. If it be God's will, then so be it. For what did they ask?"

I sensed Kelley poised over something monumental.

"We follow everything they demand," John prompted him

"Everything? Well, if we wish harmony with spirits," Kelley announced, "Then we must obey."

I held my breath, as Kelley continued.

"We are to sacrifice that which we have promised our wives."

My heart lurched like a hound catching a scent.

"Sacrifice our wives?" John's voice was horrified, "As Abraham sacrificed his son...?"

"Not *sacrifice*," Kelley reassured him, and my belly righted itself.

"Nay, but sacrifice of sorts, the sacrifice of marriage, of honour..." He tailed off, although I noticed anticipation in his tone. He was carefully not saying too much.

"We are to share our wives," Kelley said finally.

"Share our wives, with whom?" John sounded weak.

My mouth was dry. For such an intellect John could be

slow sometimes. I heard the lust in Kelley's voice clear enough, even if my husband did not.

"With each other. For carnal use John, contrary to the law of the commandment, or of spiritual love. We are to swap our wives for a night."

John mumbled something I could not hear.

"I too struggle to believe God approves," Kelley added, unconvincingly. "But this is for what they ask."

The servants below began to disperse, presumably bored by lack of understanding English.

"Did Uriel command this? Speak your mind," John was growing irritated. "They would demand no such thing."

"I report only what they speak."

"Yet in my absence Edward. How can I be sure? This is corrupt, you used the sigillum, while I slept?"

"I ensured the communion remained protected."

I leaned against the stairwell, moss damp against my back. I was glad for its support.

"This is why we must always scry *together*..." John said.

I felt dizzy, my stomach twisted with turmoil. My body slid down the wall, until I met the cold steps. John would not stand for this. He would deny Kelley his cunning scheming, of that I was sure, yet I sensed the shadow of lust in my own belly that I already feared. Was Kelley playing us all?

March 22nd 1587

I was alone in the room with John's journal. His writings are impossible to understand, even when not keeping one eye on the door. He describes an angel stepping forward, to reveal the 'og' in the square before the y/15. An angel called Uriel then approached, to reveal the t/11 for the square just *after* the y/15. It was gibberish, so I turned the page. An angel called Michael then apparently stopped the process. I looked at a translation:

Ymago tua (mors), est amara. John had scribbled out an English translation beside it, 'Your image, death, is bitter'.

I had not seen John all day, which in such a small castle was impressive. I spent the morning watching children learn archery from the bored guards, but I was less easily distracted. I was disturbed by Kelley's claim. I had lost my appetite to a flickering thrill.

I joined Joanna Kelley at lunch. The children tucked in around us, but the men were most probably sleeping.

"I eat with you more frequently than Edward," Joanna Kelley said, tapping her broken tooth. Like most people she was attractive enough until she opened her mouth. Not that she said much. She was a quiet soul, a surprising choice for Kelley.

"More for us," I agreed, while my stomach turned again at the daemon's demand. I poured mead to quench sudden thirst.

"Dr Dee has promised to teach the children after noon," Joanna explained.

John had helped prepare a makeshift schoolhouse in the yard. I had watched his preparations for lessons, consisting of jottings about his experiments, describing salts and earths suspended in water, horse manure and menstrual blood. I did not envy his young students.

The fleeting intimacy between Joanna and I presented the ideal opportunity for me to mention what I had overheard. I pulled pork from the bone, deliberating what to say.

"There be more for *me*, if you're not eating?" Joanna asked.

I looked up, surprised to find her talking. I broke off some bread. This had gone too far.

"The men are asleep?" Joanna asked.

"Of course, if the sun's up, they're sleeping…" I dipped the bread with poppy oil. "They led us here. They demanded this trip..." I allowed *they* to linger, but Joanna failed to pick up on the hint.

"It's Edward's head," Joanna explained, "It burns morning and night," she paused. I sensed tears. "Your husband. He's driven...What's going to stop him?"

I frowned. Perhaps there was more to Kelley's wife than I had thought.

"I concur, we can't continue like this," I replied.

Joanna's eyes reddened, before filling with tears. "We're on the edge of the world.... He wants children, wealth. I seem to give him neither..." She stopped, to cough tears away. "What are we doing?"

It was a good question.

I nodded for Joanna to pass the mead, as an idea grew.

"Perhaps we can stop them," I suggested.

"We?"

"I'm unsure anyone else can."

I watched Joanna pouring herself a glass of mead, before downing it. We stared at one another.

"They need to be parted. But how?" she asked.

"If we work together, as they do," I was firm. "Then pr'haps these times shalt cease. You are willing?"

Joanna nodded, "We live in dangerous times."

I poured more mead, a plan shaping that I pretended was not already fully formed.

"I overheard them this morning. Their angels made new demands. If fulfilled, it will divide us all." I sipped. "It will split our families in two." I allowed a smile, "If the men are correct, it *always* takes two. If you and I do this, we shalt never speak again."

"What do you suggest?" Joanna leaned forward.

"To do *exactly* as they suggest." My stomach flipped excitedly.

"Which is?" Joanna's eyes were wide with anticipation.

I hesitated, before imagining John fucking Joanna.

"No. I can't do it. I'm sorry. We must find some other way..."

I left her to her bafflement.

March 25th 1587

The midnight sky was cloudless. John watched the North Star as we rode. He shivered, and reached across to my saddle alongside, but I declined his hand. My gloves held firm the reins. He understood my feelings; how could he not.

I had accepted his suggestion of swapping wives as calmly as expected, as though I had not expected it. It was a good thing the chamber pot was empty when it shattered against the wall. I put on a good show.

Following our argument, we rode a track following a valley through the hills. Its high sides cut off the stars. In the darkness a sudden thunder of hooves startled us. It was deer. Despite our disagreement, we rode closer. The children remained at Trebon, to follow later with an escort to the border. I had demanded we leave immediately. It was time to abandon the scryer. Kelley's eyes had lain upon me for too long. If he was so ready to play big cards, then so was I. Kelley had smiled, as he reported the angels' request alongside John.

Our horses followed the track upwards, as it climbed through thinning trees, where open pasture lay behind high Hawthorne hedges tracing the roadside. We stopped at the summit, where a junction split the track in two. We made out the silhouette of a stone cross. Its left arm was damaged from lightning. We paused to confirm the road returning to Prague. John glimpsed comets. No doubt it was another good night for angels.

Our returning to Prague contravened the Papal Nuncio, but we had little choice but to pass its gates. Besides John would no longer be scrying. He had already sent a messenger ahead with our intention. From Prague we could better arrange our journey home to England. I looked back at the stone cross and the choice of roads leading into the night. The horses quivered their manes. They were glad for rest, more used to sleep at this time of night. We strained to see the signpost pointing right to Prague.

"And left?" I asked, with the economy of a woman spurned.

"Returns us to Trebon, if the sign is believed," John replied.

"You've believed lesser signs." I froze. "What was that?" I whispered. John had also heard something.

"More deer?" I asked, but it was unlikely. We heard it again, A footstep, or hoof.

"What *is* that?" I hissed. My horse stamped its feet anxiously, while John's whinnied nervously. It rubbed against the haunches of my own. John pulled its bit tighter. The horses nuzzled one another, eyes flashing white and fearful in the dark. John leaned forward in his saddle to pat their necks.

"I'll look." He dismounted with his usual lack of grace, somehow catching his boot in the stirrup. Were I not so afraid, I would have laughed.

"Be careful," I whispered, as he got up. Cold fear was now eclipsing my anger.

He ran his hand along my horse's flank as he passed. It shivered. Branches of trees lining the high hedgerow to the fields rustled, but there was no wind, only the smell of damp undergrowth. John looked around, but there was no one there. As he turned to reassure me, he glanced down and gasped. In the mud was a claw print, twice the size of his hand, which the hair prickling on my neck instantly recognised as not deer. My breathing stopped.

"What is it?" I called, but his reply caught in his throat. We had been followed, but it was impossible to see where the talon imprints led. They stopped dead.

"Oh Lord," he whispered, "Dost not abandon thy humble servant." He pulled his folding knife from his pocket.

"John?"

He looked up, pale beneath his beard, his mouth mumbling more hasty prayers, hoping words might bolster his bravery.

"John!" I screamed, as something passed close by in the darkness, my fear echoing down the valley. "JOHN…"

He stepped to my flank, his hand stroking the horse. His mouth was moving, now without words. His face was petrified in shock. He looked at the ground ahead. The claw prints picked up again, leading clearly to the left junction of the track. There was a gust of air, and our horses reared against their reins. I clung to the saddle, barely remaining mounted. Against the brilliant sky the stars disappeared, replaced by blackness, as a dark silhouette of huge wings spread open, obliterating all stars…

"It's impossible," he whispered, mentally measuring the distance between the claws. Something embraced my back, and I screamed. He crouched down, to find a feather twice the length of his arm. He held it up to show me, but I waved it away. I wished not to see it.

"It sat behind me, its hands, they…" I said, choking on fear again.

John squeezed my hand, murmuring gentle reassurances. We were a long way from books and candles.

"We cannot leave. It is clear. We must respect their demands, sinful though they are…"

I nodded vaguely. I saw we had no choice. He stepped away, to the stone cross, behind which he secreted the feather.

There is only one option remaining to break the men's union remaining to Jane and I.

I watched castle life from the window. The presence at the junction haunted my every thought. I spotted a stables marshal taking a break in the meadows. He sat astride a fine courser. Nearby a man was flying a hawk. It swooped low over men digging fishponds. Kelley was returning from a ride. He approached the castle and looked up to see me. He winked, and was about to move on, when Rožmberk galloped in.

"Kelley," he pulled up holding his hat. "How are you? The laboratories productive today?" Kelley was about to answer, but Rožmberk interrupted before he could answer.

"Any developments. Any shiny stuff?" he asked.

"Moving apace."

"Good," Rožmberk's spurs dug in, "I grow impatient." Hooves kicked the dirt, and he cantered through the castle's gate.

John folded his clothes into the chest by the bed, before lying on the furs beside me. I could still smell the broken piss pot. We looked up. The ceiling held as many answers as the heavens beyond. He sighed so heavily that God must have heard, when a knock disturbed us, and Kelley stepped into the room.

He looked tired, and went to sit in the window. He did not look up, as John swung down his feet, narrowly avoiding spilling the replacement pot.

"This cannot proceed as is," Kelley began, silencing John's response with a raise of his hand, "My debts catch up with me."

"Your debts are not my concern."

Kelley shook his head, "My dearest Dr Dee, indeed they *are* your concern. The time has come for us to ask the angels for what *I* desire."

"I know which sin you *desire*."

Kelley said nothing.

"And now gold as well?" John said, glancing at the crystal concealed beneath its cloth behind the door. "Gold is your price for the company of angels?"

"Do not cheapen your tone Dr Dee, you need me. You have returned, and this is my price."

"For your diminishing youth?"

"Indeed, it *would* appear you require younger scryers."

"Youth is plentiful Edward."

Kelley looked around,

"Not around here it isn't, certainly none as blessed as mine."

John's eyes narrowed. Kelley looked to the window. The thin glass distorted the distant hills of Trebon skirting eastern lands.

"Very well. You leave me with no choice."

Kelley cleared his throat. "Our journey from here is back west, from whence we came. This is journey's end." His voice echoed in the window's alcove. "You want to see this through? Then we shall open the curtain on our final act."

I watched and listened at the gap, where the door failed to find its frame. Kelley sat by the crystal and black mirror. Within an hour, his face dripped with sweat and paled. John, having murmured his prayers, lifted the quill from its rest. The room's temperature dipped. John's eyes searched for the angels, but saw nothing.

"All sins committed in me are forgiven. He who goes mad on my account, let him be wise," Kelley said, as Dee scribbled. "Thow commyttest Idoltry. But take hede of Temptation. Dee, what woldest you have?"

"Recte sapere et Intelligere?" John defaulted to Latin, I suspect alarmed at the change in tone of the angels.

"If you swap loved ones, then thy Desyre is granted. It can never be undone."

"What desire? What are we promised? *What* are we granted?"

I heard fear in John's questions. The wind picked up, a window rattled and the thatch whistled. What had been granted that could not be undone? The window shook loose and John stood to close it. He glanced outside, at trees bowing to the wind, at the moon coursing its way through the heavens. We were a long way from home. He rubbed his hand down his face, to tug his beard's point.

"John?"

He looked back, to where Kelley gripped his belly in pain. The crystal sparked with intent. Kelley's forehead twisted in a terrible frown.

"They still demand the adultery. I am sorry."

"Pray continue." John held his eye.

"They promise that if so, then he be blessed for eternity and receive the heavenly prize."

"For the heavenly prize they request this?" John sighed, nausea threatening his own balance, "This exchange of wives? For eternal life?"

Moonlight caught Kelley's face and hair, which tied back, exposed the scar tissue around his ears. His white streak glowed.

He nodded. "They do not request, they demand."

"They test our commitment," said John quietly.

Kelley fell back, hands falling by his sides. "These are fresh waters John." His eyes were shrunken and black, "Our time together is ending."

John sat alone. I stood at his shoulder. Kelley had long since retired. John crossed his legs to the draught, staring at the covenant in front of him. Its ink still drying:

O Almighty God, at this present, [we] do faithfully and sincerely confess, and acknowledge, that thy profound wisdom in this most new and strange doctrine (among Christians) propounded, commended, and enjoined unto us four only, is above human reason.

Such cost, I thought, but to what end? And for what heavenly prize?

We sat in a circle at the dining table, all awkward despite our months of jostled intimacy. I glanced at Joanna Kelley, but she looked away.

"At this present, [we] do faithfully and sincerely confess," John read, "And acknowledge, that thy profound wisdom in this new and strange doctrine shall be given in return for union of bodies. And accept this wisdom given in return."

Glances are exchanged between us, but none are met. The quill is dipped to sign the covenant. From beneath his hood, Kelley barely constrains himself, grinning as he scrawls his name flamboyantly across the parchment. John's signature is more considered, while Joanna's appears to be her first. I write as though with someone else's hand, recalling the stone cross at the junction and the devil upon my back. Yet I am angry; how has it come to this? Has it always been Kelley's plan? I refuse to make the eye contact I know John seeks. We stand back and John coughs self-consciously. It can be delayed no longer.

Kelley invited me to leave the room with him. I had little choice, so followed. He licked his lips, which I hope John missed. I glanced at my husband as we passed. My hand hovered over his shoulder, but did not settle.

We had agreed neutral bedchambers, and it was only fury

that led me to the ground floor bedroom. How had it come to this, so far out of sight, so far from home? Kelley followed me, too closely. I turned, to catch John glancing awkwardly at Joanna.

Our room was small, and a fire crackled in the corner. Kelley looked like an auctioneer promised a stallion.

"Be gentle. I've seen how you ride," I said, and he grinned unlike I had seen before.

I sat on the bed and pressed on the eiderdown. The castle had woolen mattresses after all.

Kelley misinterpreted my smile, and sat beside me. He smelled of the same wood smoke and chemicals of my husband. Food and grease clogged his hair. Even its white streak hair was grimy in the poor light. I was glad for the gloom. Treachery discourages light.

Fasteners caught the material as he negotiated my petticoat. I pushed his hands away, to loosen the drawstrings myself, allowing him to pull open the dress, exposing my breasts. I shivered, before gasping at his cold hands, at their savagery and hunger. Before he planted his mouth on mine. I tasted rosemary where he had brushed his teeth. His tongue charged into mine. I resisted, before pleasure found its inevitable voice, and my tongue sought his with shameful desire. Forgetting myself, not to mention the grime, I grabbed his hair, twisting it into a fist and pulled his head back to kiss him fully.

"We shall make it count," I whispered breathlessly. "It's *once*." My hands slid into his trousers, to seek his hard cock.

I later lay on the bed, my arms thrown back in surrender. My breathing had finally slowed. My cunt throbbed with discomforting warmth that battled a deepening guilt. I found some of his hair twisted around my fingers. Seeing me unwind it, he took it from me.

"I cannot mislay it." He packed the black hair into his

leather pouch.

"Are you Hindu now?" I asked. "You hoping to be reincarnated and not return bald?"

"Don't mock ideas."

"I wouldn't dare." I stood to adjust my dress. "What do you think this has gained?"

"Only time shalt reveal."

I tamed my disarrayed hair beneath a headdress. It was done. I stepped to the door.

"Such heavenly creatures demand such lowly behavior? Whoever knew," I said.

"'Tis between us and God."

"And my husband and your wife."

"Oh yes," he grunted from the bed, before turning over to sleep. His lack of interest, his hunger now quenched, was as insulting as I feared he intended. From outside I heard pigs snuffling in the courtyard. How long had we been? I opened the door, shivering in the fresh dawn. Everything felt wrong. I was glad for no mirror glass, as I was unable to look myself in the eye.

I did not see him immediately. His tall shadow merged with the colonnade's columns. He was nervously tugging his beard, but hearing me, he swept back his cowl and sniffed in the cold. He was as solemn as a tree. He took my hand and I heard the morning's first birdsong. We said nothing. We climbed the outside steps to our quarters and I squeezed his hand. I had done as asked; his somber mood already suggested it had not been worthwhile.

Dee's diary: 21st May 1587. Pactum Factum. (Pact fulfilled).

Chapter 27

Jet trails caught the sunset as they dissected the sky. At street level the shadows had already won. A stag party passed by, taut with forced hilarity. We gazed up at the crumbling façade of the medieval, half-timbered house. The first floor windows overhung the street. Their glass wore pollution with dirty determination. Above them, gargoyles glared down, their features worn smooth by rain, growing younger with age. Since my chat with Foxe, something had been bothering me. Whilst understandable for hippies to glimpse angels between spliffs and *Escape to the Country* re-runs, he was not alone. Research for my book knew Foxe was in company that even included George Washington. Men with reputations actually worth losing readily admitted to visitations from angels. Research showed 13% of people claimed to have encountered an angel, but then another 99% would claim they had never been asked. Foxe joined me in looking up at the carvings and darkened windows, and swotted away a fly.

"The whole damn world and it buzzes me." He sounded irritated, before studying us for a moment. "Take my lead, even you Scott." He *was* nervous. The front door was oak and likely to outlive even the house. Foxe tugged a chain dangling from the doorframe.

"You're students," he reminded us. Regrettably, I passed as one, but Scott's polished boots and Oxford shirt less so. We leaned into the door; the echo of *Deutschland* drifted incongruously from further along the street.

"It'll be a big house," Foxe coughed authority into his voice. "They're built on sites of 12th Century houses, with deep basements."

He had not seen Oliver for thirty years, and it showed. As though realising this, he pulled the chain again. There was a creak, and the door swung inwards, dragging an ancient groove into musty gloom. It halted, before a hand rested on the frame. It belonged to a woman with a fixed perm, and teeth that needed fixing. She had established her look early in life, and was aged anywhere between 30 and 70. She looked at us like we'd burped in her face. They settled upon Mr Foxe.

"Hle me? Mohu vám pomoci?"

I panicked, and considered using Siri on my phone, while Scott appeared similarly surprised. Thankfully Mr Foxe stepped into the breach.

"Ano, anglitina," he explained, "Jeste my tutaj, aby odwiedzi stron Turner. Mam nadziej e jest?" His accent was flawless.

"*All* English?" she clipped faultlessly.

"Yes, madam." Mr Foxe switched to English, "Students researching Prague," he motioned at us. "And the emperor Rudolph." With distant amusement, her narrow eyes looked down the street, as though to suggest there were other doors to try.

"We *are* expected," Foxe added. "I am Professor Foxe, of UCL. University of London," he explained. "I understand a Mr Turner lives here."

At the mention of the employer's name her eyes widened with surprise. Seeing Foxe extract a business card from his wallet, Scott delved for a LAA one, but Foxe quickly stopped him, holding Scott's arm to discourage any impromptu marketing.

"He knows me," Foxe said, "He might even be expecting

me. Please let him know that Professor Foxe is here."

Foxe's card disappeared into her apron, before the door closed, leaving us alone again.

"Well, would you allow historians into your home?" Foxe asked.

"It might appeal to my vanity," Scott said.

"Well let's hope Oliver Turner shares your sense of importance," smiled Foxe.

"That's unlikely," I said,

"You've not met Oliver Turner yet."

I then noticed something. "Whoever lives here likes a low profile, it's not numbered..."

"From the revolution days..." Foxe started, before being interrupted by the door bolts sliding across, and the fixed perm reappearing.

"Come in," she said with a tone implying it had not been her decision.

We stepped into a hallway, and I wondered if the gloom and furniture polish reminded Foxe of Mortlake as it did me. The first room we passed was a dining room belonging to someone who ate from the fridge. A sheet covered the table and dust lay on the windowsills. She hastily closed the door opposite, through which I glimpsed stacks of packing cases. I was curious, but we followed her down the hallway that revealed itself as a portrait gallery. Foxe stopped briefly at each poorly executed oil painting.

"Scryers," he whispered. The house demanded muted tones. The portraits were young men, all wearing the same glassy look in their smudged eyes, as though aware of the painter's ineptitude. At the end of the hallway, a doorway led into a garden, but we climbed a narrow staircase. Halfway up, from a half-painted window, I spied an overgrown garden shared with another house, but the housekeeper's feet tapping on a landing smelling of snuffed-candles discouraged lingering. Foxe remained quiet. We followed her to a closed door. She knocked, before showing us in.

It may have been the dark, or the smell of damp clothes mingling with oil paints, but we found ourselves standing closer together than I liked. It was less of a united front and more of safety in numbers. The woman moved past us into the room, and someone moved near a patch of daylight from a window. I heard a tap, and tiny splash of water, before a flash of white appeared as someone stepped away from what appeared to be an easel. Foxe coughed. I wondered if the dimness excused the poor craftsmanship in the hallway.

"I didn't know you had friends," a voice spoke like it required a recharge. A desk lamp clicked on, behind which a man shrugged off a paint-smattered smock. He had a young face, beneath long thinning hair that needed to admit defeat. His build suggested the metabolism of a hummingbird.

"Professor Foxe," he said, and who I presumed to be Oliver Turner stepped around the huge desk stacked with magazines, and held out his hand, which Foxe shook with a sense of relief.

"Some men enjoy company," Turner said, "But, as you know, I'm not one of them. Unless they're talented." He stood in front of Foxe, his eyes glistening like marbles. "My, you *are* looking good. I fear only one of us has aged." His flattery was genuine. He then looked at us, "So, which one is he?"

"Scott Wildblood," Scott proffered his hand. "Student of Mr Foxe."

Turner's smile disappeared like iron filings losing magnetism.

"And, I'm Ben Ferguson-Cripps," I added.

Turner's handshake had the impact of a falling leaf. I

anticipated more. He was younger than Foxe, and shorter, yet older than I expected, like he had caught up with Foxe somehow. Perhaps angel chasing was a damaging lifestyle choice.

A pigeon cooed on the windowsill, and Turner slammed his fist against the glass. We all jumped, and a portrait that even the sitter might struggle to recognise slipped from its easel. Turner was a man spending more on paints than he'd ever earn from painting, much like my laptop's relationship to writing.

"I received your proposal," Turner said. "But you had your chance. You should be careful of what you let go." Turner studied Foxe again. His eyes, murkier than the English Channel, outstayed their welcome. He nodded to worn leather chairs facing the desk, which he returned behind. I had taken immediate dislike to him, although I was unsure what annoyed me the most – a desk even I wanted to tidy, his artistic ineptitude or simply the contents of the bookcase, containing titles like *The Holy Vedas* and *A Beginner's Guide to Assault Sorcery in Arctic Norway*. He was someone with little need for a beginners guide to anything but manners. I spotted several copies of his *Crystal balls and crystal bowls, of modern scrying and ancient seership* by O. Turner. I was glad Scott hadn't seen this bookcase before listing services on our business card. Mr Turner was a man who either knew a lot, or wanted people to think he did. The claw of a broken light bulb watched from the ceiling. The years sat heavily upon him.

"So," he said, reclining in his chair. "How do you find Prague?"

He sounded like a man who had once been interested, but since forgotten why. I wanted to answer 'by following a university lecturer obsessed with Elizabethan scryers', but even I realised it was a poor moment for flippancy.

"The sister Paris never had," Foxe replied, still looking around, at the portraits. Clocking his interest, Turner asked if we had noticed how he'd captured the light. We couldn't. The sitter looked tired, as though knowing how awful the portrait would be. Turner's painting smock interrupted our appreciation by falling off his chair, which he reacted to like an assassination attempt. We were not alone in feeling jumpy.

"London?" he recovered, "Not what she once was?"

"Impressive library," Foxe changed the subject this time.

"A dying breed, men who read books."

I thought I glimpsed *Mirrors and Lies*, but couldn't see it again.

"Depends what they read," Turner said, his eyes flaring. "I put little faith in the Internet, it's an awkward distillation of conjecture and lies. Besides, I struggle with my broadband connection."

I was unsure if this wasn't a stab at humour.

"I read your treatise on Paracelsus with interest," Turner continued. "How is Renaissance history surviving your absence? Or perhaps they prefer a Head of Department with less enthusiasm for the *occult*?"

"I couldn't say," replied Mr Foxe.

"You're suggesting more prosaic pursuits bring you to Prague?" Turner was playing games, and distracted by the pigeon struggling to roost on the windowsill, he banged the glass again. "Bloody things, crapping over my city." He inhaled deeply, eyes twinkling. "Alchemy's a cheap science."

"That's never stopped you before."

"Nor yourself. Your wife embraces your renewed obsession? I thought you told her you'd buried it all." He grinned at the in-joke. I sensed he was digging.

"God forgives," Mr Foxe said.

"But the wife's always a good start."

Quietness filled the room; even the pigeon gave up trying to get in.

"Is he a recent departure?" Foxe asked, looking at the half-finished portrait.

"Well, you know the difficulty in finding partners better than most," Turner replied. "Your skill in losing them is a rare talent." He sighed, as though weary of the inferences despite having started them. "Now, your letter..." He instantly regretted looking for it on the desk. "Your knowledge of a dead language remains impressive. Ah." As he held the letter up, a business card flew from its paperclip. I frowned, thinking I recognised the impact font of a Life Assistance Agency card, but it disappeared into the darkness. Scott coughed.

"Sore throat?" Turner snapped, before looking at Foxe. "Your *students* share our belief in angels?"

"Yes," said Scott.

Turner nodded. "*You* might, but salesmen are notoriously easy to sell to. It's an unusual belief. And your companion?"

"He's seen them," Scott replied before I could counter.

"You both have?" Turner looked momentarily interested.

"I'm not so sure about that," I said.

"Not the one in Deptford," Scott corrected me. "The one at Vital Marketing, when I nearly died."

"You saw your angel when you *died*?" Turner asked interestedly, before looking at Foxe. "You've found him? Is this *him*?"

A dull mood filled the room, the history between them too stretched to understand.

"You spring up like this, like all is forgotten," Turner tapped his fingers together. "You think I'll make it easy for you? I think not Mr Foxe. For many years I might have agreed, but not now-"

"If there is some way-"

"There is *no* way Mr Foxe. You're not here for me. You just want your bloody crystal ball back."

"That you stole."

"And how did that bloody feel?" Turner shouted, demonstrating how lightly the pigeon had been getting off. "You can't do anything without it. Apparently it's *my* turn to shut windows we should never have opened."

Foxe looked perplexed, but Turner shook his head.

"No more scrying," he said, relishing Foxe's disappointment. "And apologies for derailing *your* plans."

Foxe hesitated like a boxer choosing his punch.

"Oliver, it isn't only scrying skills I'm offering." He reached into his jacket pocket. The shadows of trees flickered in the window. Foxe leaned across, to tap a small metal ball on the desk. Turner watched him carefully, as Foxe raised the sphere, before deftly twisting it open. With a crack, he allowed a small stream of red powder fall to the desk in a neat heap. Turner gasped; eyes agape.

"Where did you get that?"

Chapter 28

"But there's no tincture left?" Turner whispered. "None since Kelley."

"You think Dee trusted Kelley?"

"Evidently not." Turner stared at the red powder, eyes wired greedily. "Where did you get that?"

"Nature hides her secrets well."

As Turner rose from his desk, Foxe deftly scraped the powder across the table and tipped it back into the sphere, which he plugged.

"Your taste for experimentation changed?" Foxe asked, stashing the vial in his pocket.

Turner stepped past his desk, pausing as the powder disappeared from view, "A fool might turn their back on this, but what am *I* to do?" he asked.

Foxe remained silent.

"But how did *you* find that?" Turner continued. "It's impossible. They turned Europe upside down-" Turner stared at Foxe. "You're bluffing. This powder's tricked too many people." His eyes bore into Foxe's. "Very well, demonstrate its so-called power and we'll prove it a farce. The laboratory's next door."

"Next door?"

Turner shot a lizard-like smile, forced and fleeting. He walked to the door, "Too many people know I live here. Follow me."

"You have my crystal?" Foxe asked.

"If it's not sold on eBay." Turner waved us past and smiled. "Of course I have it."

The garden was a jungle. We followed stone flagging obscured by long grass. The fresh air revived us from the oppressive house. Turner, who had found a long-sleeved jacket, walked like a man weighing decisions. Trees blocked views from neighbouring houses. A bat swooped invisibly past. Turner reached into the grass to pull on a rusted chain. With a yank, a wooden cover broke the undergrowth. A trap door opened. Stone steps descended into thick gloom.

I followed, as we stepped carefully into the dark. Turner warned us to mind our heads on a beam. Foxe's swearing suggested the warning had come too late. Descending in procession, I held Scott's shoulder, but was puzzled when he shrugged it away. I guessed the cavern was the basement of where a house once stood, as though the city had risen like dough.

"Mind the steps Scott," Foxe warned. Our feet slid on damp stone. The words of the ruddy-faced man in the British Museum rang in my head, recalling: *'caverns in the bowels of the earth'*. The spiral staircase finally levelled out, and darkness bruised our eyes. Turner stepped away, to pull on a long flex from the ceiling, and light bulbs crackled to life.

We were standing in a large, domed cavern. The chamber was cool, damper than outside. The steps hugged the wall, to where black soot surrounded the hatch leading to the garden. It doubled as a rudimentary chimney from the fire occupying the centre of the room. On the lofty ceiling were faded colours of black, white, yellow and red, reminiscent to those in the Alchemist's Tower. Tapestries and rugs hung from the walls, while symbols etched walls skirted by benches of embroidered cushions. Oliver Turner cleared his throat. His coat contributed to an unfortunate wizard-like presence. He appeared at home.

"Mr Foxe? You journey here to *tempt* punters with some ancient powder?" he announced. "We're under 8 Jansky Vresk, an abode of Mr Kelley. There used to be a house above…"

I leaned against the rugs.

"*Don't* lean on the tapestries Ferguson-Pipps." he snapped

"Kelley returned to Prague?" Scott asked.

"Once he dropped Dee, Kelley went anywhere that tolerated his experiments," Turner replied.

"Actually, I think it was Dee doing the dropping," Foxe sounded defensive. "Kelley was useless without Dee."

"Let's agree that *neither* was complete without the other…"

Turner threw firewood into the hearth. With a splash of lighter fuel, he threw in a match, and with that satisfactory *whump* familiar to arsonists, the pile burst into flame. He sat down, and motioned for Foxe to begin.

Foxe breathed heavily beside me, before opening his Gladstone to find some crucibles. He allowed the fire to settle, before juggling small bowls, test tubes and crucibles with the deftness of a circus performer.

"The red powder alone did nothing…it was a trick," he mumbled so only I could hear him.

"Do you have *any* idea what you're doing?" Turner interrupted, pretending to be bored.

"You have rainwater?" Foxe asked, and Turner pointed to a bucket by the wall.

While Scott and Turner watched, I sat on the bench: an extra without the script. Scott's insistence that an angel had appeared in Deptford smacked of overtiredness, just as my own hallucination reeked of drug-related flashbacks. As to him having seen one when he died, well, surely that was chemical compensation for crushing disappointment at no afterlife?

The smell of burning foil and nutmeg announced some

progress. Turner stood in the shadows, watching while Foxe, despite the occasional magician's flourish, frowned with concentration. He withdrew the test tube, which he tapped into a dish, unconcerned by the heat from the fire. He stood in the warmth of the furnace like he was born to be there.

Turner was growing impatient. "As above, as below," he said. "Let's see."

"Patience, please," Foxe whispered, reaching tongs into the smoke billowing from the main pot. We stepped forward as he withdrew them, which even to my disappointment, were empty.

"Mr Foxe, you fail us," Turner's thinning tolerance reminded me of Rožmberk's in Jane Dee's diary.

Foxe nodded his acquiescence, before inspecting the other crucible hanging over the hearth. "My friend," he said, with the grace of man who had won the argument. "I allow actions to speak," he pulled the tongs again from the deep bowl, "Louder than words."

We glimpsed a dull glint as he dropped a lump into the bucket of water with a fizz. Turner moved forward, staring, silently rapt, into the bucket. He reached in, and withdrew something. He opened his palm, to reveal a beaten chunk of gold. The atmosphere blew like a fuse. He stared between it and Foxe with stuttering bewilderment. The world I knew shivered. Turner looked like he had scratched his eye forgetting a knife in his hand.

"I can't...I'd never have believed it..." Turner managed, while Scott offered similarly befuddled admiration.

I closed my mouth, looking for the strings. Gold is a natural element. It has no constituents. What Foxe had just done was impossible.

"How did you manage that which took Dee forty years without success?" Scott asked.

"I've had longer to practice."

"But Dee lived into his 80s," I added, but was interrupted by Turner with more prosaic issues.

"Is that the last of the powder?" he asked urgency melting his voice.

"That's the last of it," Foxe confirmed. "You want more?" There was silence. "Then we scry."

Chapter 29

Turner looked snatched of victory.

"That's all of it," Foxe declared. "Unless we ask the missing angels," he added.

"*Missing* angels?" Turner replied, puffing out his chest. "Mr Foxe, don't think my time here's been wasted. Exhausting yes, costly, certainly, but not *entirely* unsuccessful."

Foxe found a poker leaning against the wall to break up the embers. "So your scryers have been successful have they? It doesn't appear so. My crystal ball alone isn't enough and you know it. You don't have the tables, the black mirror, the wax discs. Need I go on?"

"The sigillum *has* been troublesome since it was destroyed," Turner paused, "By an arrogant fool."

"You've not been scrying *without* it?" Foxe was in shock.

"Who said without it?" Turner said. "I use my own design, based upon the original."

"*Based* on the original?" Foxe was furious. "It's a Faberge egg. It's perfect. You fucking idiot, you can't mess with it. The seal of truth is intricate."

Scott and I stepped back. Foxe was losing his cool.

"Its design was provided by *angels*. You can't adlib," he continued, "They struggled for angels' authenticity *with* it."

"*You're* the one who destroyed it," Turner defended himself. "You're the one who refused anyone else the original. I recalled the grids the best I could."

"The best you could? For fuck's sake. You're opening the

doors to hell if you're not careful."

It was getting so dramatic I struggled not to laugh.

"Where is my crystal?" Foxe asked.

"Did the Society follow you?" Turner asked.

"No, we lost them two days ago, near Olomouc." Foxe neglected to mention the car shredded with vintage light machine gun fire.

"And the British Museum's wax discs?" Turner asked.

"Remain at our hotel," Foxe replied firmly.

"Then we have almost *everything* we need," Turner paused. "Unless you were the successful bidder for the obsidian mirror in London." He looked at Foxe, who was failing to suppress a smug smile. "You were, weren't you?"

"There was a slight hitch, but yes."

Turner sighed, and sat down to think.

"And, I also have the *correct* tables for the sigillum," Foxe said, so smugly that I actually sympathised with Turner.

"You do?" Turner frowned, clearly still thinking. We looked around awkwardly.

"Very well," Turner announced. "We'll do it. It's safe enough. The Society presumes to know where I live." He looked to the ceiling. "But, these foundations are absent from Google maps." He studied Foxe again. I was unsure what Turner saw, other than a tussled prospector.

"They won't find us?"

"No. Now, collect what you need, and ensure you're not followed," Turner said. "But Scott's staying here."

'I am?"

"Yes." Turner pressed a button, an intercom crackled. "Maria, show them out."

I was glad to leave. Maria had either revised her earlier manners, or they now compared favourably to Turner's. Passing along the hall, I saw the storeroom door off the hallway had drifted open. Once again, she closed it on a room of trunks stacked with the finesse of a hoarder. This time she clocked my interest.

"Private," she warned.

The portraits stared down. There were similarities beyond their pained expressions.

"They believed in angels," she said sadly. "And you?"

"No."

She nodded like I was the first sensible person she had met for a while, which was unnerving. We reached the front door.

"Your friend?" she asked. "He's staying?"

"Yes," I nodded. She allowed me out. "Look after him." I said, unsure whom I was advising.

A breeze hassled crisp packets and cans. Passersby ignored me, lost in the humdrum, while my head span with fresh rules. I heard footsteps and someone calling my name. Mr Foxe caught up and fell into step. We walked down the hill in silence.

"What're you thinking?" Foxe asked.

This took me my surprise; Foxe had plenty on his plate. In my experience people with loaded plates tend not to notice other people even have plates. We passed a bar ruined by Elvis mirrors. I felt strangely lonely, like I was still staring into the Thames from Hungerford Bridge again. That felt a long time ago.

"My mother," I admitted.

"Your mother?"

We passed human statues appealing for small change. I wondered how fast they would move if their tin was nicked.

"Why didn't you change names in your book?" Foxe asked. "Not even your mother's."

"There wasn't much point. They were all dead. Clairvoyance killed her."

"It was the booze that killed her, Ben."

"You didn't see her face when the punters failed to arrive."

"The danger of practising magic means you're the only one not believing it-"

I was sure I'd read that in Jane Dee's diary, but he disappeared into a cloud of Belgium tourists.

"How did you make that gold?" I asked when he reappeared.

"It's nothing but a cheap parlour trick. There are more impressive things than that Ben. Gold just catches the headlines."

His face told me nothing, and we walked in silence.

"We can't call upon you...to assist?" he asked. He meant scrying.

"No. Anyway, you're the one warning about scrying burning."

"It does. Even if you *do* know what you're doing."

"You're not making it any more tempting," I laughed.

"But you and Scott. He's convinced you've got something, a *partnership*."

I shook my head and we walked in more silence.

"How about Turner's grids? You sounded pissed off," I asked.

"His ad-libbed sigillum? Having it inaccurate could've killed him, or his scryers. It may even have done so. The angels demanded a filter. The co-ordinates spelled the words that Dee wrote down. The Sigillum Aemeth filtered the signal, like a polarizer. You can't stare Heaven in the eye. It annihilates you. That's why I brass-rubbed the original sigillum. It's good to make insurances."

"How did you know it was on that brass disc in Krakow?"

"A secret." he smiled. "Dee was also instructed to make four seals for the table's feet."

"The ones you've stolen from the British museum?"

"Borrowed. Besides, they're more use to me than they are to gathering dust and disinterest, Ben. As you know, many people have tried to scry over the years, but they've never had *everything* they need. This is the first time for that in a very long time."

"Dee and Kelley succeeded?"

"They had something. And any descendent of Kelley will be similarly skilled."

"But he had no heir."

Foxe stopped. "Jane Dee gave birth nine months after they swapped wives," Foxe paused. "Theodore Dee, born February 1888. He was born in Leimbach. Dee named the boy as his own."

"You think Theodore inherited Kelley's scrying skills?"

We reached our hotel; its carpet was welcome relief from cobbles.

"Think about helping," he advised, as we split to our rooms. "Wrongdoing's your angel leaving the room," he said, with a gravitas that I feared was for dramatic effect. "Let her back in."

I swept through our rooms, grabbing what we might need. Scott's wash bag jangled with pills, so I brought them.

I should come even cleaner about my reluctance. The occult *is* a dangerous pursuit; it breeds dissatisfaction with the real world. You chase shadows for colours, and hope for fact. If I'm honest, my cynicism had thawed a *little* in Deptford, after I seeing the shimmer on my curtains. Hope is what triggered my writing; hope that I would succeed in capturing what I intended. I knew the hope that it might be a success and not self-indulgent twoddle. I recalled the joy of getting Kathleen as my agent, until it was just someone else not calling me.

You don't see an angel and walk on in life; it changes you. It is declaration of things you'll never see or feel again. It's a peak, and the only way is down. And I saw what that did to my mother.

Shoving Scott's tablets into my pocket, I met Foxe in the hotel lobby. He was keeping an eye on the door. He handed me the mirrors' satchel, looking at me for a decision. I know he saw my fear, but we said nothing.

Maria met us at the door, eyeing our bags. Foxe handed her his bag, which she looked through. She held up the vitamins, shaking her head.

"You must be pure. No additives, medications," Foxe explained on her behalf.

"No meat, no washing," she continued.

"We must also abstain from coitus and gluttony," he whispered.

"Well that wrecks *my* plans."

My joke was lost in translation, as she searched through my wash bag, removing shower gel and vitamins, before doing the same to Scott's. She shook out meds and a facial scrub. My blood stirred at the invasion.

"Scott might need his medication," I argued, but she shook her head, indicating my satchel. I flashed the heavy black mirror at her. She waved us through, before stopping.

"Your pockets?" she asked.

Just past Scott's stray meds, I found a handkerchief, so held back the meds. She pulled a face as the handkerchief landed on her tray.

We found Scott and Turner enjoying leather armchairs like old friends pretending they still had things in common. Turner still clutched the gold.

"He's perfect," Turner announced as we entered. I endeavoured not to catch Scott's eye. He was the last person needing such praise.

"Where *did* you find him?" Turner asked, as a police siren wailed in the distance.

"Hiding in clear sight," Foxe answered.

Turner stood to pull books from their shelf. He handed one to Scott. "And you Ben, get reading. There's time to practice before the Swift-Tuttle. It peaks in two days. You can use the lighthouse."

"Lighthouse?" asked Scott.

"It's upstairs. You won't be disturbed." He looked to Foxe. "Help them Thomas. I need Scott pure."

I was afraid he'd start patting Scott's knee.

"And him?" Turner looked to me.

"He's pure like cynics always are," replied Foxe.

"I want the statue, not the sculpting." Turner added. Maria was ready for us at the door.

"And be careful what you ask for," Turner added, in the tone of someone habitually ignoring that advice. Scott, seeing the bag, asked after his pills.

Turner shook his head. "No medication, I'll pray for you."

"When's this comet?" Scott asked Foxe.

"In a day's time," he replied. "These things aren't as definite as astrologers like to think. I have further calculations to make."

"Like why I'd be willing to do this?" answered Scott.

Turner smiled, "I think almost all of us know why you're doing it Scott."

Chapter 30

We sat in a room at the top of the house with glass on three sides. Prague's traffic lay below in flows of stars. We moved various telescopes and calibrating equipment aside to position the crystal ball in the centre of the room, on top of the black mirror. It was beautiful. Foxe looked at me expectantly.

"Ben?"

I shook my head, telling them "I bet no one asks Richard Dawkins to take communion." I looked around at Scott's alarming sincerity and Foxe's fresh excitement. "You're seriously asking me to join you? You both *read* my book. Didn't you, Scott?" I didn't wait for an answer. "This is *exactly* the mirrors and nonsense that people deceive themselves with."

"I read it, Ben," Foxe reassured me. "And contrary to its sales figures, it was very good."

"Flattery isn't going to work," I warned him, knowing if he carried on I'd be eating out of his hand, or at least scrying.

"Come on, Ben, we're a long way from home, what else are you going to do?" Scott said. It was an annoyingly good point.

"You may question it," Scott added. "But you *understand* it."

I hesitated, always a mistake. Foxe guided me down opposite Scott.

Foxe polished the crystal. "Welcome back," he whispered, placing it between us. "Take it slowly," he warned, as though promising something more impressive to come. He began mumbling what I supposed were invocations.

"Five times to the east," he explained. "And as many to the west."

My greatest concern had once been not pulling my writer face while scribbling in cafes. Before then it was developing ways in which to attract women. It was this that led to writing. Before that, it was hoping to secure a mother that might provide me a *Star Wars* AT-AT, or at least a father. It was now not disappointing two alchemists more desperate than either would admit. My stomach rumbled.

"Be *very* careful what you ask for," Foxe advised us, echoing Turner. They apparently agreed on something.

"Even in your head," Foxe continued. "We want to avoid any historical mistakes. If you see them, ask only their names." He shut the window.

"Right, empty your minds," he demanded like he was ordering bar snacks. "It's kenosis. Empty your *will*."

The drone of planes flying in landing patterns overhead had stopped. I glanced at my watch. We had been at it for three hours. My head throbbed with concentration. Not that it was helping. Nothing was happening, just as I had expected. We stared into the ball. This was a fourth attempt.

"To allow God in, we must leave," whispered Foxe.

I recalled the Ouija board. Time erodes novelty and that evening's hallucination had grown as unreal as my night with Ronnie. Scott caught my eye, and frowned. I *had* to clear my mind, this, whatever it was, required purity. I sensed the Ronnie betrayal scolding that ice with alarming ease.

The weariness sitting on Scott's face had switched from road movie cool to long-haul fatigue. He was a blink away from snapped-matchsticks. He looked up in surprise, as though concluding an internal conversation. I exchanged a look with Foxe from which I felt short changed.

"What's wrong?" Foxe asked. I could have told him what

was wrong. To the east, I saw the rising sun; when the sun rises, my heart sinks.

Foxe was losing patience. "You said you've done this before?"

"We have," Scott looked at me. "Something's changed."

The room swayed, or was it me? Ronnie shot through my mind in a blaze of guilt.

"Nothing's changed has it Ben?" Scott asked.

"Your conscience is clear?" Foxe also asked, looking worried. They were staring at me like Nazi hunters. I nodded, I hoped convincingly.

"Perhaps we should rest?" I suggested, but it was a too obvious change of subject. Empty words hung in the air like sitting ducks. My words were losing the will to live.

Scott stared at me. "What've you done?"

My deep breath marked the line of a new future. Scott's face dropped, as rumours were marked true.

"I..." I stammered without having planned where I was going.

"Ronnie," he said, staring at me. "Oh my God."

"I didn't-" I blushed, in place of denial.

"Didn't what?"

The room did that swimming thing.

"Who's Ronnie?" Foxe asked,

"*My* girlfriend," Scott replied, his eyes not leaving me. The last time his skin had looked so pale was before his heart attack. He held the table like a train hand loop while hitting a bend.

"Are you alright?" I asked.

"Am I alright? You being serious?" There was silence. "Fuck off Ben," Scott said.

Foxe looked away.

"I *knew* it, I *bloody* knew it," Scott shook his head.

I groped for an excuse, but found nothing. Scott looked at me with a disappointment I might never recover from.

"It was obvious Ben. God, it was *so* obvious," Scott said.

"I'm sorry."

Prague's rooftops and spires were developing form in the lightening dawn. The drop to the garden was inviting. My face burned with tiredness. I swayed with internal fury. In the growing light, the crystal ball looked pointless. Foxe took the appearance of a discounted wizard. What was I doing?

"*You* dragged me here," I spat pathetically, like that excused anything.

I had to leave. I stood up, and paused at the narrow stairs. Everything shared since joining the Life Assistance Agency was a farce. *I* was a fucking farce. Another apology bubbled up, an armband for a drowning elephant. Scott rose to follow me, to press further, but Foxe stopped him. As I stumbled down the stairs apologising, I heard them arguing. I had fucked up.

Maria had done her best with our rooms, which was unimpressive. Disuse hung in the air. The bedspread puffed with dust as I landed upon it with what I feared was petulance. That was how I felt, childish. Furious at my stupidity, I stared at the ceiling. I cross-examined myself, until testimony drew blood when I punched the wall above the bed. No one heard. I lay still, my numb hand as ignorant to its pain as I had been of Scott's. Blood seeped through the bandage. Had Ronnie told him? I finally dozed off, once the infernal dawn chorus retired to bed. I wasn't sure the past mattered now.

To rub things in I had an email from Ronnie, she signed off with another kiss; the trouble people can cause with a single kiss. I opened the email to find what she claimed was the last diary entry of Jane Dee. I read it with a heavy heart, while welcoming the distraction.

BACK WEST

May 1588

The following day was greyer than death. A persistent drizzle blew in from the mountains that the castle walls predictably failed to keep out. Everything was damp and cold. I'm certain that John has no idea *what* he's asked his angels for, nor the cost. My own feelings are too tumultuous to pin down. I know if God asked me what I most desired, it would be fuller cushions, new teeth and a trip home to Mortlake. I certainly wonder if he should have been more careful for what he asked.

Kelley left for Prague four days following our exchange. I stood by his horse in the courtyard, holding the stirrup. Its fresh leather creaked softly. Before Kelley mounted, he pressed his hand to my belly. Realising why, my mouth dropped open.

"Look after him," he whispered so only I could hear.

I stared away, unable to speak, which I now regret. He spurred his ride, and with a kick of mud the horse galloped away, saddlebags flapping its rump. I watched him, until he mingled with the trees. He did not look back. I clutched my belly that now burned with familiar feeling.

Rožmberk watched him leave from the gate. John later admitted to watching the farewell from the castle's outer bailey, before returning to his room. I later found him amidst the chaos of a man having turned his room upside down.

"What are you looking for?" I asked.

"The crystal ball," he replied. He looked broken. "He's taken it."

He sat on the bed and I perched beside him. I put my arm around his shoulders. But he shrugged it away, staring into the distance.

"That rogue's bloody taken them. It's the key. Without it we cannot see anything."

"We? There is no more 'we', there is only Us, John."

He looked at me. "I have you then?

"Yes," I nodded. "You have me."

We remained sitting there for a long time, a long way from home, alone with our thoughts together.

November 18th 1581

We left for England a few days later. It was hard to be interested in the same roads, tracks and lanes we had travelled before. John insisted that we retrace our journey, for 'spiritual reasons.'

We were in Germany by the time I was seven months pregnant. It did not require a man as versed in mathematics as John to draw conclusions. The true father was obvious, but John determined to not discuss it. As we travelled, he continued in attempts to contact the angels with Arthur, but without success. The creatures had apparently abandoned him as readily as Kelley. His self-pity had worn me thin before we even reached Krakow; the esteemed Dr. Dee had come a long way to learn not to swap your wife.

He blinked into the easterly wind that had buffeted us since departing Trebon. Leaving that bedraggled castle had been easy, but I saw John was hurt. He was the last to see Kelley's true colours. It was at a junction populated by abandoned pottery sheds that John insisted that we divert to Krakow. I groaned, before capitulating for what I swore was the last time.

Krakow was gloomier than I remembered. Its glamour now unimpressive compared to Prague's grander designs. Its smoking chimneys, stinking stables and shuttered windows provided little charm. A sixteen-day detour for our two-day stay seems pointless, but then I am not the alchemist.

John had only one destination in Krakow. I accompanied him to the steps below the Wavel's battlements. He held my hand to help my balance, as I'm carrying more heavily than before. At the entrance to the crypts, rats scurried into dankness. John ducked below a beam, but banged his head anyway. I smiled, but he said nothing. I had no interest in seeing his Monad, in situ, and knew not why he needed to. I hoped door lintels might knock more sense into him than I ever had.

"Why the insistence, John?" I asked, peering around the gloom. "Seeing your gift will surely upset you."

"The Emperor stockpiles gifts, but he's never ignored one so important as this. Both the Envoy and Sendivogius claimed it was installed here," he smiled. "It's an insult, yet one that serves me perfectly."

We looked past recent excavations in flooded pits surrounding the forecourt. The ground glistened from recent rain.

"What's all the digging?" I asked.

"Drainage I believe. No one likes rotting kings, not even rats."

I followed him down newly laid steps, and shivered in the dark. To our left, a chamber had been freshly whitewashed. A few candles lit our way. John's eyes traced fresh flagging covering a drainage channel. Then he stopped. There it was; the brass disc of his Monad embedded in the floor, its gleam already dulled by damp.

"It's the *ideal* place," he chuckled, "Amongst such noble company it is unlikely to be disturbed,"

"What's that?" I asked as he pulled a copy of the same brass plaque from his bag. It clanged against the stone flagging, and we paused to listen, but there was no one around.

"Insurance," he explained, "From that which I hope the angels have granted. A decision that I may one day wish to undo." He turned over the new brass disc. Its flip was covered with intricate engravings of tables.

"These tables are the way in. Wax and wood will perish," he explained. "Everything but gold. *That* is eternal, the reason for its worth. But brass shalt last well enough." He paused, as I kissed his cheek, in an unexpected rush of love.

"Now if you could..." he began.

"Watch the door?"

"My dearest Earwig, how well you know me-"

He knelt, and laid out his tools. I nodded, and stepped away, allowing him to prise the disc from its position in the floor, to be replaced by the heavy chink of its double-sided companion.

February 1588

With gentle disregard to political affairs and the darkening enlightenment, the Austrian mountains gave way to Bavarian hills and well-mannered valley vineyards of France. Our smiles grew as we recognised the better-shod roads we had previously travelled.

In central France, we passed mounds of compost and manure, from which women spread across fields. Other than the occasional glance, smallholders and peasants ignored our diminished wagon train, but John noticed wealthier road users keeping their distance. Our son interrupted his thoughts, "Where art Kelley, father?" Arthur asked. "I miss him."

Arthur was growing broad, less the boy who left England and more the man returning. Perhaps it was he who was most changed by our travels.

"He succeeded, in vanishing," John explained. "Perhaps I will learn from him. But to abandon his unborn child is cowardly in the extreme."

I said nothing. It was the last time I heard him admit the child was not his.

We approached the crossroads I recognised as Leimbach. The church was now almost built, although the giant boulder remained. A wooden scaffold surrounded the stone building. Men were breaking rocks for the perimeter wall.

John stopped the horses and dismounted. Arthur resumed his latest pastime of drawing; sketching the scene on his father's paper. Despite the scaffold and oxen cart stacked with quarried stone, a makeshift sign informed pilgrims that the church would soon by ready. The smell of burning enveloped the road, as black smoke drifted across the path ahead.

"Crops?" I asked.

John helped me down from the wagon to stretch my legs. I felt a twinge. The stonecutters, wrapping their tools for the day, looked up.

"No, heretics," John corrected me. "It's a burning." He shook his head disapprovingly, before extracting two of the wax tablets and tools from his saddlebag. My shooting pains were rapidly increasing, but I said nothing.

As Arthur continued to sketch, John entered the churchyard. I watched him find a young yew with a split trunk. He rattled a small tin, before pushing it as deep as possible into the tree's Y. He returned with wood shavings on his sleeves and a fallen bird's nest, which he handed to Arthur.

"For good luck on a new birth. A new start."

I was as surprised as Arthur at his father's reference to superstition. John then kneeled, to triple wrap the wax discs in muslin cloths and an oilskin, before investigating the new tombs. He paused at the largest, and braced himself to lift the lid.

At this point I winced in pain, and sat down, a cramp

searing through my stomach. The horses whinnied.

"God, not now?" John asked, returning from the headstones without the discs.

"I fear so," I gasped, instantly afraid.

We named him: Theodorus Trebonianus Dee. Theodore. God's gift at Trebon.

May 21st 1588

We found passage, and the Dutch coast slid noiselessly past. I listened to cattle, which had strayed too far onto the mud flats. They groaned forlornly in the dusk. The coastline was flat and the sea a miserable grey. The sky lit up in flashes of lightning further inland, illuminating everything for a moment, before darkness returned. Moments later the gentle discontent of a storm arrived. At this distance the thunder rumbled like the snores of abandoned gods. The flashes of light, of hope and the enlightenment, struck dimmer behind the clouds. A sailor yelled for a pulley, and someone replied. With a creak of ropes, the sails billowed, catching the offshore wind. The boat surged and I braced myself against the balustrade. Theodore whimpered in my arms. Much like Kelley we were not leaving Europe empty handed. I prayed John would not hold the theft of the father against my son.

1st June 1588

The farms hummed with bees and ripening apples, while more woodland was cleared than I remembered. Our war with Spain clearly needs more ships. We had picked up a cart from Gravesend, and passed through Kentish orchards, before finally approaching London's wall. What a sight it was! We waved away the pleas of the homeless husbandmen, begging since evicted from their land. Some even still carried tools. The world was changing. I was absorbed with baby Theodore, but I knew John had one eye on the reunion with his books.

I shouted first, as our wagon pulled up by Mortlake church. The churchyard had been extended, with fresh mounds lying near the perimeter walls, and headstones marked with the red cross of plague victims. Our house had also slumped into the ground with deathly resignation. I dared not guess how many times the Thames had flooded its banks since our departure. Any surviving doors swung on snapped hinges, while windows and shutters lay smashed on the ground. From the living quarters a squirrel negotiated loudly with a jackdaw, while the thatch, black with damp and possibly a fire, was barely intact. Even the beehives lay cracked and empty on the grass. John pulled his horse quietly up alongside.

"Another shadow, and darkness will prevail," he said. "My books," he gasped.

He dismounted his horse, and gathering his cloak, he ran through the neglected orchard to the laboratories. The long grass was strewn with shattered apparatus. A sideboard jutted from a blackened pyre, amongst other abandoned furniture. The western wall had collapsed, and he joined it, falling to his knees, where boots had trodden mouldy parchment and books into the earth. He heard squawking herons on the river, the chink of a gravedigger in the churchyard striking rock, and the sound of our crying baby. It was no glorious homecoming. John's hopes for a better future lay trampled in the Mortlake dirt by what appeared to have been a mob.

The double doors of his reading room hung limply from their hinges. The rugs and carpets were gone, along with the desk. John groaned; Mercator's globes, all so carefully marked with his own discoveries, now lay in other hands. A chair lay collapsed in the corner beneath the weight of a large bird nest. Wet weather had made significant inroads into the room. Only the stone chapel stood untouched. He closed the door sadly behind him, on the chaos of a house turned over by local intolerance and suspicion, and prayed.

I returned to the wagon, cradling Theo. The world had changed. Even I could see that. I thought of Kelley in Europe charming castles' courts, and bragging of his obsidian mirror and crystal ball. John had lost everything, but me.

Chapter 31

A spider floated on its webs. I wished sleep had smoothed my turmoil, but it hadn't. I emailed Ronnie thanks for Jane's diary. I did not add a kiss. I hoped a shower might wash, if not my sins away, then the grime of this old house. I stripped off the jeans I'd slept in and found Scott's pills in their pocket. I remembered his face, drained of its tan and cursing me. He might need his meds, so I had to find him. I stood shakily and used the corridor walls to guide me.

I knocked on the door, but to no answer. I was in the process of creeping in, when Scott arrived. Descending the stairs from the glass room, his hands held the walls to support himself. He looked at me like someone finding another side to exam papers with a minute to go. The man brushing past was not the Scott that dragged us here. He fell upon his bed. Barely able to open his eyes, he unbuttoned his shirt, and lay there clutching the silver cross around his neck. His face folded in on itself, tiredness exposing worry lines and sleep frowns. I apologised again, hoping I might have produced something better once I opened my mouth

"You're an *adult* Ben, you can't *move* without consequence." He peeled off his shirt. "Get out."

I threw his pills on the bed and returned to my room. He looked shocked, like a man stung for the first round of drinks in the City. What's so good about being a philanderer? I asked myself. What's the true cost of the sound of a belt buckle hitting the floor of a one-night stand? I felt a long way from home. I called Daisy, but only got her answer phone. It was probably for the best.

A damp breeze from the garden woke me. I stared down onto undergrowth bordered by high walls topped with barbed wire. I could see the outlines of old foundations and grass we had trampled leading to the trapdoor. I was partly relieved Scott had found out. Secrets erode self-esteem, and I was in bits. I was regretting everything I'd ever done. I checked my phone, but there were no messages.

Scott's room was quiet as I passed, as was Turner's study. The ground floor was equally deserted, but I hesitated on the stairs, remembering glimpsing our business card attached to Mr Foxe's letter on Turner's desk. Had I imagined it? I crept in. The study remained gloomy, but there it was on the floor. It was indented with a missing paperclip. I held it up, wondering how the hell our business card had reached a study in Prague when we had struggled to distribute them in London.

I went to the bookcase, where I had also not been mistaken. *Mirrors and Lies* was there, in hardback. I opened it, to find I had once signed it. I frowned. I had done so few signings I could probably remember them all. Inside was a slip of paper: **an interesting read** it read in handwriting I did not recognise. I left before I was discovered.

The rooms leading off downstairs gaped privately. It felt like a Hastings hostel, laminate wood peeling away from the crumbing plaster it intended to hide. I was not alone in falling apart. I found the front door locked with the size of key you don't want with you on thin ice. I needed a drink, and no one would hear me leaving. The house was deserted, particularly the room Maria had warned against entering. I stopped outside it. Only the mournful portraits gazed down upon me. Floorboards creaked as I stepped in. I paused, but heard nothing. It was musty, and brimming with clutter that had never reached the attic. I weaved my way through. Surprisingly, towards the back, was an open space with a writing desk. Legal filing boxes were stacked alongside, labelled by year, dating back twenty years.

The desk was piled with letters. I sorted through, recognising one with Foxe's handwriting. The letter was in Enochian, with some kind of chart paper-clipped to it. Could Foxe have sent our business card too? A frown was establishing itself, and I shoved it into my pocket just in time, as a hand grasped my shoulder. I gasped in fright. I was still refilling my skin when I turned to face Maria.

"What you do?" Maria asked. She was apparently exempt from the special diet. I could smell coffee on her breath. She was wearing glasses that looked broken, but weren't.

"Get out." She ushered me out, towards the stairs. I started to climb, was there anyone I wasn't pissing off?

"Your friend?" she asked. "He is ok?" Everyone was concerned about Scott.

Still breathless, I stopped. "He's resting, I think."

"No, he's awake. In the lighthouse."

The stench of school dinners filled the house, and it was dark outside. I was hungry enough to follow the smell downstairs. I found the front door locked and the key gone. In the unused dining room, Maria had prepared food apparently rescued from a boat wreck. Mind you, a recipe's most important ingredient is appetite, and I was almost enjoying some dank spinach and tofu, when Foxe arrived. He slopped food clumsily onto his plate. He looked as robust as the tofu.

"My calculations are a little wrong," he said, sounding amazed that this might be possible. "Damned calendars," he added.

There was no sign of Scott.

"The comet's tonight," Foxe continued. "Celestial activity must be *incoming*."

"They hitch a ride?" I asked through spinach.

"Your sense of romance prevails," he smiled. Guessing he referred to Ronnie, I appreciated his restraint. It didn't last.

"One must be careful with friends," he said, wiping dust from the chair before sitting down. "Ignore foundations at your peril."

He sounded like Turner, who startled us by appearing at the door. A flake of paint fluttered from the doorframe.

"Food to your liking?" he asked without interest in our reply. "How's the sigillum?"

"Well it can't be any less accurate than you had it," Foxe replied like a parent.

Turner shrugged, before looking to me. "Upset your friend?"

"Apparently so," I answered.

Turner shook his head, and left.

"He's not alone in chasing the powder," Foxe tutted, as Turner left. "It's *always* bloody gold." He shook his head. "People are so disappointing." He looked at me. "Even the Emperor made Edward Kelley Marshal of Bohemia, and not because he was short of marshals."

"So what're you both after, if it isn't gold?" I asked. "And what's the risk of Scott scrying? Or is he in as much danger these 'others'?"

Scott was an unlikely victim, besides this is how he enjoyed living, without a safety net. I pushed the spinach away. As I stood to leave, I noticed the front door key on the sideboard and swept it up as I passed, to join Foxe's letter from the study in my pocket.

On the way upstairs, I paused at the garden door. I guessed the day's horoscopes made no mention of Swift-Tuttle's influence on three men that evening. The sun was tucking in for the night. The trees lining Mala Strana silhouetted against a reddened sky. From my window, I watched Foxe stride across the garden, consulting papers. He had fresh focus. I imagined the cavern beneath the grass. He reached down, opened the invisible hatch, and disappeared.

Thinking of Fred Perry, I buttoned my shirt to the top and pulled the heavy front door key from my pocket. I paused, allowing an idea to form. It was a fleeting shudder of anticipation, a significant improvement on self-loathing. Downstairs, legend and wishful thinking had never danced so close, and I wanted no part of it. I grabbed my bag, wallet and passport, before creeping downstairs.

I peered round the dining room door. Maria was clearing plates. She had her back to me. I stepped past, and paused, listening for the scuff of plates. I slipped the key into the front door, wincing as it clicked loudly. The dining room was silent. I held my breath, until the sound of clearing resumed. I gripped the handle and pulled the heavy door. It creaked, but remained shut. With both hands, I tugged, and with a groan it opened inwards, scratching its path across the tiles. The chink of plates paused. I held my breath. When the sound of clearing resumed, I wrenched it further open, I heard a shout in Czech. I yanked hard enough to squeeze through and ran into the street.

I soon stopped running because I looked stupid. No one was chasing me. Above me, a plane's tailfin glinted in the sunset. The streets had emptied of tourists. This was Scott's gig, and we were no longer a partnership, I had seen to that. The Life Assistance Agency was over. Street cleaners swept cobbles, as cafés hauled in tables. Gift shops were closing;

soft toys pressed against windows, their hopes for new homes shelved for another day. I found myself leaning over Charles Bridge, the river's current scooping through the narrow arches. I stared at the water, flashing white in its haste to be elsewhere. I should have been happy, but something niggled. Something was wrong. This time there was no lifeboat below me, and no policeman. I checked my phone. No signal. I needed that drink.

I found the bar with Elvis mirrors. They shared as much resemblance to Presley as Turner's portraits to his overworked scryers. The place was empty, which suited me. The beer struck my throat with satisfying sharpness. The inescapable sense I was missing something remained. Self-pity's selfish scowl fluttered through me. I ordered another drink and considered Mr Foxe, his unfaltering focus and determination that his journey was not to be wasted; a man with Bren gun tricks up his sleeve. If I wasn't careful I would hear my head pop, and I knew where that led. I stared at my glass. Thankfully it was undamaged.

I gazed along the bar, at the red ashtrays and bored barman. He stood to dim the lights. It was dark outside; the streetlights smudged the pavements. Where was I to go? I ordered more beer and peanuts, foodstuff doubtlessly banned by the moody Oliver Turner. I felt Scott's pills in my pocket, and pulled them out, to find the letter I'd filched from the desk. I unfolded it. It was headed in Enochian, but written in English. It was addressed to 'My friend?':

Oliver,
It's been a long time. You disappeared, and were it not for the Society I'd have never found you. We are not friends, not after your theft, but we are entwined because of it. Dee's angels are crucial. They offer opportunity to draw a line beneath past

*events and pursuits. As WC Fields said: if at first you don't
succeed, try, try again. Then quit. Well, there's no point in
being a damn fool about it. You want to see the creatures?
Well I assure you, you'll get no better chance than this. This
is it. I have finally found he who is 'assigned' to the crystal.
The family line has skills. You are likely to claim that I would
not be inviting you, were you not possessing my crystal, and
you would be correct. But as you do have it, I have no choice.
I need that crystal. However, there is one thing if we are
successful. I warn you – be more careful than the men before
us of what you ask the spirits...*

I drained my beer, to look at the family tree that had been
attached to the letter, alongside our Life Assistance card. It was
the same family tree from Marble Arch headed by Theodore.
My head was spinning with overstimulation. To my gathering
dismay, things were adding up, but I was unsure to what. I
needed the loo.

I sat there, my head cupped in my hands. The bar's refit
had not stretched to the toilet cubicles, but I was grateful for
the absence of Elvis. Foxe clearly believed that Scott was the
key? Was he a descendent of Theodore Kelley? What nonsense
was this? A bell tingled to announce another customer. The
barman was doubtlessly relieved to serve someone else.
Catching myself sighing, I pulled myself together, washed my
hands and made the mistake of catching my reflection in the
mirror. I returned to the bar, and caught the fading whiff of
Sobrani smoke. My jaw slackened, and I plonked onto the bar
stool like I'd been shot. I asked who had just left.

"Someone wanting directions," answered the barman.

"To where?" I was losing the will to live. I knew the answer.

"Mala Strata, the old houses up there."

I stared at my beer and considered my karma account.

Chapter 32

Heroes seldom write their own stories. They prefer adventures told through the eyes of hired pens and excitable eyewitness, while modestly exaggerating certain exploits for historical accuracy. Therefore, with a foot light upon exaggeration, I report some redemption on my part. But, I'm no hero; there's no medal for rescuing people you pushed.

Reaching Turner's house, I looked up the street. A woman watered flowers on a windowsill. Turner's door remained unlocked. I feared the Society had already arrived. I slipped back into the house and listened. It was as quiet as the *Ladies* on match day. With my heart racing, I locked the front door firmly behind me, but as I passed the storeroom, I heard footsteps coming down the stairs, so ducked in. It was Scott being *helped* down the stairs. I retreated further into the room, as Foxe opened the back door to the garden.

"You'll be fine," Foxe reassured Scott, indicating things were far from it. "Announce what you see, let Oliver locate it on the board..."

His voice faded away. I edged out, to watch them cross the grass. Supported by Foxe who was carrying the satchel, Scott's feet dragged the ground. Seeing him so fragile was weird, like seeing Kermit being ironed. Foxe carried another heavier bag. I supposed it was the London Stone. My theory of Scott's importance and family background was taking shape. Looking around the room, my pounding heart suggested that investigating the shipping crates could confirm my hunch to be right.

The Society might be imminently knocking at the house, but I had to risk it. The further into the storage room, the more crates I found. And the further the years on the stickers went back. There were boxes from the 1970s, and 1980s. Streetlight through a half-painted window illuminated my attempts to prise the lid from the nearest crate. It broke with such a crack that I paused, breathing shallowly, but there was no response. I eased off the lid, to find four portraits inside. In the next crate, I found the same – another four paintings. How many scryers had there been?

I estimated over twelve portraits, including the six in the hallway. Clothes differed, but Turner's artistic ineptitude was unwavering. As I hauled one from its crate, the scryer's name scrawled up the side, something caught. An envelope was attached behind the painting. It contained a contract of employment. It was home-typed in English and I was shocked to find it included a disclaimer: '...*should harm come to me*'. The faded signature on a dotted line matched the scryer's name, and a date: 1986. Shadows passed outside the window. I thought I heard English voices. I froze, but they moved on. I returned to the box of letters on the desk. They were again headed in Enochian, but written in English. It was another letter from Foxe, and dated recently.

Oliver,
In reply to your letter, yes, I am certain I've found him. He's been lost in the crowd. I've contacted the agency. It's incredible synchronicity; we couldn't have planned it better. I've secured their services. I'll collect my equipment and head your way. I'll bring them with me if I can, but it might be tricky. He's a horse – he'll refuse if approached directly. We'll be canny. We'll get

him to you under the false pretences you suggested. We'll use his Life Assistance Agency, we'll take them to their word, that they can assist with anything!

They clearly thought Scott was a descendent of Kelley, or Dee? A passageway through taller crates leading to a wooden chest at the end of the room soon revealed exactly who they suspected Scott to be. The chest was the size of an armchair. I was no longer concerned about the possible emergence of the Society or Maria. Noticing manila files from the shelf above the chest I pulled them down. They were profiles of people. The first was labelled: Franklin Kelley (New York City). It was dated: (b) 1867, another was labelled Stephen Kelley (Sussex) dated (b) 1872, and then Max Kelsey (unknown) dated (b) 1943. They were character profiles of descendents. I guessed of Scott's family. It was time to find Scott. If what I feared was true, then he needed me, like Foxe and Turner needed him. He had no idea what he had let himself in for. It was my chance to make amends.

…The rap at the window rattled like Bren gun fire. I stumbled against the chest. My soul dropped an inch with shock. More hammering on the glass finished me off. I tripped backwards into the crates.

"Ferguson-Cripps?" It was Fred.

Before I could answer, there was a crack as the window exploded with a plant pot flying into the room; lead and glass shattered across the floor. Maria almost immediately arrived in the room, shouting over the crates, whilst a pistol butt knocked in remaining shards of glass from the window frame. With a gush of colder air, a leg swung over the windowsill. Fred suggested we stand back, as he followed his pistol into the room. Standing, he straightened his Harrington, still looking like he washed his hands before taking a piss. He looked around with the disdain of someone wishing to touch nothing.

"Ferguson-Cripps *again*," he announced. "Good God, we need to stop meeting like this. How's your hand?" he grinned. "Thought we'd bought it?" he asked, shaking his head. "Nope. Now where's Scott?"

Even knowing why they were so persistent in chasing us, didn't help with how they had survived the car crash. The next leg swinging in required Fred's help. It was Beard from Marble Arch, although the facial hair had gone and the denim wisely ditched. He wore agent black, and his head gleamed in the light. He landed with less grace than he would have liked, and glanced around still chewing his gum. The only positive was the absence of Dougal, whom I rather guilty guessed might have perished in the crash.

"Archives," Beard murmured, which rather flattered the hoarding. He pulled out a portrait, before letting it fall back against the wall. He looked past me to the trunk.

"Where are your friends?" he asked, seeing the files in my hand.

It was poor timing to suggest we were agents, not friends. I was still stammering when Maria decided not to let their weapons intimidate her.

"Get out," she demanded to little effect. Fred's hand pushed me ahead through the crates. Maria's face implied she had expected this.

"No," she said in the hallway, "Leave this man alone." She glared at the intruders.

"Where are Foxe and Turner?" Fred asked.

She hesitated, as though seeing their guns for the first time. "They're in the lighthouse." she admitted, motioning for them to follow her up the stairs. They frowned up at the narrow staircase. I flinched as Fred raised his gun. I wish I hadn't.

"Stay here," Fred demanded. "He's no hero," he reassured Beard of my unimportance.

Maria winked, as she followed them upstairs. The sound of their feet on the stairs spurred me to prove him wrong. No hero? I legged it out into the garden, before the Society realised Maria was stalling to buy time. The outside air smelled fresh, of grass and darkness. I traced the path to the hatch, which I found with greater ease than I hoped the Society would, and closed it after me.

Chapter 33

In the centre of the candle-lit cavern, an altar now replaced the swept-away fire. Under the eye of Turner, Scott watched Foxe unpack his bag, revealing what looked like two cheeses in enough wrapping to survive a nuclear winter. Foxe brushed dust off the pair of wax tablets, before they joined those he had stolen from the British museum on the floor.

"You found these where Dee concealed them?" asked Turner. "I won't bother asking how you knew. But what a honeymoon that must've been, I almost feel sorry for Mrs Foxe."

Turner replaced them carefully, before looking up at my arrival.

"We have visitors," I announced.

Rather than waiting for me to negotiate the stairs, Foxe lifted the altar's legs upon the wax tablets and gently placed the crystal in pride of place atop the dark obsidian mirror.

He looked at me without surprise. "Then we don't have long."

I glimpsed an anxious smile, as though my arrival confirmed something. Scott ignored me.

Dee's crystal was central again, multiplying the candles. It looked magical enough even for an agnostic to find otherworldliness in its depths. The lump of London Stone stood more prosaically below.

"Scott," I descended the steps, out of breath. I was worried at how shattered he appeared, and why he was allowing them to abuse him. "Are you ok?"

"I need to see them," he mumbled.

"Maybe, but you've got to…" I wanted to alert him to who they thought he was, but Foxe forcing Scott to sit interrupted our reunion. Scott waved me away. I perched on the chair, glancing upwards. At least now I had company. I felt safer.

"So, your sigillum tables Mr Foxe?" Turner challenged. "Let's see them."

His own leaned against the wall, facing away from the room, where Foxe had despatched it in disgust. Foxe nodded, producing a similar shaped board from behind the curtains. He walked it to the altar, and laid it down. Turner studied it, his fingers delicately tracing over the squares.

"Perfect," he admitted. "And the London Stone? You're sure?"

"Dee used it. It's a missing link, 'though not *the* missing link."

"Scott…" I tried to get Scott's attention again, but Turner pointed at me.

"If you interrupt us again I'll silence you." His tone suggested he meant it, but the revolver that he placed with elegant carelessness on the altar confirmed it. Foxe studied his partner with interest, before positioning Scott with his back to Turner.

"This was Kelley's seat," Foxe murmured to Scott, who stared glassily into the sphere. He looked exhausted.

Turner sat a few feet away, admiring the grid of numbers and letters that Foxe had clearly transcribed from his wax rubbings. His hungry eyes betrayed the years since he had last seen it.

With his pen poised over a ledger, Foxe sat beside Scott, praying quietly. Rainwater dripped from somewhere, when Scott's face contorted like he'd been electrified. He fell forward, to grip the altar for what were not spiritual reasons.

Foxe pulled him back. "Focus," he whispered. "Lose yourself. Let them in."

Scott's hands held the altar edge like he was at sea. His eyes sprang open, glassy and without focus.

"Feel the shadow, not the object," Foxe advised. "Feel your genes."

"Look, I know this isn't a great time-" I started, but Foxe silenced my interruption, although not without clocking my glance upwards, to where the hatch door remained closed. He frowned, but let it go. Turner asked Scott who was there. Scott seemingly allowed the question to echo in his mind.

All I could hear was the heavy breathing of four men. Scott's fingers tapped and he called out numbers. He repeated some, which he repeated again, but more weakly. Turner located them on the tables.

Scott paused, so Foxe nudged him. He may have fallen asleep.

"Anything?" Foxe whispered.

Scott's eyes shut tight. He shook his head, "No, I don't think so."

Turner read the writing he had so far transcribed.

"This is no further than *I've* been," he said. As his pen tapped the paper. "Any fool can get here. And I include myself in that."

"So, what do we have?" Foxe asked in a tone sidestepping hope.

"Death is the lesson," Turner read quietly. "Yes. Death is the lesson, life the path, and death the gate. Fools would think otherwise." He tapped the pen. "There's nothing about any red powder."

Scott looked paler than anyone should. He gazed weakly at Foxe.

"He who is assigned to the crystal." Foxe said like it was a mantra.

Scott winced, before calling more coordinates.

Turner wrote down the letters to translate. "*Only* he who is assigned," he said. "They're *insisting*. That it be the one they've assigned."

"How can that be?" Foxe frowned. "He's here. They're playing, as always. Press on Scott."

But Scott shook his head, "They've gone."

He was in a poor way. It was painful to watch, but Foxe held Scott's head firmly to stare into the ball.

"We're not giving up," Foxe declared. "*Ask them.*"

"Ask for the red powder's ingredients," Turner suggested gently, while Foxe snorted in disgust. Scott closed his eyes again and after a few minutes managed some vague co-ordinates.

"Carmot," Turner translated.

"Doesn't exist," Foxe declared. "It's mythical."

"If he's not assigned then who is?" Turner demanded.

Scott slumped forward, clutching the table for support.

"Mr Wildblood," Turner said, "If you might indulge us, *please...*"

Scott rasped further coordinates, before collapsing drunkenly to his side against Foxe.

Turner stuttered with disbelief. "Are you playing me?" he said, reading what he had translated. "It suggests Ferguson-Cripps." He looked at me. "And why do you *keep* looking at the trapdoor?"

"I told you. You have visitors," I reminded them; aware they had not fully registered my warning about SPR.

Turner reached for his revolver, and pointed it at Scott.

"Get Scott to call something he can't possibly know," Turner demanded, "Something to prove their authenticity. And his for that matter-"

"I can't. It's too much-" Scott whispered.

"*You can,*" Turner shouted, pulling the hammer back on the revolver. For someone with a gun pointing at him, Scott looked even worse than he should. He was gurgling, and bunching his shirtfront into his hand. His eyes rolling back and forehead dripping with sweat reminded me of his collapse at *Vital Marketing*. I had no choice; I had to help my friend.

"Why don't *I* do it?" I announced.

I mentioned heroes should never hold pens, only Manila folders full of answers. Foxe stared at me, his face tense and licking his lips strangely.

"Ben's mother *was* a medium," Foxe reassured Turner. "He's likely to have *some* ability." Foxe stared at me. "Don't you Ben. Deep down, you've always known."

I smiled at his confidence. "If you say so."

Turner, finally acknowledging the state of Scott, relented. I eased Scott aside, who slumped further along the bench, while pushing the family tree and files into his hand beneath the table. He gripped them, but barely.

"You want me to stare into the crystal?" I asked, the audience volunteer expecting to disprove the magic. There was still no sign of the Society. If they appeared it wouldn't hurt to make myself indispensible.

Foxe closed my eyelids gently with his hands. "Listen to the whisper of history, to the shadows," his voice dropped. "Find the spark. It's all there."

I looked again at the trapdoor, before trying to relax. I was unsure how to blag this. I thought of my mother, allowing the candles and echo of Prague's depths to dance in my mind. I determined to see something. Lights in the crystal swelled and darkened, before my head seared with pain. I winced, falling forward in shock. My eyes dotted like I'd stared at the sun.

Foxe held me, suddenly interested. "It's OK. Just relax."

I was lightheaded, so inhaled, like Daisy had shown me after yoga. More shooting pain sparked through my brain, my eyes ached. I glimpsed a face, or the shape of something forgotten, but shook it away. Turner started praying, or chanting, in Latin.

"Mitte lucem tuam...."

Letters started flickering like ticker tape in my mind, but nothing definite.

I struggle to explain what happened next. More numbers sparked like map references. I called them out, to a gasp of surprise from Turner, who pulled the face people reserve for when pigeons unexpectedly fly in their face.

I held my head. It may have been an image, or suggestion from the crystal, but coordinates rattled through my mind like lottery results. I barely had time to repeat what I saw before another number replaced it.

"A in the 21st table," I whispered. "85, H 49 ascending."

The numbers hammered through my mind. I couldn't hear myself, all I saw were digits, followed by stabbing pain, as each flared like a strobe. I held the table for support, wincing in agony as Turner demanded for more.

"Two thousand and fourteen in the sixth table," I said. The room was quiet. There was only me mumbling what sounded like tongues; dark incantations dredged from some pre-historical place.

"What are they saying?" Foxe asked.

"It spells Rožmberk," Turner whispered.

"So? The small time baron?"

"Yes, but it's not just that," Turner stared at the paper.

"Well?"

"Who had wooden teeth?"

"What?" I heard a tremor in Foxe's voice. "How could *he* know that...?"

They didn't know we had read Jane Dee's diaries, but even that didn't explain the visions of the moth-eaten nobleman grinning in my head. Foxe stared at me. I'll always remember his eyes, a swirl of frantic anticipation. Then he winked, and I slumped forward, tension disappearing from my body. The sharp crackling had stopped, replaced by an unreachable pain between my ears.

"They say," Turner cleared his throat, hesitating as he completed the translation. "Oh ...my... God." He sounded as though announcing his own name for the gallows.

He joined Foxe in staring at me like I'd conjured his house keys from a lemon.

"It's impossible. It's *him*?" Turner said.

But I was no longer listening. I frowned. From behind them, shadows on the wall flickered together like magnetised filings taking shape. I gasped, as a pale, emaciated figure emerged from the darkness. Its wings were translucent as though from malnourishment. Its thin skeleton traced dark lines through its stretched skin, forming wings splaying between hands and ankles. What I had previously thought were horns on the head were in fact ears, like a bat's. Its fingers were long tendrils, stretching to impossibly narrow points at the edge of paper-thin wings. Its eyes sprung open with a puff of dust. Bloodshot whites punctured the darkness. A bony finger pressed against its slit of a mouth. '*Shhhh*'. There was a creak and gust of stale air as it stretched to full wingspan. Ashes stirred on the ground. Bones as narrow as tent poles flexed impossibly wide. Some candles extinguished in whisps of smoke, while others flickered through the transparent skin stretching from the arms to its torso. I fell silent, or screamed, I will never remember.

It stared angrily at me, like I was responsible for its

presence, before shaking its head and hugging itself like a pterodactyl perched upon some prehistoric cliff. Beneath the wings' hem were ragged talons on its feet. I thought of my scratched floorboards in Deptford.

"We *were* once pterodactyls," it spoke, in a parched voice. Had it read my mind? "It's our secret, Ben Kelley. We're the hum, the roar, the silence and the scream. We always are and always will."

"It's there isn't it?" Foxe followed my gaze without focus.

He looked desperate, like he'd waited his entire life for this.

"Did it speak to you?" Foxe asked eagerly. "What did it say?" He stepped forward, towards where I was staring. "What did it say?"

"*You*," it declared, staring murderously at Foxe. "It's been a long time since we saw you." The angel leaned towards Foxe; its face wrinkled like volcanic rock. "It's been a *long* time. What d'you call those things? Centuries?" Its voice creaked inches from Foxe's unseeing eyes. "Have you had enough?"

"What did it say?" he asked me.

"Have you had enough?" I repeated, finding fresh energy.

"Well? Have you?" it hissed at Foxe.

"It's Uriel?" I said, without knowing how I knew.

The angel nodded.

"Uriel." Foxe dropped to his knees. "Please undo what was done," he pleaded.

The angel's mouth opened. "Thy Desyre was granted. It can never be undone," it hissed.

"This was not my desire, but Edward Kelley's…"

I joined the creature in staring at him. Scott recovered himself beside me.

"You what?" asked Foxe. "Who *are* you?"

But the angel interrupted, and I swear we all heard this time.

"You sought profound wisdom in this most new and strange doctrine of eternity," it said.

"Which was a mistake." Foxe nodded, "We were bound by the velocity of promise, caught on the streams of stars."

The angel frowned. "Indeed you were."

"But," Foxe continued, "Immortality, it's above all human reason. I cannot bear the weight of more loss, of children, of loved ones," Foxe's voice cracked, "Of friends. All life must end. This is unnatural, an abomination…"

The angel leaned forward, its flared nostrils flaring inches from Foxe's face. "Immortality is indeed a weight upon my shoulders too, yet your desire remains strong," it said. Its arms reached out, long fingers trailed across Foxe's heart.

He frowned. "Is she, *touching* me?" he asked.

I nodded.

Foxe looked suddenly older, his eyes weary and full of too many days. The angel looked at me, its eyes dark above the sharp cheekbones and long snout. It belonged to freak shows, to the gothic monstrosities of murky nightmares and dusty corners. I was unable to look away. Universes and blurs of comets swam in the bleakness of its mortified eyes.

"Please," Foxe's voice broke with hope, "Recte sapere et Intelligere." His Latin was fluent. "Quaeso, ait, ista maledictio abrogare."

The angel's head tilted, as though hearing distant prey. We all stared at Foxe, at his desperation.

"Please, undo this curse," he pleaded blindly to the room. "I can't watch Constance die too, not like I did Jane." We stared at him, but the angel growled.

"Dr Dee, be careful of what you pursue."

"Dr John Dee?" someone, or all of us, said.

Foxe nodded distractedly, the news less monumental for him than the rest of the room.

"And a few men since," he admitted, looking around without focus. "Is it still there? Did she hear? Is it undone?"

It was gone.

Turner was the first to speak.

"You're John Dee?" he said slowly enough to suggest this might help him comprehend matters. "You're Dr. John *Dee*?"

His disbelief spoke for us all. Foxe nodded, before staring at me.

"Is it still there?" he asked. There was nothing left but a faint outline.

"I think so." I said, but I was losing it, in more ways than one.

"Is it undone?" Foxe, or rather Dr. Dee asked the air.

There was silence. The angel had merged with the background. I was losing focus. I winced as my head contracted with electrical pain.

"It's undone?" he asked again, "I can die?"

The angel reappeared to nod, but was growing indistinguishable from the background. It retreated further, blending with unfinished walls. Another candle snuffed out with a string of smoke.

"And my friend, Kelley?" Foxe asked. "Did he perish from the tower in Trebon? Or did he prevail...?" he raised his voice. "He *can't* have survived. We'd have met, surely his inquisitiveness would have got the better of him...?"

The angel's finger returned to its stony lips. "Hush," it whispered, before pressing its mouth close to mine. "Never scry for us again. It is not permitted. Men must know their place." And it disappeared.

Blackness filled my head with such terrifying intensity that my body tensed as though falling. There was a yell, as the trapdoor above opened, and the Society arrived. They descended the steps two at a time. Scott groaned beside me, and I lunged to catch him before he hit the ground. Actually I didn't, he was shattered and it wasn't a film. I missed him, and he hit the floor like humans tend to, with a terminal thud. My head hurt like my brain was bouncing inside it. As I lifted Scott from his armpits, I was afraid I'd join him. He was enormously heavy, but I dragged him clear.

"Water?" I demanded purposefully. Turner nodded distractedly as he greeted our visitors. He was traumatised by Foxe's announcement. He waved vaguely towards a tap, from which I filled an alchemy flask. I shook some of Scott's medication into my hand.

"They allow themselves in," Maria said, as she followed them down the steps.

Chapter 34

"What is this?" Turner demanded, but he had lost all authority. Sounding shell-shocked, he eyed Fred's holstered automatic pistol guardedly.

"It's our *business* is what it is," Fred said, eying Turner's revolver with similar wariness, before taking in Foxe, the crystal and myself. "What the fuck's going on here?" he asked, eyes shining dangerously.

Scott's eyes flickered. He couldn't speak, but still clutched the manila files that I had handed him. The angel had gone, leaving my head throbbing like a war room at critical threat.

"Mr. Foxe, you assured us you'd stopped these pursuits," Fred said, edging behind Beard, and out of Turner's line of fire.

Foxe shrugged like it didn't matter any more, which failed to discourage Fred.

"I'm sorry we're late," Fred said. "Mind you, we'd have never found you had your woman not shown us the view from upstairs. It's a well-hidden path... but clearly trodden."

Beard looked displeased at his role as providing cover. They both appeared to think we weren't taking their entrance seriously enough, which in light of Foxe's revelation was understandable.

"What brought you out of retirement?" Beard asked him.

"Developments," Mr Foxe, or rather Dr. Dee, replied. "But mirrors and lies mainly." He smiled, aware that Turner and I were staring at him with growing disbelief. I could see the wisdom, if not the years.

"Developments? You're not a fucking Audi," Beard snarled, nodding to the crystal, "We've come for that." Beard's voice levelled. "And there's little need for pistols Mr Turner."

"I guess not," Turner's narrow smile flickered. "Maria, please enlighten our guests."

From her long skirt she produced what I recognised from *Tintin* comics and the *World at War*, as a Schmeiser German machine pistol. What was it with Second World War hardware? Fred and his companion laughed.

"What're you going to do with that? Throw it at us?" He laughed, but Maria pulled back the bolt and in a flash of noise and sparks, fired a burst over their heads. I winced, as my head split at the explosion. The room stank of gunpowder.

"Ok." Fred surrendered their pistols.

"Thank you Maria." Turner lowered his revolver, sighing like a man finally able to concentrate. Scott was recovering interest. He opened his eyes, to look at the papers I'd handed him.

"So?" Turner's voice remained weak with disbelief. "Mr Foxe, or should I say Dr Dee?"

Fred laughed, until he realised it wasn't a joke.

"I've not answered to that name for a while," Dee replied.

"Your angels have returned..."

"They were never mine, but yes. I am Dr. Dee," he nodded to Turner. "And perhaps we might next ask more important questions, not request frivolities like eternal life. Ben, perhaps you might, well ..." He smiled. "Assist?"

I shook my head, while Fred looked confused. Dr. Dee held my shoulder more firmly. I tried to stand but his fingers tightened, hurting my neck and keeping me seated. I tried to shrug him away, but his grip tightened.

From the shadows, Scott, clutching the family tree, seemed about to admit something.

Dr. Dee smiled. "No one's been here since...Well, since me. They're dusty lines, but we've made contact. You saw her, Ben?"

"I saw something." It felt churlish not to admit it, but I had to get my head around things first.

"So, the Stone remains assigned to *a* Kelley. Those genes survive." Dee peered more closely at me. "If not *the* Kelley."

The sound of rain pattered the trapdoor above, its dampness sinking into the chamber. I was wondering what he meant.

"What d'you mean? Who's Ben?" Fred asked, having recovering his cool, as though meeting 400-year old men was something covered during the Society's induction. "Is Ben who I think you're saying he is? How did you find him?"

Dee nodded. "His mother changed their name. She distanced herself from Kelley's bloodline without even knowing she had done so. Although it had already been done with Theodore all those years ago. We *all* lost Ben, even he did."

My head buzzed as though electrified. Numbers, grid references and lightning strikes cross-patched my vision, and pain throbbed my eyes. I needed to lie down. Scott tried to stand, to intervene.

Dee stared, eyes narrowing. "I suggest you sit down Mr Wildblood, your enthusiasm is dangerous in such contained places. Do not forget who's paying you."

"Paying you?" I asked, as a darker mood stung the air. For some reason I remembered Scott pretending to have been on the phone to Ronnie at the petrol station. I faced him to better engage with whatever the hell was going on.

"What's this about?" I asked.

"It's about you Ben," Scott began.

"Scott, I suggest you stop," Foxe warned, but Scott pressed the family tree into my hand. Foxe snatched at it, and Fred stepped forward, but Maria waved her Schmeiser at him, reminding him to stand down.

My hands trembled as I opened it. It read clearly:

Theodore Dee had reverted his name to Edward Kelley's alias Talbot in 1605, and it remained unchanged through his children and grandchildren, until 1780, when the family immigrated to New York from Ireland. It was then that a Franklin Talbot reverted to the old name for a new life. Had Franklin suspected his true roots, or simply met a Kelley on the boat? Either way he reached New York harbour's gangplank as Franklin Kelley; a new name for a new life. Kelley had mutated to Kelsey by the family's return to England's south coast in the 1880s. And *his* son, Max Kelsey was born in Hastings in 1943. Ben was born thirty years later.

The file also contained pages ripped from *Mirrors and Lies* that I had not noticed – my autobiographical passages were highlighted for Turner's attention. My stomach lurched. I reached out; unaware of whose hand I caught.

"Your mother married Max Kelsey in 1968," Dee clarified, tapping the papers.

"Max Kelsey was my father?" I felt sick, and joyous; I'd never had a name before. "Max Kelsey," I repeated. "Kelsey."

"We lost you when your mother renamed you Ferguson-Cripps," Dee explained, "We were close, but when your father disappeared along the coast we lost him, like he lost everyone. We never reached you. It was sensible conjecture that he might've had a child, if not more. Kelley's make a habit of abandoning their sons."

I was struggling. We had been chasing Foxe, but were actually being led? By Foxe himself, and...I looked at Scott, who looked sheepish, and cleared his throat to speak, but Foxe shook his head.

"Not now," he whispered.

"What've you been up to?" I asked Scott. "Are *they* paying you? *You* knew all this?"

"Not all of it." Scott looked at Foxe, "I certainly didn't know who he is..."

Things were slotting into place at an alarming velocity. "You didn't see anything, in the crystal just now, did you?" I asked Scott.

"We rehearsed co-ordinates upstairs."

My anger was erupting; our betrayals matched. "You knew about this?"

"We're life assistance Ben. Consider yourself assisted. You've found out who your father was. You're a Kelley"

I leaned against the wall.

"Mr Foxe," Scott continued, with disbelief, "Or rather Dr Dee, read your book, and realised who you were. You joining LAA was *particularly* fortuitous, the sort of synchronicity the agency was based upon. Anyway, Mr Foxe tracked you down to your agent Kathleen, where he found our business card." He smiled. "In your copy of *Great Expectations* left in reception."

Things were falling into place, such as that tall man ducking down the stairs as he left our office and Dr Dee's constantly sore head. The supposed phone call to Ronnie...

"Scott," I snapped. "Shut up..." I paused "You're buying some crap about me having Kelley's mystical abilities?" Glancing at the crystal again I winced with pain.

"Of course Ben," Dee interrupted. "Traits *survive*. You've proven it. We're only custodians of our genes. You can't deny what you saw. I read your book. I sent it to Turner. I recognised your father, and we traced him to Hastings-"

"Kelsey, Kelley?" It sounded warmer each time I said it.

"We got close, but for thirty years you vanished." Dee shook his head, "Then I read *Mirrors and Lies*, and rang your agent...well, I didn't bother seeing Kathleen once I found your Life Assistance business card in reception." He smiled, "I walked past you, on Hanway Street, as you came in that morning. Remember, I hit my head on the gas meter?"

I nodded dumbly

"I read your blog and book. I met you at a book signing," he continued, but I couldn't ask you to scry on the street. I heard your cynicism, you'd have laughed in my face. I had to be canny."

That was an understatement

"You're faced with the chance to be where no one's been since me and your forefather," he said.

"My *fore*father?" It was monumental enough to discover my father's name, much less ancestor. Realising that I came from a generation of fraudsters struck home. I clutched the wall to combat the dizziness. How many words had not been my own? How many of my steps had already been trodden? But disappointment wrestled with blossoming pride that I had *any* heritage at all.

Dee smiled, "You're *skilled* Ben." He stroked the crystal ball, "You're *chosen*. Every new line has a start, that's you. You're the *one* assigned to the crystal. I've never worked out *why* Kelley had such ability. No offence," he added, "But he wasn't exactly upstanding."

I thought of my mother missing my unsavoury father. Deep down, had she known?

"I used my honeymoon to replace my equipment," Dee continued. "I'd finally given up. Connie snagged me despite my caution about falling in love, but it's good to keep options open. It's something I've learned over the years."

Turner was still staring at him like he'd just announced he was a 400-year old Elizabethan alchemist and angel caller.

"Now what?" he asked with a newly found reverence.

"We spend the remaining time I have left alive to ask the angels from where they came. And where we go. We *have* them again." He glanced at me.

The room darkened. I imagined my future – a crystal ball, a rotting boardwalk, and footsteps never stopping. I saw my mother's signage: 'Psychic Readings here today' in rain-smudged chalk. I finally knew who I was. I was tense with identity.

Who is to say family traits don't hop around, jangled by years and aging blood? Foxe's eyes were dark. Turner flashed what he thought was an encouraging smile. I shook my head, as *certainty* shot through me. I had never been so sure.

There was a smash, followed by the dull explosion and shattering of heavy glass, as I rolled the crystal ball off the table. It shattered across the flagstone floor. Fred leapt out of the way with a cry, while Dee groaned as though shot.

"No, no…" he said, dropping to his knees, and clawing at the glass, as though he might reassemble it with desperation alone. Turner joined Dee on the floor. The two of them, on all fours, scooped up shards of the glass.

"What have you done?" Dee spat. "We *had* them."

Before they had time to stop me, and before I changed my mind, I pushed the black mirror too, which split in two as it collided with the flagging. They stared at me with impotent fury, but I felt an electrical shimmer, as a sense of self, shoot through my being. I knew who I was. My sense of belonging surged, and my eyes burned with great fat tears. I knew where I was. I knew who I was.

We left the cavern, and walked to the house as different men with different names. Maria secured the machine gun in its cabinet, before showing the Society agents towards the front door. My head was spinning. Foxe was Dr Dee. I knew it was true. I was unsure where this left me. My cynicism was in tatters. My mother had been right. Such mysteries did exist? With so much trickery, was I to ever know what I saw in that cavern? Those moments would join the swirl of memories: of sepia picnics and first days at school, until reality would erase it completely. I had plenty of questions for Dr. Dee, which predictably Scott was already asking. I had not yet fully computed his deceit with our so-called Life Assistance Agency either.

"What sort of man forgoes immortality?" Scott asked.

"One who's tired of watching the world die around him." Dr. Dee paused. "Yet, I was never going to kill myself, like Kelley must have done."

The breeze from the broken window in the front room had strewn papers everywhere. We looked around at the crates.

"We'll be archiving," Fred said, already starting to pick through them, "Returning what's survived to the Society of Psychical Research." He sparked a familiar vanilla cigarette. "Turner owes us."

"How about your car crash?" Scott asked.

"We jumped." Fred rolled up his sleeve to show a still livid long wound on his forearm. He looked at my hand. "Quits?"

Chapter 35

It was raining. Dr Dee drove the Jaguar without speaking. There was too much to say. His spirit had dulled since the crystal smashing. He stared ahead, grasping for solace or reassurance in the road spray as we returned to pick Ronnie's Saab up from Krakow. I looked through the window, and the reflection of Kelley stared back as housing estates and roadside embankments fought for shape in the rain.

"What was Kelley like?" I asked.

"Like someone drinking from the fountain of youth, only to later discover a dead fox floating in it. Kelley was a deluded man," Dee replied. "Like many bright men he made the common mistake of underestimating the intelligence of others."

As a relative, I tried not to take this too personally.

"So, what do you miss the most?" Scott asked.

"From those days?" Dee answered. "Not much, even the stately homes had drafts measurable on the Beaufort scale, there was ice inside the walls, and the Wi-Fi was terrible. But the world was smaller. Less crowded. More trees. God, there were *far* more trees."

I asked Dee about Mrs Foxe's wanted poster in Mortlake that Daisy had found.

"Connie wasn't in on it," he replied quietly. "I couldn't tell her. I had to go missing. It's not a conversation I'm particularly looking forward to."

"She doesn't know who you are?"

"No."

I didn't envy him that chat.

"And, I'd appreciate your silence on this matter. Love doesn't conquer all," he continued, "Death does. It steals everything. Don't judge me Ben. I've seen too many people die. Connie got septicaemia, and that was it. I made a decision." He paused. "I mean who *really* wants to live forever. Life steals. That *is* life."

"It's why people need a Life Assistance Agency," Scott said.

"I thought it was *the* life assistance agency?" I smiled, before looking at Foxe. "You weren't tempted to approach me directly?" I asked.

"A stranger asking you to call angels? Claiming you're descendent of a powerful spiritualist?" He glanced at Scott, "Even he might have baulked at that."

"When I found your Life Assistance Agency card I thought God was finally smiling," he added, looking older under the café's fluorescent lighting, which couldn't be blamed on the foul tea alone.

"You do realise what you've done, Ben?" Dee asked. "Smashing the crystal. That was our only way in."

I recalled their insistency. "Or their way in-"

He glared at me.

"What did the angel say?" he asked again, and I told him: that they were once pterodactyls. It didn't seem enough, even to me. It occurred to me they were winding us up.

Motorway traffic roared around us. Dr. Dee had resolved himself to his loss.

"You can see why I needed you. I never could contact them without Kelley."

"How did it all start?" I asked.

"I guess it was the necessary advertisement I printed to quell rumours. I should have seen it'd only fuel them. '*Against the untrue and infamous reports of Dr John Dee*'," he repeated the words we'd seen in Jane's diary. "'*Refuting slander and loose tongues that claim he is a caller of devils and spirits. Dr Dee is not, as some have claimed, the arche conjurer of the kingdom…*'" He laughed, "God, I sound *so* old. It was a long time ago, when Jane answered the door to Mr Edward Talbot." He paused. "I remember the dogs barking. I was in the laboratory."

He unzipped his holdall. "Read this. It's from my diary."

John Dee (1527–1608 or 1609)

Barnabas Saul suggested meeting near the porch of St Clements, beneath the Three Kings sign in Covent Garden. My low expectations were fortunate. The building was deserted. The print works had relocated closer to Kent's pulping factories, but the smell of oak apple still lingered, as did the stench of mucked fields off Tottenham Court Road.

Saul looked older than I remembered. He frowned as I emerged from the shadows.

"The road has suited you Dr Dee. You've not aged a month," he said.

Rain dripped from the roof truss, as we set up the table and dark obsidian mirror. How I missed the crystal, and wondered how effective Kelley was without me. I will live to rue my lack of vigilance allowing Kelley to rob it. Hickman and I sat down and focused.

Following numerous attempts, we had vague success, as something shimmered in the black obsidian. Hickman smiled. The light in the mirror rippled between us. It was Raphael.

"I have now, here, in this pearl entered possession, to serve you at all times," I said. My heart pounded, but the light faded.

A cart rumbled past and a night watchman called at the sound of a fight breaking out in the Three Kings next door.

Saul yawned, his eyes wide, white as pearl. I consented. It was time to conclude the session.

It was first light when I left an equally wasted Hickman at the edge of Lincoln Inn fields. A butcher was opening alongside a still-shuttered wheelwright. The sound of cleaver sliced through the morning dawn.

"I wish to view the river," I explained, as we parted. Saul shook his head, like a man who if he had not seen too much, had certainly thought it. He walked away, his collar upturned to the morning wind. I was not to see him again.

The fields quickly gave way to gardens of the houses skirting the Thames, creeping establishment competing with the darker alleyways and lanes leading to river steps and small quays. The tide was up, its current sloshing the embankment under construction. On the southern bank, a beacon flickered at the entrance to a dock; a few dung-boats and wherries bobbed between.

I pulled the lump of London Stone from my leather bag. I had considered returning it to the menhir on Candlewick Street, beside the notice '*carts be advised to collide at the risk to axle*', but how could I reunite the chunk chiselled away at midnight all those years ago? The lump of Stone looked like any piece of sandstone. I felt its weight and power in my hand and looked out to water that had passed Mortlake seven hours ago. Without another thought, I heaved it into the river. With a deep splash it crowned the surface, before plummeting to the riverbed.

I knew Jane had stopped posting my letters to Kelley. Nor did she tell me the news, when in 1593, she heard of Kelley's fall. It's not in the corridors of power, but in sculleries, mews and kitchens, that news travels. She stood in feigned shock when I told her of the news that Kelley had died several months since she had known.

1604 required all the tears I held. I had successfully secured position as warden with Manchester's Christchurch. It was below me, but times change. Queen Elizabeth had died and my escapades were slipping from folly to danger, as a friend visiting from London had warned. 'King James has no time for witches' were his blunt words of warning.

It was when exploring the flatlands of Cheshire with Theodore, where I dig the salt for the alchemical *aqua pennanens* along certain dragon lines, that Kelley's son first shocked me. Theodore was tall, with his father's nose. I sometimes sense my old friend Kelley walking alongside me. We were loading the cart with buckets of salt when Theodore asked if they meant harm. I was unsure what he meant,

"The creatures…?"

I pulled the horses tight. The cart creaked to a standstill.

"What creatures?" I stared at what I had long considered to be my son.

"At night. The winged girls, in my chamber."

I looked at the hawks floating on updrafts and the trees bending away from the wind. Concern for his future weighed heavily on my soul.

"Do not mention this to anyone," I warned him. "You hear me?" I clutched the boy's thin shoulders so firmly the lad was alarmed. "*No* one. It's dangerous times."

We moved on in silence, my mind sparking with unbidden desires.

Manchester

Jane had been in bed for a week, holding on a few days longer than most.

Plague doctors survived little longer than the victims of Black

Death they treated. Daily contact with the dying leads to an end that their bird-like beaks and heavy leather trappings do little to prevent.

Beneath his wide-rimmed hat, the doctor swerved through the doorway, his beak catching the frame. He cursed, but no one heard. He quickly adjusted it, before twitching mint hanging outside the door, mingling the leaves closer to lumps of camphor and vinegar sponges. Mud, and what appeared to be blood, caked the hem of the man's overalls; only the glimpse of a buckle attaching the mask to his head reassured us that he was human. He stepped carefully through the gloomy room.

"Fear not my beak," came a muffled voice, "I'm no demon, but a plague doctor." He prodded the bed-ridden Jane with his stick. She groaned, and whispered what sounded like 'dodo'.

I recalled my wife's fondest memory of our travels. The doctor's leather gloves were stained, but from marking doors with red crosses, not strawberries.

"Try not to speak, nor breathe," the doctor advised.

"We want her to breathe…" I corrected him.

The beak arced from left to right, surveying the room. "It's in the air."

I was less sure about that, but it was no time for theories. I knelt to hold Jane's hand.

"Step away," the doctor warned, but all I could see was Jane. For once my eye on earth, not the heavens, as she always accused me.

"You can cure her?" I asked.

"Cure her?" the doctor's beak swung towards me. His eyes blinked behind the mask's cheap red glass. "I provide care, and I register her death." He tapped the beak, releasing a fresh whiff of laudanum and camphor.

The doctor uncapped the gourd on his belt. He spilled myrrh, and what I guessed were pulped rose petals onto a rag.

He let it flop across Jane's face. She said nothing. I rearranged it, brushing her face raging hot with fever. The doctor asked me to move away, but I saw Jane's breathing grow shallow. Her face grew pale beneath the black sores.

"You have nothing more to provide?" I asked the Doctor.

The beak shook from side to side. "No."

"Then leave us."

"But, you shalt grow infected."

"My health is not your concern," I declared, as Jane reached for my face. I leaned down and kissed her full on the mouth. Saliva hung between us as I moved away. I looked from her, to the strange looking bird doctor. "That there *is* my life."

A tear burst, hot and heavy in the corner of my eye. Jane reached to rub it away, but her hand never reached me. My teardrop fell to her face, as her hand felled onto her chest, beneath the weight of a thousand words never spoken.

"Keep the boys safe," she said, before managing a smile. "Protect Theo from his father's path, I beseech you."

The doctor hovered above us, and waited, before prodding her again with his stick for that purpose. He nodded, and mumbled a prayer.

Mortlake

I lay the vial carefully in the drawer of my desk.

"What's that?" My son's voice shocked me so close. Theodore is ten. He has the same quick eyes as his father and even the beginnings of the distinctive white streak in his hair. He already speaks more words than he understands.

"Red powder?" he asked, his mother's inquisitiveness combining with Kelley's intuition. It is a lethal combination.

"Yes. The very last of it," I said.

"It once made gold? As mother said?"

"It did." I replied, and I swear he noticed my mood dip.

"You miss her?" he asked.

I nodded, daring not to speak; it would bring tears. Manchester's plague had stolen more than Kelley ever had. I closed the drawer on the vial.

"Enough to make gold only once again," I admitted. "But no more," I lied, thinking of the secret tin embedded in the French tree trunk at Leimbach. "Pr'haps one day, but not in your time Theo. Your path must lead to safer pastures."

We were quiet for a moment, and it seemed an appropriate moment to announce my plans.

"It's time," I tugged my beard nervously, "It is time for you to leave."

The boy looked confused, but expectant,

"We need you safe," I continued. "*I* want you safe. I've booked your passage." I pulled out some papers, an itinerary to Antwerp. "Travel, as I did. See the world, read, learn and escape these times. King James has no time for the curious." I sat down. "We'll say the plague took you. I'll register your death." I held the boy's shoulder, "Your name will be chased."

"Dee?"

"Yes," I smiled. "But, fear not. You know your true blood."

The boy nodded, before looking closer at the documents with puzzlement.

"But these papers are not for a Dee or Kelley, but a Theodore Talbot."

"Indeed they are. Get used to it, for a while. But don't forget to return, perhaps to your old name, when times are safer. But, a word of warning, don't chase things thou cannot see." I sighed. "I have learnt that by tough means. And remember, eventually, every new line has a start."

Chapter 36

Over the road drone, my favourite band came on the radio: the itchy drumming, scuzzy guitars and pristine electronics of New Order. Our heads nodded, but no one clocked the song's name. In typical enigmatic fashion, its title is barely mentioned. As Hooky's bass line strutted pylon-like across perfectly swept synthesisers and strings, I murmured its opening line: *We're like crystal, we break easy / I'm a poor man, if you leave me / I'm applauded, then forgotten…*

Dr Dee was quiet, as though having an exclusive on tomorrow's bad news.

"Who did I think I was?" he broke the silence. "You don't conquer death. It always wins. It takes everything, even the gleam in your children's eyes. Those moments break your heart because you'll never claw them back." He sighed like I'd never heard anyone before.

"It has taken everything, and it can now have me," he finished.

Krakow is a mini Prague. Trees had turned autumnal red to match the roofs. Women circled the town walls, walking their dogs knee deep in mist, watched by men on benches blowing cigarette smoke over their newspapers. Dee stretched by the car. He had been rubbing his joints since leaving Prague, as though the years were catching up, a physiological hangover I suspect he hadn't anticipated.

He left us at Ronnie's Saab, before going to settle our hotel bills and replace the brass disc in the crypts. He held my shoulder and stared into my eyes. I saw forgiveness. He looked much older.

"Kelley disappeared, and I should have learnt from him. In 1609, I took the church records from Mortlake. I've faked my death more times than anyone should. Connie and I can die together now. And perhaps I'll finally confront what lies beyond this life, the place from which the angels come." He peered closer at me and gently tapped my forehead. "Edward, I know you're in there." He smiled, "Welcome back."

I laughed; what did he expect me to do? We drove the Saab off before stalling, and agreed to meet him in Mortlake the following week.

Chapter 37

Our Hanway Street office appeared abandoned. Our only visitors destined to be disappointed in looking for a massage. It should've been on our business card but we didn't have strong enough hands.

"Daisy left a message. She's done the website." Scott said.

"She's webbed it?"

"I like the *us* Ben, congratulations. We now have Foxe's money." He paused, "Oh, and this."

He held up a cheque for £5000.

"What's that?" I snatched it from his hand. Kathleen had signed it.

"Your agent owes you this. They said you owed them four thousand, six hundred and fifty pounds. Well, you never owed them a thing. Dr Dee arranged the debt, to help persuade you to join the Life Assistance Agency. He promised Kathleen there might be another book in it. One that'll sell."

"You what?" I felt anger brewing.

"You should be flattered. Dee needed the Life Assistance Agency but only with you on board. We had to persuade you. He needed you needing money."

I wanted to be more furious, but Scott's positivity soaked up anger quicker than a meditation retreat.

"Daisy can man the phones," he continued. "While you're being interviewed."

"*What* interview?"

"We need you out there." He looked to he window. "We

have a *story*. The Fortean Times are interested in it. It'll bring us business."

I met Daisy that evening.

"Right," she said, unravelling the scarf she once again should have begun earlier. "No small talk, what happened?"

"Firstly, you owe me an apology, but beer's a start," I replied.

She relented and returned with a beer. Since discovering my true name I had been calmer. I didn't need any badass moments, not Denzel's, nor anyone else's.

"I might have a new book," I explained. "Mr Foxe wants me to write it." I decided against revealing his true identity.

Dr. Dee was happy for me to write this book. 'Just change the names like you didn't last time,' he advised. I pointed out that he still lived in Mortlake. 'It'll be a novel Ben. No one will believe it. Besides, I can look after myself.'

"You've changed..." Daisy smiled. "Your shirt." She looked closer, "And what's this? You stopped dying your hair?" she laughed, but closer inspection in her compact mirror revealed a white streak I had not noticed before.

Of course Daisy wanted to know more about what happened, about what I had seen. And I too wondered about the dusty apparition I saw in Prague, that strangely sad and undernourished creature.

"You'll scry again?" she asked. "How can you not?"

I thought of the angel's warning and shook my heads. "I don't think so. Most walls are high for good reason. And at least Scott hasn't put scrying on the Life Assistance Agency business cards."

"Not yet he hasn't."

This book exists because I had something to write about, which is all writers' need: throw them something to scribble and they'll peck away, happy as ducks and other metaphors.

Scott and Dee had changed me. Like railway points, something had switched. I was no longer on the siding. Do I accept angels exist? I have little choice now, and besides, it means my mother's in a better place, which considering her empty booth on Hasting's pier isn't particularly hard. I blogged a few times – Scott insisted, for promotional purposes, but how many people are in need of scrying assistance?

Scott woke me up by taking Hanway Street's stairs two at a time. He arrived too soon for me to look purposeful beyond lifting my head up from where I'd been dozing. He threw a box of business cards at me, which I somehow caught.

"Ben," he looked at me. "Remember, never chase the rainbow. Let it chase you."

"So now what?" I asked.

"Take the lid off."

I took it off and picked up the top card...

Ben Kelley
Life Assistance Agent.
Your problems, our assistance
Where telephone banking and dietary supplements fail,

The Life Assistance Agency succeeds.

Private investigation, sick day excuses, situation manipulation, people: lost and found, Life advice, coincidences arranged, hits arranged, soul mates found (special rates apply), final Will and testament re-writing, fear of death minimalisation, account massaging, Swimming lessons, Feng Shui and Bonsai trimming. And Scrying.
0208 333 21-0   07873 643 338

THE END

ACKNOWLEDGEMENTS

You learn a number of things writing a novel, and I don't just mean justifying reasons for staring into space. I used to think a single name deserved to be on a book cover, in fact so many people help with the process that there should be twenty.

I'd like to thank the authors of those first novels I read as a teenager: Douglas Adams, Stephen King, Sue Townsend, PG Wodehouse, H Rider Haggard, and the sporty types at school, who made it clear that I'd need to enjoy areas in life that didn't involve chasing balls.

More specifically, I'd like to thank Suzy, the mother of our two beautiful boys, my parents Norman and Jenny, and sister Alice, for all their support.

Also Barry Blake, my now deceased English teacher, who disregarded the curriculum and instead made us study more screenplays and novels than we could ever carry into class.

There are many people who read drafts of the Life Assistance Agency, most of whom might better recognise it as the Karma Account. Thank you, all of you, in particular Frankie, who can take credit for what is, I hope, a successful plot twist. If it fails I can similarly blame her.

I'd like to thank Nikki Dupin for her beautiful cover, Michael Rowley at Penguin Random House for his encouragement, Rowan Pelling, Alex Hannaford, Charles Brotherstone, Richard Skinner, Clare Conville, and of course Matthew Smith at Urbane Publishing, who has taken a punt on me.

Lastly, I'd like to thank those I know who've survived life, and those that did not. You are always inside. Living on. Thank you.

Thomas Hocknell is from Kent and lives in London. He has been a social worker, car salesman and gardener. He attended the Faber Academy and The Life Assistance Agency is his first novel. His regular Idle Blogs of an Idle Fellow aims to embrace random topics of modern living, but mostly complains about other people's inability to make decent tea. He also writes for Classic Pop magazine, the Good Men Project and The Line of Best Fit.